W9-ATY-639

The Bullet Catch

The Bullet Catch

Murder by Misadventure

AMY AXELROD

DAVID AXELROD

Holiday House / New York

Acknowledgments

Many thanks to the Harry Ransom Center at the University of Texas at Austin for allowing us access to their wonderful Houdini collection.

HOLIDAY HOUSE is registered in the U.S. Patent and Trademark Office.
Printed and bound in December 2014 at Maple Press, York, PA, USA
www.holidayhouse.com
First Edition
1 3 5 7 9 10 8 6 4 2

Library of Congress Cataloging-in-Publication Data
Axelrod, Amy.
The bullet catch / by Amy Axelrod and David Axelrod. — First edition.
pages cm
Summary: In early twentieth-century New York City, in the golden age of magic, Leo, an orphaned magician's apprentice, becomes involved in a murder mystery when he trusts a dishonest man.
ISBN 978-0-8234-2858-8 (hardcover)
[1. Magicians—Fiction. 2. Apprentices—Fiction. 3. Orphans—Fiction. 4. Conduct of life—Fiction. 5. Murder—Fiction. 6. New York (N.Y.)—History—20th century—Fiction. 7. Mystery and detective stories.] I. Axelrod, David (David Jacob), 1985– II. Title.
PZ7.A96155Bul 2015
[Fic]—dc23

2014023522

For Michael,
who took me
to India—A.A.

For Jessica,
my Chinatown partner
in crime—D.A.

Contents

In this book I have told of the methods of criminals, and held them up to your gaze, not as heroes but as malefactors; not as examples to be emulated, but as corruptions to be shunned, as you would shun a plague.

—Harry Houdini, *The Right Way to Do Wrong*

CHAPTER 1

The Doctor Smells a Rat

A small crowd had formed in front of Pershing Wadlow's Wonder Museum. The stained and torn banner stretching the width of the building advertised the attractions. Amazing things were promised: a two-headed lady, a genuine mermaid from the far-flung coast of Fiji, a woman with a beard down to her waist, an alligator girl.

Without ever having seen the exhibit, Leo knew the mermaid was only a stuffed monkey stapled to a fish, the bearded lady was really a man in a dress and the alligator girl's skin was plastered with thick glue that had dried and cracked. Rattling cold steel bit at his back through his thin black coat. He glanced up and saw through the slats of the tracks the mechanical guts of the Third Avenue el train as it came to a stop.

The usual lot came filing down from the train: sailors in bell-bottom trousers practically running to the closest saloon, a few sad-looking men searching for a pawn shop to sell whatever gold they had for next to nothing. Some ordinary folks mixed in as well, just looking for a new hat or a cheap suit. The Bowery was no ritzy neighborhood, but Leo was most comfortable working there. It was easy for him to blend in.

The last person to descend to the gray pavement was Murph. Under his opened jacket he looked like a strip of jerky. His suspenders hung loosely over a plain white shirt, holding up baggy pants hiding deep pockets. A newspaper carried by the wind whipped around his feet. He shook it away and passed by Leo, giving him a slight nod.

Leo left his post and crossed the street. He settled near the back of the crowd. A "talker" dressed in a shabby tuxedo rushed out of the doorway of the Wonder Museum. He stepped up onto a low platform, twisted the ends of his moustache into points and adjusted his bow tie.

"Start talking, already," Leo shouted out.

"Ladies and gentlemen," the talker began.

"Louder!" Leo yelled.

"*Ladies and gentlemen,*" the talker said louder, "presenting Dolly Dimples!"

A woman in tight corkscrew curls, with rouged cheeks and a body like a rhinoceros, wobbled through the door and onto the platform. The wood creaked under her footsteps. She was dressed like a little girl, in a pinafore, and carried a doll. She pouted, then turned around and flipped her ruffled skirt to the audience.

The talker waved his hands like a symphony conductor. "Our Dolly Dimples was a beautiful baby. She's now the great fat lady. Don't make her mad or she'll make you sad. Earn your worth, guess her girth. Free admission if you're right."

"Three hundred, easy," someone called. "Bigger! Three-fifty!" another yelled.

A stagehand wheeled an industrial-size Detecto scale onto the platform. The talker cued Dolly Dimples, and she stepped up onto the scale. The needle swung across the face of the dial, but before it could register her weight, a man standing in front of Leo cupped his hand to his mouth, about to yell out an answer.

Murph and Leo had passed Pershing Wadlow's dozens of times, and they had seen the man now standing in front of Leo guess Dolly Dimples' weight every single time. The scale was fixed, like everything else at the Wonder Museum. The man was a shill planted in the crowd to get people warmed up and ready to fork over their dimes. Everyone likes a winner.

Just as the shill took a lungful of air, Leo kicked him hard in the back of the knee and he stumbled forward.

"Four hundred thirty-seven pounds and not one ounce more!" Leo yelled. The needle stopped and the talker pointed into the crowd.

"A winner, we have a winner! You there —the small gentleman in the brown cap. You, sir, must be a genuine clairvoyant! Come inside, come inside. Your admission to our curio hall of curiosities is free."

Leo pushed through and went straight up to the platform. The talker dangled the ticket in front of Leo's face.

"What's the big idea?" the man said through his teeth.

"Idea?" Leo said loudly, watching Murph circle the crowd, whose eyes were all fixed on Leo. "No idea at all. I'm just a good guesser. Ask anyone between the Hudson and the East River and they'll say that I'm the best guesser they've ever seen put up against a conundrum. The sphinx himself is no match. No riddle is too twisty or too tough. Really, it's not your fault. My Aunt Gertie was one fat lady. She was from Rochester, never got out much. So you see, with all due respect and deference, et cetera, to what you're doing here, mister talker, a good guess isn't really a guess at all. It's just putting two and two together."

Leo swiped the ticket from the talker's hand. The talker leaned down so close Leo could see the grease shine on his moustache.

"You are quite the talker yourself. After you come out the other end of the museum, I won't see you around here again. Understand?"

Leo smirked and turned to go inside, waving the ticket high in the air.

With his free hand, he retrieved a small piece of soap from his pocket. Right before he got to the entrance of the museum, Leo stopped. He made a fake cough and popped the soap into his mouth, working it into a lather with his tongue. The bitter taste made him spit up a little. When his mouth was so foamy it was overflowing with bubbles, he turned back to the crowd, which was now lining up to pay for tickets. People began to stare.

"Oh, my. Are you all right, boy?"

"Poor thing is having a fit! Somebody get help!"

"Why, he's convulsing! He's gone mad!"

Leo started to shake and jerk as if he had been struck by lightning. He rolled his eyes and fell to the ground, kicking and moaning the whole time. A circle of concerned people formed around him. Through their legs he could see Murph's shoes shuffling. It was working beautifully. Leo figured he would wriggle around for another minute or so. Plenty of time for Murph to dart his hands into pockets and drop whatever he found into his own.

Without warning, a hole opened up in the circle. A tall, bald man wearing wire-frame glasses pushed through. Leo opened his eyes wide as the man knelt down.

"Everyone back away. I'm a doctor. Give me room."

Leo shook his head and tried to say he was okay, but with the lather in his mouth, the words came out as a gurgle.

"Don't fight me, son. I'm here to help."

The doctor pinned Leo against the sidewalk. Panicked, Leo looked around for Murph's shoes, but they were gone. He was alone. Leo tried to get up but the doctor pushed him back down. The doctor leaned in. He smelled Leo's breath. Then he patted his back pocket. His eyes narrowed. "You dirty little . . ."

The doctor grabbed Leo by the shirt and hoisted him up off the ground. Leo's feet pedaled in search of concrete. "Everyone, check your pockets," the doctor yelled as he dragged Leo through the crowd. "Look in your purses, make sure your valuables are still on your wrists and around your necks. The kid is a thief!"

Leo spat the froth out of his mouth.

"Honest, I ain't!" Leo cried. "Let me go! I'm epileptic, apoplectic. I get the shakes. I have a condition, I need my pills. Where's my mother? Take me to my mother, she's waiting for me just 'round the corner. Please, doc, let go."

The doctor did not loosen his grip. They were only a few feet from the talker now. His face was red and puffy like a burned thumb. Leo heard the shrill of a police whistle.

Never before had he been so close to being caught. There was no mercy in New York City for street thieves, regardless of age. The inmates in the Tombs would not hesitate to stab you in the eye with a fork for an extra slice of bread. He knew that from the Mayor, and the Mayor's knowledge on such topics was as strong as his fear of going to jail.

Leo thought fast. There was only one thing to do. The idea made him sick, but he had no alternative. Leo shoved his hand into his pocket and grabbed all the money he'd stolen earlier that morning. The lump of bills and coins was heavy. He closed his eyes, said a short prayer and then cursed both Chapter Seven and Harry Houdini. *The Right Way to Do Wrong* promised this would happen to a thief eventually. It was the only part of the book Leo had chosen to ignore. Then he flung the money up into the air.

The people went wild, and in the confusion Leo wrestled his way loose and ran off through an alley, jumping over passed-out hobos and piled-high trash. He ran several blocks more, until the frigid air tore his insides to strips and he stopped to catch his breath.

CHAPTER 2

The Right Way to Do Wrong

On his way to the West Side, Leo paused on street corners, casually looking over his shoulder to make sure he wasn't being followed. He was in no rush to get back to Hell's Kitchen. Murph would explain to the Mayor and Boris what had happened. There was no way they could hold it against him. Still, he knew there would be some grumbling. Especially from Boris. The money Leo had thrown to the crowd was supposed to be for dinner, and if dinner wasn't plentiful, Boris turned sour. Leo hoped that whatever Murph managed to hold on to would be enough to feed them all for the next few days.

The clouds grew dark. A few early flurries drifted in front of him, the flakes disappearing as soon as they touched the ground. In his mind's eye he saw that frostbitten field upstate that he had left behind two years before.

He remembered the fire clawing at the stars dotting the night sky. The orphanage was already caving in on itself. The sound was like bones cracking. Tree branches blocked the light of the fire, creating shadows that looked like a spider web stretching across the Mayor's face.

That was when the Mayor pulled out the book and handed it to Leo: *The Right Way to Do Wrong: An Exposé of Successful Criminals* by Harry Houdini. Leo knew all about Harry Houdini. Who didn't?

Newspapers constantly blasted headlines of his latest amazing escape: from a jail cell, from a locked and shackled steamer trunk dropped to the bottom of a river, and even from a casket buried six feet under the ground.

Leo opened the book to the first page. An illustration of a demon dominated the top half. He flipped through the rest and found it was exactly what the title suggested—a book explaining how criminals executed their crimes.

"Well? Are we in this together, like always?" the Mayor asked.

Leo looked toward the burning building and thought over his future prospects. The nuns would ship three of them off to other orphanages by morning. But not the Mayor. He was almost sixteen. They would force him to become an apprentice carpenter or a baker's trainee or something similar. And before long they would force Leo to do the same. Most of all, Leo knew that he did not want to be separated from his friends.

The Mayor, Boris and Murph had made life in the House of Providence tolerable. The Mayor looked out for his brother, Boris, and had taken Leo under his wing as well. He offered friendship and protection from bullies. When Murph arrived at the House of Providence, it was Leo who brought him into the fold and showed him the ropes. Sometimes he and Murph would fake sick and stay in bed all day while the others went to class. Leo would whisper-read dime novels. And Murph, sitting in the bed next to him, would act them out. Soon their bond became just as solid as the one shared by the Mayor and Boris, who were brothers bound by blood.

Leo gave the book back to the Mayor. He liked what the Mayor had in mind. He'd be with his friends, living an adventure. It would be exciting. It would be all the things they'd daydreamed about—being pirates, explorers, bandits. Hadn't he and Murph stayed up many nights weaving stories of bank robberies and armored-car stickups that they'd pull one day? The timing was perfect.

"I'm in," he said.

The four boys spat and shook on it. Then the Mayor led them through the field, away from the fire. They hitched a ride into town, and from there they hopped trains traveling down the east bank of the

Hudson River until they reached New York City, where they had been living ever since.

In two years, a lot had changed. But some things had not. Ahead, Leo could see the abandoned tenement they called home. The Mayor promised them all that once they had enough money, they would get a real place to stay. It would be heaven. Soft sheets and fluffy pillows, three hot meals a day, pretty maids to come and clean up their mess. But there never *was* enough, and Leo was beginning to understand that the Mayor's promises for a better life weren't necessarily promises the Mayor could keep.

The abandoned tenement had a large sign nailed to the front door: CONDEMNED. A chain and a broken padlock were draped around the handle, but it was all for show. The boys slipped in and out unnoticed, and the only ones who knew they were there were the rodents crawling along the rafters and the pigeons flapping from window to window.

Leo walked through the small foyer, which blocked the view of the inner entrance. The stairs leading to the upper floors were rotted through. Every apartment except the one they occupied was completely gutted. At least they had a closet-sized washroom with a faucet that spurted cold water. What the boys jokingly called the bedroom was in reality a hallway with four cots set up along the walls, left over from previous squatters.

At the door to apartment A5, Leo gave the knock—three hard raps, two quick pounds, three hard raps. There was just one key to the front door, and it never left the chain hanging around the Mayor's neck. When they'd first discovered the building, they'd found the set of keys for apartment A5 and its mailbox sticking comically out of the only intact door on the first floor, as if someone had left for work and forgotten them.

Leo was let into the apartment. The Mayor was screwing a rusty hot plate onto an exposed gas pipe. As he put his ear to the pipe to listen for the whoosh of gas, he looked up at Leo. "Got a match?"

Leo took one out of his pocket and struck it against the wall. He knelt down and touched the tip to the hot plate, and a crown of blue flames burst out. They all sat around it to warm themselves. Boris's wooden leg was placed a safe distance away. There was a deep stillness in the room.

"Why's everyone so glum?" the Mayor asked.

Silence.

"I've got a riddle. First person to get it gets a nickel."

"This is stupid," Boris said. "I'm starving. Let's just get to the greasy spoon for the blue plate special, already. We already had to wait for Prince Leo's return, and now we're just sitting here like a bunch of idiots."

"I want to go to Horn & Hardart," Murph said. "How come I never get to choose?"

Boris gave him a shove.

"You can choose when you grow a brain."

"This brain scored us six bucks today. And a pair of silver cuff links."

"Six bucks barely covers Prince Leo's *laundry* bill. You can't eat cuff links, and ten-to-one they're only silver plated."

"Knock it off, the both of you," the Mayor said. "Leo needs clean clothes. He can't be a *good* crook if he's walking around looking look a *rotten* crook, can he? Anyway, who wants to hear the riddle?"

Leo kept his mouth shut. He hated that the Mayor had to apologize for him. The way Boris said the word "laundry" made him gag. He *did* need those clean clothes. He had earned them. His work was hard. Harder than whatever Boris did all day, anyway.

Leo picked up the copy of *The Right Way to Do Wrong* from the floor next to the Mayor. They had all read it so many times the spine was cracked and the pages were loose.

The Mayor liked Chapter One, "Income of a Criminal." He was fond of late-night stickups in dark downtown alleys. When an opportunity presented, he would jab an unsuspecting Wall Street banker in the back with the Louisville Slugger he had found. Nobody ever suspected that it was not a shotgun.

Murph, wiry and fast, was a natural for Chapter Two, "Professional Burglary." He broke into people's apartments while laundry was being hung on a line or while the woman of the house was out shopping.

Sometimes, when he was feeling especially impatient, he would take advantage of a distracted clerk and reach over the counter to empty the contents of a cash register.

When Boris was ten, he'd snuck out of the orphanage with some other boys and lost a game of chicken against the South Buffalo Railway. Since then he wore a wooden leg. But when he went out to work, he would leave it off and hobble with his crutch on crowded subway platforms. His best days were when he put on sunglasses and groped around the stations pretending to be blind. Chapter Eight, "Beggars and Dead Beats," suited him perfectly.

Leo, to his own surprise, turned out to be the most gifted of the four. Part of it was from studying Chapter Seven, "Pickpockets at Work," over and over. The other part was natural talent. While Murph was fast on his feet, Leo had invisible hands. The entire city was his oyster, from Sugar Hill to the Battery. Everywhere he went, people practically begged him to take their wallets and jewelry—on buses, in waiting rooms, in the park, standing in line for a bank teller so they could get more money which Leo would then take.

"What's put on a table, cut, but never eaten?" the Mayor asked.

Nobody answered.

"Anyone?"

"Whatever we rob?"

"Good guess, Murph. But no. A deck of cards. Get it?"

They all groaned. Leo was only half listening. He was still unsettled from the close call at Pershing Wadlow's Wonder Museum. But it wasn't only one close call that worried him. Lately he'd been wondering how much longer he could do this. There'd been a gnawing in his stomach that wouldn't quit. After two years, getting nowhere fast had become exhausting. He flipped to the back of Houdini's book and skimmed through the last few pages. These were the pages he'd ignored because Houdini's preaching sounded just the same as the nuns at the House of Providence. And he figured that if he didn't think about getting caught it would never happen. But this time certain words jumped off the page: "evil-doing", "sordid life", "disgrace", and "punishment". He slammed the book shut and set it on the floor.

"Leo!" the Mayor said.

Leo looked up.

"What?"

"Hey, cheer up. Today didn't go quite as planned. So let's just move on. Okay? Everybody happy now? You happy, Leo? You happy, Murph? You happy, Boris?"

"No, I'm not happy," Boris said. "Leo messed up today."

"You weren't there, Boris. I'm telling you it wasn't my fault," Leo said.

"Really? Seems to me that Prince Leo has lost his magic touch."

Leo stood up. He felt like grabbing Boris by the collar and shaking him. But the Mayor's eyes told Leo to let it go and that he was still in charge of the gang. He didn't know how much more he could take of Boris's criticisms or of this life they were living. The rope that bound the four of them from their days at the House of Providence was steadily fraying. Something would have to give pretty soon.

"You go on to supper without me. I'll catch up with you guys later," Leo said.

He slipped out the door, leaving them behind. He just wanted to be alone.

Horn & Hardart was bustling, as usual. Leo went in, grabbed a tray and got in line. Leo liked the automat, with all the food selections right there for you to see in glass cases. When he came to the sandwich he wanted, Leo dropped his last nickel into the slot and opened the door of the case to grab it. He settled near the back at an empty table. A few minutes later he saw the Mayor walk in alone. The Mayor piled his tray with macaroni and cheese, beans, sliced steak, two types of pie and coffee. He found Leo in the back and sat across from him.

"Just a cheese sandwich isn't enough. Eat some of this."

Leo took a forkful of beans.

"Where are the others?"

"Boris won out. They went to get the blue plate special. I thought it would be best if everyone took some time and cooled down a little."

Leo appreciated the Mayor coming in and treating him to a big dinner. He smiled. Even back in the orphanage, the Mayor used to save some of his food for Leo, and it had always lifted Leo's spirits. By the time they were mashing their forks in the pie crumbs, Leo felt like his old self again. "Thanks," he said.

"Not a problem."

The Mayor took a gulp of coffee and rolled up his sleeves. The two-inch tattoo of a cricket on his forearm seemed to jump as he did it. The Mayor pointed to it.

"Remember when I got this? At Coney Island?"

That was the day the gang took the Sea Beach Line Express to Surf Avenue. It was a day meant only for fun. They walked to the Dreamland Circus Sideshow and each paid a dime to get into the Congress of Curious People and Living Curiosities. There was Lionel, the Lion-Faced Boy, who had a thick mane of auburn hair growing on his face, and Baron Paucci, the world's smallest man at twenty-four inches tall, and Rob Roy, the albino wonder. They were the real deal. Not like the trash exhibits at Pershing Wadlow's Wonder Museum.

"Of course I remember," Leo said. "Boris threw a fit in Luna Park because they wouldn't let him ride the elephant. And that magic show at the Eden Musée. The guy chewed up sawdust and spat out fireballs. It was incredible. But the whole time you were complaining about how much your arm hurt!"

They laughed together.

"That's right. I never told you guys why I picked the cricket. The tattoo artist told me it was a sign of good luck. I thought we would need it."

He crumpled his napkin and dropped it on the tray. Leo got up to leave but the Mayor grabbed his arm.

"I need you to be working hard."

"I *have* been working hard," Leo said.

What Leo really wanted to say was that *he* was the only one of the gang who had been working hard. Boris was too old to keep on begging. No one sympathized with a grown-up cripple. And Murph was getting soft, losing his nerve, afraid to work solo. The only reason he'd scored some money and cuff links that day was because of Leo's epileptic diversion. And the Mayor. He had stopped going out at night altogether, and when Leo questioned him about it, he grew surly. Now he just gave the orders and did the bookkeeping. The weight of everyone depending upon him was making Leo's shoulders droop. And by the Mayor's accounting, there was never enough savings to make a move, because each week there were a few dollars less than the week before. It seemed more and more like a losing enterprise.

"I know that," the Mayor said. "And I know that Boris gets under your skin. I know him better than anyone. He's my own flesh and blood. He doesn't mean anything by what he says."

"So then what's the problem?"

"Leo, you're smart. Where do you see this heading? We can't stay in that tenement much longer. We'll die. I wake up so cold that I'm afraid my teeth will crack if I bite too hard. Believe me, I've got a plan to change things. The next step is up here," the Mayor said, tapping his head. "But we're not there yet. Soon. Any day."

"You keep saying that. But it's getting harder to swallow each time you say it. And the thing is, I've been thinking maybe there's something else we could do."

"What are you talking about?" the Mayor said.

"I don't know. Maybe we could get money some other way."

"You mean get jobs? No, Leo. My way is easier and faster. It's the best way. It just needs a little more time. I'll roll it out soon enough. But it's not for tonight. I told Boris and Murph we'd meet them at the Orpheum. There's a double screening of *20,000 Leagues Under the Sea* and *Sherlock Holmes*. You're coming, right?"

To Leo, a flat screen was lifeless. And too much sitting still in a theater made him want to run, jump, kick the chair in front of him. The only exception was magic shows. Ever since that day at Coney Island he'd been hooked. But tonight he would go to smooth things over with his friends.

"Yeah, sure, of course I'm coming."

Outside, the newsies were screeching the headlines from the evening paper. Most of them were Leo's age, and some even younger. They hawked papers by day and slept on the sidewalk at night, waiting for the next delivery of bundled newspapers. One of them called out a headline that made Leo stop and turn.

"Extra, extra! Houdini straitjacket escape in Times Square!"

Leo grabbed the *New York Times* from the newsboy's hands.

“H*ey!*”

Leo shoved two pennies at the boy. He scanned the columns full of World War I news about the Western Front and German U-boat aggression. He found the notice about Houdini buried at the bottom of the first page.

Houdini to Perform in Times Square

Harry Houdini, who has several times been prevented by the police from attempting spectacular feats in public, will be strapped into a straitjacket and hauled aloft by the heels at Broadway and Forty-sixth Street at 12:30 o’clock on November 10th. Permission for the feat has been given by the Police Department, as the stunt will be done for the purpose of advertising a patriotic performance to be given at the Hippodrome next Sunday. Houdini will be hauled up by a derrick on the north end of the Times Square subway construction buildings. While in the air he will endeavor to escape from the straitjacket.

Leo imagined Houdini dangling upside down above thousands of people as he struggled his way out of the straitjacket to freedom. The scene in his head was much more exciting than any movie. Nothing would stop him from being there to see it.

CHAPTER 3

Mysteries of the Yogi

On the morning of the show Leo left the tenement while the others slept. The sun was just inching over the buildings. He walked to Times Square and waited by the platform that had been set up for Houdini's stunt. A sea of men in overcoats and felt fedoras swelled around him. Angry motorists blasted their horns in frustration over the gridlock. There was undeniable excitement in the air.

Leo waited for hours as more people packed Times Square. And then, exactly at 12:30, Houdini appeared. An escort of three policemen pushed a way through the throng and led Houdini up to the platform. The crowd cheered, but Leo felt a slight twinge of disappointment. The King of Handcuffs looked nothing like the posters of him outside of theaters. He was shorter and older, with thinning hair. Leo also noticed that he was bowlegged. His face was intense and his mouth drooped into a scowl.

Houdini was not wearing a coat. He removed his necktie, then unbuttoned the top button of his white dress shirt. Houdini presented his arms and two of the policemen slipped on the straitjacket. Leo watched closely as Houdini took several deep breaths, and held the last one until the policemen fastened the back buckles of the straitjacket. *Of course. Makes sense,* Leo thought. Houdini puffed up his chest with air so he'd have more room to wriggle out of the straitjacket when he exhaled.

Next Houdini sat on a chair while his ankles were secured by ropes that hooked onto the crane. The policemen supported his body as the chair was slipped out from under him. They propped him up until the winch lifted him high enough in the air that he was hanging upside down. It lifted him about fifty feet above his audience, where he swayed like a chrysalis in the middle of the city.

He started to thrash and jackknife his body upward. Leo looked around. Everyone in the crowd was straining to watch. As Houdini spasmed and twisted, Leo's pulse raced. What if this was the one time he couldn't get out of the straitjacket? Or what if the ropes slipped free from the crane and Houdini fell to his death? Houdini was a famous magician, but this was not magic. It was more like a circus daredevil act.

The crowd cheered when one of Houdini's arms slipped free. It was then that Leo noticed the man standing in front of him. He inched closer to get a better look. The man was tall, and well-dressed. The strong scent of the tonic in his slicked-back hair reminded Leo of pine trees upstate. Leo could hear the rustle of Houdini trying to break out of the straitjacket above. But now he was focused on something else. A perfect opportunity to make up for the disaster at the Wonder Museum.

Instinct took over. Leo pushed into the man. While pretending to peer over his shoulder to get a better look at Houdini, Leo slipped his hand into the man's pocket. When he had the wallet he shoved his way backward through the crowd toward Broadway. The Palace Theater had a real magic show going on in half an hour. Leo turned around for a brief moment. The man whose pocket he'd picked was patting down his coat and trousers.

As Leo reached the edge of the crowd he heard the spectators yell, "He's done it!" Leo looked back.

"Two minutes and thirty-seven seconds," a man on the platform announced through a megaphone. Houdini was lowered to the stage. He took a bow and was promptly escorted from the platform by the police officers.

Leo rushed to the Palace Theater. The show was expensive—a quarter for a seat in the upper mezzanine. But if the *Black Magic Mys-*

teries of the Yogi was half as good as the program promised, it would be worth it. Everything inside the Palace Theater was golden and ornate. The columns were intricately carved and the walls were painted with scenes of Greek gods on Mount Olympus. The deep red carpet was thick. At the top of the stairs an enormous chandelier hung from the ceiling like a colossal jewel.

Leo walked around the people idling by the doors and gave his ticket to the usher. He kept the stub and slid it into his pocket next to the wallet he had just stolen. The usher escorted Leo to his seat in the middle of the mezzanine, where he had a clear view of the stage. The soft velvet seat enveloped him. People were chattering all around him and a spotlight raced across the crowd that packed the orchestra level. After a few minutes the lights dimmed and the audience got quiet.

A screen dropped down from above the stage and bright lights flickered behind Leo. The organ player in the orchestra struck a few dramatic chords as a newsreel about the war blinked onto the screen. The first title read OUR BOYS IN THE FRENCH TRENCHES and was followed by footage of soldiers at ease, leaning their rifles against trench walls. Their helmets covered their faces as they ate greedily from tins of food. The next title read GERMAN ARTILLERY STRIKES and the screen cut to clouds of smoke and dirt blowing over the trenches and rocks flying every which way. An ambulance streaked across the screen. The organ reached a fever pitch as the title on the screen read THE ALLIED RESPONSE, which was followed by scenes of soldiers in the trenches lining up cannons and loading them. Together the cannons recoiled and smoke filled the screen as the shells were shot off into enemy territory. The organ player stopped and the newsreel sputtered to a halt. A few moments passed while the projectionist changed reels.

Leo took out the wallet. His usual practice was to clean out the contents and toss away the pinched wallet. But this one was nice. It felt expensive, with raised bumps over the tan leather hide. Why not keep it? Maybe they could get a few bucks for it at thieves' alley. He hunched over and peeked inside. It contained some folded pieces of paper and at least thirty dollars in cash. He slipped the wallet back into his pocket, happy with his morning's work. The Mayor would be pleased, too. Thirty dollars would feed them for a good while.

Suddenly, a countdown was thrown up on the screen. 3. 2. 1. A Chinese man stood in the center of the frame. His long robes hung to the ground. He stared intently at the camera. His gaze did not reveal any emotion, but his stare was hypnotic. A title came up: THE GLORIOUS CHUNG LING SOO, WORLD FAMOUS MAGICIAN, ENDS HIS STAY AT LONDON'S ALHAMBRA THEATRE.

The next screen told the man's life story.

> *Chung Ling Soo, the Chinese conjuror, is a combination of East and West. His father was a Scotch missionary named Campbell, and his mother a Chinese girl from Canton. The name Chung Ling Soo means* "Extra Good Luck." *Chung Ling Soo has been around the world more times than Columbus.*

The screen cut to a scene of two men loading rifles. The title read CHUNG LING SOO PERFORMS DEFYING THE BULLETS. Chung Ling Soo held a ceramic plate against his chest. The men raised their guns, aimed, and shot. After a burst of light, Chung Ling Soo staggered back a step, then steadied himself. Leo stiffened in his seat. Onto the plate Chung Ling Soo spat out one bullet, and then, with much fanfare, the second bullet. The final title read CHUNG LING SOO WILL TRIUMPHANTLY RETURN TO AMERICA SOON. Then at once all the lights in the theater went off.

Leo watched the stage for any movement, half hoping the Chinese magician would materialize right then and there. The theater was as black as a coal mine. A violin struck up a sweeping theme and out of nowhere a yogi appeared. He wore a white turban and a flowing white tunic. His long black beard made a V shape over his clothing. From Leo's perspective the yogi looked like he was floating in the middle of the theater, since everything else was black.

The yogi raised his arm. On the ground a white wand emerged from the darkness and floated into his open hand. With the wand, the yogi tapped the air in several spots. Each time he tapped, a white bone was left behind. After a dozen taps, a skeleton stood next to him. The yogi turned and walked across the stage, with the skeleton jangling behind. He turned left and right and the skeleton matched his every move. He could not escape, pacing the stage frantically, trying to avoid the monster he had just created. Finally he swung his wand at the skeleton and it fell to pieces. The yogi pulled a white cloth from his sleeve and draped it over the mound of bones. When he pulled it off the bones were gone.

"Hey!" a raspy whisper broke Leo's concentration. "Hey. Psst. Leo!"

Leo knew the voice but ignored it, hoping Boris would just go away. Leo's ear was flicked. He turned around in his seat. Boris's mouthful of stale breath caught him in the face.

"Get up. We need you."

"Quiet!" Onstage the yogi had created a window with his wand and was about to pull something through it. "I'm watching the show."

The man sitting next to Leo gave him a shove.

"You two, shut up!"

Boris yanked Leo's collar. Leo sighed. He got up and shuffled into the aisle. Leo heard the audience gasp and then clap so loudly it sounded like a thunderstorm inside the theater. He turned around but the trick was already over. He turned back and helped Boris onto the stairs. At each step Boris swung his wooden leg wide.

"How did you know where I was?" Leo said.

"It's Saturday, Palace Theater magic show day. Where else would you be?"

"You bought a ticket just to get me?" Leo asked.

Boris laughed. "Of course not. The usher took pity on me when I showed him my war injury," he said, rapping on his wooden leg. "Although he told me if there were no seats left I'd have to stand. Jerk."

When they hit the street Leo walked briskly to annoy Boris, who could move only so fast without the help of a crutch. He was angry about being dragged out of the show. At the door of the hideout, Leo gave the knock. The door cracked open and an arm with a tattoo of a cricket shot out and pulled Leo inside the hallway. The Mayor beamed at Leo as he sat down on his cot. Boris finally caught up and limped in. He slammed the door behind him and took off his leg.

Leo turned to the Mayor. "Whatever it is you cooked up this time, I'm sure it could have waited. No one interrupts *you* when you're playing cards in the saloon. No one drags *you* by the collar while a yogi is onstage."

"*Yogi?* Leo, get your priorities straight. Everything we've been waiting for . . . it's happening now. We're about to move into a mansion, practically. I'll lay it out just as soon as Murph gets here. He should have been back an hour ago."

The Mayor paced back and forth through the parlor, rubbing his hands and tapping his feet, seeming to count time with all his body. The chilly November air leaked into the building from tiny cracks in the walls and loose windows.

Then, a sound at the door. A knock. The wrong knock. Leo's guts tied up into knots. This was how it was going to end. The knock came again, the person now pounding at the door. Boris cursed.

Leo imagined what must have happened: Murph running straight into a cop and falling backward, all the cash he had just stolen falling out of his pockets. Poor Murph, he always got so nervous. When he started talking he never knew when to stop. Leo figured that after five minutes of interrogation, Murph probably spilled the beans about everything—the gang, the hideout. The cops had come to arrest them all. He could feel cold handcuffs circling his wrists.

The Mayor's massive arm reached out toward the Louisville Slugger leaning against his bed. He gripped the bat and stood up. The sounds of people hollering and bottles clinking could be heard from Keeley's Saloon next door. Small slow-moving flies buzzing in the slants of light shining through the boarded-up windows were the only other things moving in the room. The Mayor crept toward the door with the bat raised over his head. If it was the cops outside, Leo didn't want to get nabbed with the wallet he'd just stolen, so he slipped it under his mattress.

"Hey guys, it's me, open up!"

They all let out a sigh of relief as the Mayor opened the door. Murph looked around at his friends. "What took you so long?"

"You didn't do the knock, numbskull," Boris said. "We thought we were getting raided."

"Huh? The knock is stupid anyway. What's the point? You bust in, or you don't. I knock, you guys say 'Who is it,' I say 'It's me,' end of story."

The Mayor dropped the bat and grabbed Murph around the neck, holding him tight. The tattoo of a cricket on his forearm squirmed as he dragged Murph into the hallway. The Mayor pushed him down onto one of the beds, then dug his fingers into Murph's shoulders, squeezing the pressure points. Murph winced.

"Remember when I came up with the knocking system? Do you remember why? It lets us know that whoever is on the outside knocking is one of us," the Mayor said.

The Mayor leaned closer. His face was inches from Murph's. "I'm just trying to look out for everybody," he whispered.

"That's enough," Leo said, pushing the Mayor away from Murph. "Knock it off."

"Don't interfere," the Mayor said, poking a finger at Leo's chest. A vein trembled under the tight skin on his forehead. Leo had seen the Mayor get like this more often lately. Just as Boris always had it in for Leo, the Mayor vented all of his frustrations on Murph. And Murph was an easy target who never fought back. But Leo hated seeing Murph pushed around by the Mayor. This was the opposite of why they'd all gotten together in the first place.

Murph got off the cot and rolled his shoulders.

"Just lay off. He gets it," Leo said.

"Yeah, I get it," Murph said. "Besides, I brought presents."

The Mayor stood back. He let his snarl relax and composed himself.

"Well, that changes everything. Let's check the books."

He pulled a chain of keys from under his shirt and walked out to the hall to the row of bronze mailboxes built into the wall. He opened the box for apartment A5, took out a black box and brought it to his cot. With another key from his chain he opened the box. Boris, Leo and Murph crowded around. Inside was a thin roll of bills, maybe twenty bucks all in, and a ledger book and a pencil. Murph handed over some loose change and a few bills. The Mayor counted it up and wrote it down in his book. Boris frowned.

"Not much."

"Wait, I've got something else," Murph said.

He fished in his other pocket and pulled out a pocket watch. "This pocket watch might be worth something. I think it's gold. Look, it's got some guy's name engraved on it—Horace Chadwick, June 3, 1882."

"Which means we can't sell it to a pawn shop," Boris said. "Since we can't prove we're Horace Chadwick, it will be obvious that the thing is stolen."

"Well, then we won't go to a pawn shop, genius."

"It doesn't matter," the Mayor said, lowering his voice. "Forget the watch. Tonight we're making our big move. Thousands of bucks on the table. You'll see."

CHAPTER 4

Don't Disappoint the Dropper

When the singing finally died down in the saloon next door in the late hours of the night, Leo and the Mayor found Jack the Dropper waiting for them at a table close to the wood-burning stove. The barman wiped up spills on the other side of the room, paying them no attention as they entered. Leo's feet shuffled on the sawdust-covered floor. Jack's pudgy face remained unchanged, bored and distant, when they sat down.

Jack the Dropper's reputation was well known. He was a gambler and a gunman, a con man and a slugger. He was all the things that Leo didn't want to be. Stealing was an art, a delicate balancing act. The only art the Dropper knew was the bicycle-riding Cupid on the back of a deck of cards.

The three of them sat in silence until the Dropper croaked a groggy *har har har* and fished something out of his teeth with a splinter from the table. The stove next to them crackled and threw off intense heat. Leo felt flushed.

"The neighborhood kids I've heard so much about. Here they are right in front of me. That's what I like about the youth these days. They have the entrepreneurial spirit."

"Thanks for giving us the opportunity," the Mayor said. "We're ready for the big time."

"All right, Mr. Big Time, wait here a minute."

The Dropper left Leo and the Mayor alone. Leo was angry. When Leo began picking pockets for the Mayor, he'd never felt like he was doing something bad or illegal. He *knew* it was, but it had never *felt* wrong. *This* felt wrong.

"You should never have agreed to this without asking us first," Leo said. "This was your big plan all along? You said we were going to rob a card game, not join a gang."

"Maybe we didn't discuss this plan exactly, but it's golden, trust me. The Dropper told me he's got half the city police force under his thumb, especially the ones on the Lower East Side and Chinatown. He said the cops in Chinatown are as crooked as the tong members. I see it this way: if we become part of his crew, we'll have protection if we ever get pinched. We'll have no worries about ever getting locked up."

When the Dropper came back he had a piece of paper in his hand. He slid it across the table to the Mayor.

"This is the address. The password to get into the game is 'rutabaga.' Make sure yous got some dough. Yous can't walk into a stuss game without dough, even if yous are just going to rob it. Yous even know how to play stuss?"

"Sure. The thirteen spades are laid out on the table. You place your bet on your lucky number. The first card drawn is the winner, the second is the loser. If your card didn't get drawn, your bet rolls over to the next round. Easy."

The Droper laughed. "So is it correct to assume yous guys got your own firepower?"

"Firepower?" Leo asked.

He felt his foot being kicked under the table.

"Yeah, we got plenty. Don't worry about that," the Mayor said.

"Good. When it's done, you ring me up at the phone number on that slip of paper. The split is seventy-five percent going to me, and yous splitting up the rest of the take. Don't try to come in here with money skimmed off the top, because I'll know it. Sound fair?"

"Sixty-forty or nothing."

Jack the Dropper made a weak smile. "I like you, kid. You got heart. What's your name again?"

"They call me the Mayor."

The Dropper belched out another *har har har.* "Terrific. See you soon, Mayor. You won't disappoint me, will you?"

"We won't."

"Good. Because if yous foul up, and, say, Kid Jigger starts working you over, and maybe you let slip that it was me that sent yous to knock over his game, we'll have a very big problem." With that Jack the Dropper got up, put on his coat and left the saloon.

Leo looked at the Mayor. "Firepower? Are you nuts? You said the game was easy pickings. You said they don't even allow guns inside! You said we would just have to knock out the guard up front and we'd be in and out."

"Well, maybe I just sort of guessed at that part."

"So what the hell are we going to do now?"

The Mayor ran his hands through his hair and shook them, as if trying to jolt a thought loose. "I got it! Remember those firecrackers you got for New Year's last year? We've got some left, right? We'll set them off. When the guard looks to see what's going on, you'll knock him out."

"What do you mean *me* knock him out? You're the muscle. I don't want to hit somebody in the head. What if I knock him out permanently? I want out of this," Leo said.

The Mayor put a hand on Leo's shoulder. "Listen, there's nothing to worry about. Just don't swing so hard. Once you're in, you set off more firecrackers, everyone ducks and we'll take the money on the table. Easy. I'll be there the whole time. I'm not going to leave you hanging. Okay? Just do this for me and we'll be on our way."

Leo felt as if his feet were snagged on a rope attached to a ship at sea. Or worse, an anchor.

CHAPTER 5

Firepower

They stood outside the factory in the Garment District where Kid Jigger held his stuss game and went over the plans a final time. The Mayor took a deep breath and handed Leo his Louisville Slugger. They all looked at each other. A few moments passed. No one was ready to make a move. Finally the Mayor slapped his hands together.

"Well. I guess this is it." The Mayor turned.

"Wait," Leo said, pulling him back. "There's still time to back out."

"Yeah," Murph said. "This isn't how we do things."

"Don't be nervous, boys," the Mayor said. "How we do things is getting us nowhere. Now get your heads straight and stay on your toes."

He squeezed their shoulders and walked away. Leo, Murph and Boris went to a mailbox nearby and crouched behind it. Leo poked his head over the top to watch the Mayor pound on the factory door. A slot on the door slid open. A moment later the door opened wide and the Mayor walked in. Leo could feel Boris breathing heavily next to him.

Leo's hands tingled as he walked up to the door, the bat firm in his grasp. He leaned against the wall next to the door. The sizzle of a fuse came a few seconds later as Boris tossed a small handful of firecrackers. Leo counted down in his head. Before he got to zero the firecrackers went *pop pop pop pop pop* like a ghost gunfight in front of him.

Eyes appeared in the slot on the door. "What's going on out here?"

Leo yelled, "Kid Jigger's been shot!"

As the door flung open, Leo saw the enormous guard in front of him and he swung. The crack made his stomach sick, but the giant guard fell without a sound. In a second, Boris and Murph were behind him.

Leo knelt down, and to his great relief found the guard was still breathing. In fact, lightly snoring. Leo searched his pockets and took his billfold. When he threw open the flaps of his jacket, he found a large revolver sitting high up in a holster under the guard's armpit. He stared at it for only a few seconds, but it felt much longer. He didn't want the thing. He didn't even want to touch it. But if the guard woke up, the whole plan could spiral out of control. Boris would not be able to handle him alone. Leo cautiously took the revolver out of the holster and stuck it in the waistband of his pants.

Boris took the bat and used it to prop open the door, keeping a lookout while Leo and Murph dragged the guard behind a rack of coats. Leo's arms and feet were moving fast, but he felt as if he had no control over them, like a marionette whose strings were being plucked by someone high above him.

Leo and Murph crept stealthily through the rows of sewing machines and rolls of fabric, working their way to the back of the factory floor where a single lamp illuminated a table with about two dozen men standing around it. They could hear the dealer asking for bets to be placed. Leo and Murph silently nodded to each other and lit the smoke bomb and remaining firecrackers. *One, two, three,* Leo mouthed, then they lobbed them toward the table. There was barely any time for the gamblers to figure out what was going on before the firecrackers exploded.

"Everyone scram," the Mayor yelled. "It's a raid!"

Leo and Murph watched as the men scrambled like drowning rats to get out the back door. They ran up to the gambling table where the Mayor was waiting for them. The dealer remained, trying to scoop up the cash. He saw the kids and immediately figured out the score.

"You brats think you can come in here and bust up Kid Jigger's game? Get lost before you get into some real trouble. Half these guys are probably on the horn with him already. Your skins ain't worth a penny."

"Leo, gimme the bat," the Mayor yelled. "We gotta knock this sucker out!"

The bat was with Boris, propping open the door. Leo panicked. He reached inside his coat, pulled out the heavy metal and pointed it. The dealer's face turned a bluish milky color, except for his eyes, which were red-rimmed and twitchy.

"Money, now," Leo said.

"Hold on a minute, kid. Put that thing away."

"*Now!*"

Murph and the Mayor grabbed all the cash on the table and what was in the dealer's hands, then ran as fast as they could. When Boris saw them coming, he pushed open the door and grabbed the bat. The Mayor scooped up his brother and threw him over his shoulder. They ran until they were all out of breath. The Mayor put Boris down and put his arm around Leo.

"Well, I guess I can't say you never surprise me. *That* is what I was talking about, Leo. Guts."

Back in their hideout, the Mayor counted up the loot—nearly seven hundred dollars. Their portion of the money would be enough to set them up in a decent apartment for half a year. But Leo didn't care about the money. His hands were locked into a claw shape and he felt raw inside.

"Here, take this. Lock it up. I don't want it around me."

He shoved the gun at the Mayor, business end pointed down.

"Sure, sure. Take it easy, Leo."

The Mayor put the gun in the mailbox for A5.

"Time to meet Jack the Dropper. Leo, come with me. A little air will do you good."

They walked around the block and found a fleabag hotel with a phone booth in the lobby. The call was quick. They were to meet at the Dropper's hideout on Twenty-fifth Street. Be there in fifteen minutes. Don't be late.

"When we tell the Dropper how things went down, he's going to look at us completely differently. We'll have respect," the Mayor said. He tried to hide his smile but his lips curled up anyway.

"I don't care about the Dropper's respect. You promised that this job was about one thing only. Getting enough dough together so we won't freeze to death this winter," Leo said.

"You're not seeing the big picture, Leo. Just trust me."

The boys entered a store on Twenty-fifth Street and went all the way to the back. They knocked on the door marked PRIVATE and waited. The door opened, revealing a small office and two guys in sharp suits sitting with the Dropper.

"It's our friend the Mayor. Come on in. How did your stuss game turn out?"

The Mayor beamed. "Great," he said.

"Fork it over," the Dropper said.

The Mayor dumped the cash on the Dropper's desk. He counted it and placed the bills in piles. When he was done he looked up. "Yous still here?"

The Mayor let out a nervous laugh. "We'll be out of your hair once we get our cut. Sixty-forty or nothing."

"Cut, cut . . . oh yeah. Well, about your cut. You can take it one of two ways. One, I can have Johnny Boy over here cut your ears off. Or two, I can have Dopey Jacky behind you cut out your tongue. Your choice."

Leo closed his eyes and listened to the blood running through his body. He felt like a rabbit with its foot caught in a steel trap waiting for what he knew was going to come next. This was it—the defining moment in his short and wild life when all doubts vanished. He had to quit—wanted to quit—to walk away and start over, to stop the stealing and the lying, and to give up being such a low-down no-good thug.

"We did everything you wanted. You can't do that," the Mayor said, trying to sound convincing.

"Why not?" the Dropper said.

"Because if we don't show up back home, our crew will come looking for us. They've got firepower."

"The more the merrier. Hey, Johnny, Jacky," the Dropper said. "Go sharpen your knives."

"Sure, boss," they said in unison.

"Just let us go," Leo said, quietly. "We won't tell anyone what happened. We promise."

Leo's eyes darted around the room. Dopey Jacky and Johnny Boy cracked their knuckles.

"I'll tell you what," the Dropper said, kicking his legs up on the table. "I'll let one of yous go. It don't matter to me who stays. Yous pick."

Leo turned to the Mayor. "You rotten bastard!"

Leo's arm swung and his fist landed squarely on the Mayor's eye. With that, the two boys were on each other. The Mayor grabbed Leo's thin neck and squeezed, thumbs digging into the windpipe. They fell to the floor. Leo kicked and bucked. He smashed his head forward into the Mayor's nose. Bitter metallic-tasting blood trickled into Leo's mouth and he spat it back out. The Mayor released Leo's neck and began blindly swinging, hitting Leo hard in the guts, knocking all the air out. Leo rolled over onto all fours and gagged for breath. The Mayor came down on his back with a shoe and Leo collapsed.

"Get these animals outta here," the Dropper said. "They're bloodying up my floor. Buncha imbeciles. Don't you idiot kids know how to take a joke? I was gonna give yous a cut, but now I've changed my mind." He pushed them to the door. Dopey Jacky opened it.

"Get lost. And don't come back."

The Dropper slammed the door behind them. Leo limped to the front of the shop, with the Mayor close behind him. They walked to the end of the block and turned to face each other. Leo had barely gotten his wind back.

"I had it under control," the Mayor howled. "We could've come away with something. Now we've got nothing! What got into you?"

"I'm done. I don't care about the Dropper, or big scores," Leo said. "I'm not picking pockets anymore, either."

Leo looked straight into the Mayor's eyes. Gone was the look of anger. What he saw now was confusion and hurt. The Mayor seemed genuinely upset. Leo felt a pang of regret in his stomach. He hadn't really thought about what it would mean, being on his own. A few streetcars rolled noisily past them.

"What's gotten into you? You suddenly turn into a choirboy? Okay, so it didn't work out with the Dropper, but we'll figure something out. You'll see. It'll all be all right."

Leo shook his head. "You're not listening to me. I can't live like this anymore. I'm done with a life of crime."

"What are you going to do, huh? Hawk newspapers? Sell rotten apples? Work in a factory, get your fingertips clipped by some machine?"

Leo shrugged. "I don't know what I'm going to do. But I've got to do something else. All I know is that I don't want to be sent to prison or wind up dead."

The Mayor smirked.

"Aren't you the one, suddenly developing a conscience."

Leo said nothing. But the Mayor was right. It was his conscience that had caught up with him. Houdini's words from the back section of *The Right Way to Do Wrong* finally proved true.

The space between him and the Mayor seemed to grow. Leo waited for a punch or a shove.

"Well, we don't need you anyway!" the Mayor yelled at him. "I always knew you were a coward, Leo. You'll never make it by yourself. Even at the orphanage, you were nothing without me around. And you're nothing now!"

Leo felt sick. "Just listen to me," he said in a small voice. "I'll earn money some other way and I'll share it with you all."

But the Mayor had turned away, walking toward the tenement. Leo pulled his coat tight around him. The cold air stung the cuts on his knuckles as he walked. Each step seemed like a mile.

CHAPTER 6

A Fresh Start

Leo roamed the streets until early morning. It was freezing and steam drifted from manholes like phantoms. There was a hush that blanketed everything. The buildings looming over Leo were like impossibly tall mountains. Even though he knew exactly where he was, he felt lost, like he was floating in some terrible underworld. He watched the sun crawl through the valleys of the streets to the east as the city slowly stirred. He eventually made it back to the tenement. He needed to make it official. He would explain to the others why he was out—especially Murph. He owed him that much. He knew the Mayor and Boris were a lost cause, but maybe he could convince his best friend to leave the dangerous life behind.

In the foyer of the hideout, as he lifted his fist to give the knock, he heard an argument going on inside. Murph was talking very fast, and then Boris and the Mayor spoke over him. Leo put his ear to the door.

"What happened last night was proof that Leo has changed. We can't trust him anymore. Sabotage a payout? What kind of a friend does that? He's no member of this gang, not anymore. I don't care if *he* says he's out, *I'm* the one throwing *him* out. He's a danger to us all. What if it was *me* that didn't come back last night?" the Mayor said. "Think about that, Murph. Who would take care of you then?"

"I don't know," Murph hedged. " I just know that Leo is no thief. Well, at least not from us. He would never do that."

"Forget it," the Mayor said. "If we're ever going to get ahead, we need to focus and be a real crew. I've got plans for us. Big plans."

Leo could hear the Mayor's voice rise and fall as he paced around the apartment.

"But I bet if you asked him, he'd tell you why he stashed the wallet under the mattress," Murph said. "I know he's got a good explanation."

That wallet. Leo had forgotten all about it.

"Just do as you're told. We're sticking to what we discussed."

When the conversation died down, Leo gave the knock. Boris opened the door but blocked the doorway with his body. Leo looked over his shoulder into the parlor. Murph fidgeted with his hands and looked all around the room.

"Are you going to let me in?" Leo asked.

"By all means." Boris didn't move. Leo pushed him to the side of the hallway and flopped on his bed. The cushion on the cot slumped under his weight.

"Good of you to show up," the Mayor said. "Where've you been?"

"Yeah. Nowhere."

"Got something you want to tell us?" Boris asked.

"I'm leaving. I'm done picking pockets. The little taste I got last night of armed robbery is still turning my stomach. I won't be hanging around for the next job only to get picked up for attempted murder."

"What are you going to do?" Murph asked.

"I'm not sure," Leo said. "I've got a few ideas."

While he was out walking all night, Leo didn't have to think very hard to realize the one thing he liked best about living in New York City: the Palace Theater. Sitting in those theater seats, watching the Saturday magic shows, was his relief from the daily pressure of providing for them all. Once he said his good-byes to the gang, he'd find a boarding house with cheap cots, then apply for a job at the theater. Maybe he could be an usher or, if he were lucky, a stagehand.

"So this is it? Forever?" Murph asked.

"Come with me, Murph. You don't want this life, I know it."

The Mayor put his hand on Murph's shoulder.

"Murph's staying right where he is," the Mayor said.

Leo looked at Murph, trying to make him understand he had a choice.

"But," the Mayor continued, "if what you want is to leave, then I guess we couldn't change your mind if we tried, right?"

"Right," Leo answered. "And besides, that's not what you want anyway. There's no sense pretending. I overheard everything from the foyer."

The Mayor smirked. "Okay, you got me there. I was upset and I needed to blow off steam. But everything's okay now. We just need you to do us one little favor, and then you're free. No strings," the Mayor said.

"What is it?"

"We just need you to come to Chinatown with us. Since we're going to be a crew of three, I came up with a plan to help us work better. None of us wants to carry around the gun. You're right, it's too dangerous. So we were thinking we could use more fireworks, the good stuff. Smoke bombs, salutes. From now on we'll cut the fuses short and anytime we run into a close call—*BAM!* But we used up all we had knocking over the stuss game. Where did you get them the first time?"

"A little shop on Pell Street. You can't miss it."

"Great. You can show us where."

"Why do we all have to go?"

"Come on, Leo," the Mayor said. "Come with us, for old times' sake. What's another hour?"

"Okay, then. But I want to set the record straight about something. So you don't think I'm the scum you were ranting about. The wallet under the mattress. I wasn't holding out on any of you. Remember when Murph forgot the knock and was pounding on the door? I thought it was a raid, so I stashed it where it would be safe."

"That explains a lot," Boris said. "Thanks for clearing that up. After all, we're still like family."

"Sorry about what I said," the Mayor said. "Accept my apology?"

"Sure, no hard feelings. But before I leave for good, I think a few bucks coming my way is fair. I'm not asking for much, just something to hold me until I get things squared away."

The Mayor stuck out his hand for Leo to shake.

"Of course. What's fair is fair. We'll take care of you after Chinatown. Okay?"

CHAPTER 7

Smoke and Mirrors

They took the Ninth Avenue el downtown and got off at Franklin Street. The foursome walked in a staggered formation with Murph up front, Leo in the middle and the Mayor and Boris in the rear. As they penetrated the heart of Chinatown, the streets narrowed and people walked slower. Rows of Chinese paper lanterns and flapping American flags were strung above the sidewalk. Men chattered in Cantonese while hand-rolling cigars in front of a tea shop. Peddlers sold produce from the backs of their horse-drawn wagons. "Singsong girls" in brightly colored silk costumes escorted opium addicts to basement dens.

They passed a group of Chinese men standing on the corner of Pell and Doyers. The sign on the building behind them read HIP SING ASSOCIATION. Each man had a queue braided from the middle of his scalp. They wore black collarless jackets with baggy pajama pants and flat slippers with curled-up toes. The Hip Sing Association was the largest of the tongs in Chinatown. Along with the Four Brothers and the On Leong Tong, they were supposed to help new Chinese immigrants get accustomed to life in America. They started businesses, dealt with the government and helped the elderly. But they were also rival gangs with their hands in opium, extortion and countless other shady operations. Their turf wars made headlines especially when bodies littered Doyers street.

Boris dropped back from the others as they neared the middle of the block on Pell Street. He stopped at a fruit vendor to buy some apples and four bags of lychee nuts.

"Where's this firecracker place?" Boris asked as he caught up with them.

"Just up ahead," Leo answered.

"We don't all need to go into the shop, might make the owner nervous," the Mayor said.

He pressed three quarters into Leo's hand.

"That should buy enough firepower for starters," the Mayor said. "We'll be waiting for you right here."

"Here, Leo," Boris said, holding out a bag of lychees. "Your favorites."

Leo nodded his thanks, then shoved the bag into his pants pocket. He left the Mayor, Murph and Boris standing in front of the Wing Sing Teahouse. When Leo was about twenty-five feet away from the shop, he heard Boris and the Mayor laughing. He turned around and saw them pointing at a fishmonger trying to capture frogs that had jumped out of a barrel. A Chinese man wearing a business suit and a derby hat walked in front of the Mayor and took a seat in the teahouse in front of the large window facing the street.

As Leo entered the shop, bells attached to the door chimed. The shopkeeper, an old man with white hair and lined skin, was busy with a customer. He gestured for Leo to sit on the only chair in the room. Leo obeyed and a cloud of dust rose from the faded cushion of the overstuffed chair.

Leo waited impatiently, tapping a foot, while the shopkeeper wound string around packages for the customer. As they concluded their business, the shopkeeper and customer bowed deeply to each other. The customer turned around and gestured Leo toward the counter. He was dressed in a pin-striped suit. A huge diamond ring sparkled on his pinky finger.

Leo approached the counter and looked down through the glass top of the display case. He saw dried herbs and small sea creatures in jars, long sticks of incense, carved pieces of light green jade and two small shiny gold figurines displayed on a satin pouch. They looked like dogs, but with very strange faces. One had a paw positioned on top of a globe and the other had a paw resting on what Leo assumed was a puppy.

"What are those? Dogs?" Leo asked.

"Not dogs," the shopkeeper answered. "These are ancient lions. Guardians of the Forbidden City. Very powerful. They protect and keep away evil spirits."

"Can I see them?" Leo asked.

The shopkeeper took them out of the case and set them on the glass countertop. Leo picked up the figures. They were heavy and cold to the touch.

"How much?" Leo asked.

"They're gold. They come from far away. From Peking."

"How much?"

"Ten dollars."

Leo opened his fist and looked at the coins.

"Maybe another time."

"So. Do you want something else?" the old man asked. "Or are you just leaving hand prints on my glass?"

"Firecrackers and smoke bombs. As many as fifty cents will buy."

The shopkeeper viewed Leo with a suspicious eye.

"What do you intend to do with these?" he asked affably.

Leo pushed the money on the counter toward the shopkeeper.

"Some matches too, please," he said.

The shopkeeper gave Leo a few strike-anywhere matches. Leo thanked him and left the shop. He looked down the street. By now it was dusk. He could see the gang all together down the block. The Mayor and Boris were huddled around the policeman, all pointing in Leo's direction. Murph stood off to the side and looked around shiftily. Droplets of sweat formed at the base of Leo's neck and rolled down his back. His shirt clung to his skin. His fears were confirmed when Boris yelled from across the street, "That's the thief!"

A whistle blew. "Stop! Police!"

Leo grabbed two smoke bombs from the box and dropped the rest on the street. He ran past a group of old ladies to the other side of Pell Street. Leo moved quickly, trying to blend in with the crowd on the street. He didn't see the man in front of him pushing the wheelbarrow stacked with wicker cages of chickens. Leo rammed into him, toppling the cages. The man shouted and chicken feathers flew everywhere.

The Mayor and the cop chased after Leo but the flapping chickens blocked their way. Leo ran as fast as he could around the corner. The street bent at a sharp angle at the intersection, and he got disoriented. Leo turned around. The cop was closing in on him. As he rounded the bend he heard the Mayor shout, "There he is! Get him!"

Leo was trapped. He saw a sign for the Chinese Midnight Mission. He unwrapped the smoke bombs and with his left hand struck one of the matches on the sole of his shoe. The match smoldered as it broke in two. He struck another one. It burst into flame. He lit the smoke bombs and tossed both straight at the approaching cop. Leo covered his nose and mouth with his sleeve as black smoke billowed in front of him and filled the street. He rushed toward what he thought was the mission door. He pushed hard and his pants tore at the knees as he stumbled down steps.

Leo had entered some kind of underground passage. It was pitch-black. He took small steps until he lost his footing when the hallway narrowed and twisted. He squinted and strained to focus, but it was too dark. All he could do was move forward with his arms outstretched and feel for the wall. Leo gagged as the smell of decay filled his nostrils. He had no idea where the tunnel led, but there was no going back.

Leo grazed his head on the ceiling of earth. His eyes stung from the dirt falling into them. A current of air blew around him. Then he heard some sounds of the street. The tunnel widened and light came in through a hatch above a set of six wooden stairs. Leo pushed up on the hatch and walked out to the lobby of a building. He rubbed his eyes as sunlight streaked in from the open door. Someone was holding it open.

"Patrolman Quinn, look what we have here."

It was the Chinese man who had been in the teahouse. Standing behind him was the policeman who had given chase.

"Yes, Officer Chang. It appears that our groundhog has surfaced."

Leo saw the badges glint on their lapels. They slammed Leo against a wall and cuffed him. Then they dragged him outside where the Mayor, Murph and Boris stood waiting next to a paddy wagon.

"Officer Chang, Patrolman Quinn, he's the one who did it," Boris said loudly. "I saw him run like a coward after he stole my old man's gold pocket watch. It's all I have left from my dad. Go on, search him. It's inscribed 'Horace Chadwick, June 3, 1882'."

"I guess that makes you Boris Chadwick." Leo snarled.

"Shut up," the cop shot back.

Patrolman Quinn stuck his hand into Leo's right pocket and turned it inside out. The bag of lychees fell to the ground. He picked it up and looked inside, then dumped out the contents of the bag. Mixed in with the fruit was the gold pocket watch. The cop handed over the watch to Boris.

"Here you are, son."

Officer Chang grabbed Leo by the arm and threw him into the back of the paddy wagon. Leo stared out the small barred window in the back. Murph looked down at his feet. The Mayor spat. Boris raised his hand and waved at Leo as the paddy wagon lurched forward with a jolt. Through the window, with his heart in his throat and his mind frantically clicking away, Leo launched curses at each of his former friends as they grew small and distant.

CHAPTER 8

The H Is Silent

Leo was flung to the ground as the paddy wagon came to an abrupt stop. He stood and pressed his face against the bars at the back of the wagon. In front of him a streetlamp flickered, casting a warm yellow glow on the pavement. He twisted his neck up to take in the building in front of him. The Tombs was massive, like a castle. The high gray walls led to a steep roof with spires, and the barred windows were skinny like buttonholes.

Leo seethed with anger at the same time tears rolled down his cheeks. He rubbed his eyes so hard that white spots blurred his vision. The whole trip to Chinatown to buy firecrackers had been a backstabbing setup. No matter what Leo said to the Mayor, no matter how he explained how he felt, he would never be forgiven for leaving the gang. But Murph? How could Murph have been a part of this? What had he ever done to him except look out for him, care for him like a brother?

Patrolman Quinn's face appeared. Leo staggered back and sat on the bench. The lock clinked and then light flooded into the wagon as the doors were drawn open. In one fast lunge Patrolman Quinn reached in, grabbed Leo's leg, dragged him out and held him in place against the paddy wagon.

"Look what you did to my jacket," he said, pointing to a tear the length of the sleeve. "You ruined it. A new one will come out of my pay. Just for that, I'll make sure you stew. I can tell the judge all sorts of things to delay a hearing. Reports get lost, kids get forgotten about. I can tell the judge things that will make your sentence last so long you'll still be in there when they find the Titanic. Move!"

There was no way for Leo to talk his way out of this, no side street to disappear into. There was only the jail looming in front of him, blocking the setting sun. As they approached the stone archway, Leo inhaled deeply. Patrolman Quinn pushed the door open, revealing a brightly lit office and the steady ticking of typewriter keys. One police officer led a prisoner in handcuffs, his arm on his shoulder, looking like they were old pals. Another officer had his nose buried in a file. Others cops sipped coffee and casually read reports. All the routine things the cops were doing flooded Leo's senses. He noticed the squeak of every eraser rubbing against paper and the mad flutter of every ringing phone. He felt like he was about to be gobbled up by some big animal, just tossed into its mouth and forgotten.

Patrolman Quinn led Leo to a man with a droopy face and sallow skin sitting behind a desk. He had the earpiece of a telephone plastered to his head and he barked orders into the mouthpiece. Then he slammed the phone down and waved Leo forward. The nameplate on his desk was partially covered by a spread of papers, but Leo made out the letters SGT. A sergeant. He might be more reasonable, since he had more experience than Quinn. But how could Leo make a case for being framed when he had been caught red-handed?

"Patrolman Quinn," the sergeant said. His gruff tone didn't match his puppy-dog face, "What happened to you? Your uniform is a mess."

"Another punk. This one stole a gold watch and set off a smoke bomb in the middle of Chinatown."

"High stakes, I see. Big-time offender. Where's Chang?"

"Still in Chinatown."

"Any word on the street about the double homicide?"

"Not yet," Quinn responded.

"I suppose not. We have delinquents setting off firecrackers. It's pandemonium in Chinatown. Who can focus on the body parts of tong members in the middle of the street when there are kids skipping school and playing with fireworks?"

Leo liked the sergeant's sarcastic style. He relaxed a little.

"Go ahead and tag the evidence, Quinn. Let's get this over with."

"The theft happened quickly, sir. It was more despicable than it sounds on the surface. He stole from a cripple. Doesn't get much lower than that."

"I look forward to reading your full report. In the meantime, tag the evidence," said the sergeant.

"At my discretion, I gave the stolen property back to its owner, who correctly identified it," Quinn said. "It was of sentimental value to the owner, a crippled boy, as I mentioned."

"What sort of cripple was he, you say?"

"He had a wooden leg."

"And you have his name and address in case we need him to testify?"

"I didn't see the need, sir. But you have my statement. The kid was also carrying a weapon," Quinn said, laying Leo's small penknife on the desk.

"You're joking, right? All this looks good for is cleaning fingernails."

The sergeant rubbed his eyes. Leo guessed this wasn't the first time Quinn had come to him with less than perfect police work.

"Uncuff the boy," the sergeant ordered.

Patrolman Quinn reached behind Leo's back and unlocked the handcuffs. Leo's hands flopped to his sides. He rubbed each wrist and stretched his cramped fingers. The sergeant opened an ink pad and placed a blank form next to it on his desk.

"Touch the pad," Quinn said, prodding Leo in the small of his back.

Leo ignored him. Quinn bent down. His teeth were brown and stubby and his breath smelled like a wet cigar. "Listen to me, boy. You're nothing but one of the many worthless bloodsucking leeches that we bring in every day. Here is where you belong. Not on the street, not bothering the law-abiding citizens in our fair city. But you should think yourself lucky that we caught you while you are still young. If your luck holds out, you'll get sent to reform school, where you will receive a proper education. And if you don't straighten out there on your own, they'll beat it out of you."

"I don't have all day," the sergeant said. "Just print the kid."

Quinn grabbed hold of Leo's hand and pressed it to the pad. He rolled Leo's fingers on the admitting form. There it was. A police record.

The sergeant picked up a pen. "Name?" he asked.

"Leo."

"Last name . . ."

They had his fingerprints, but they wouldn't get his identity. With his last name, they might be able to trace his past. That was the last thing Leo wanted, to be sent back to an orphanage. He closed his eyes.

"H-o-u-d-i-n-i," Leo spelled slowly. "The H is silent. It's pronounced oo-dee-nee. I'm of Italian origin."

"A comedian, are we?" asked the sergeant.

"No, sir."

The sergeant tapped his pen several times on the desk.

"Listen," he said. "I can tell this is your first time here by the way you're standing. Back straight, head high, trying to be brave. But inside you're quaking. You're not fooling me. So let's start again, and this time without the wisecracks. Last name?" the sergeant asked again.

"I already told you. It's Houdini."

The sergeant sighed and shook his head. "Date of birth?"

"February 2, 1901," Leo answered. That was his second lie. Leo's real date of birth was February 29, 1904. A leap year. Leo gambled that a boy of sixteen might have better chances of not being shipped off to a reform school than a boy of thirteen. He would rather spend a few months in jail than a few years upstate.

"You don't look sixteen to me."

"I drank coffee as a kid, I never hit my growth spurt. Don't kick me while I'm down, sergeant."

"Right, right. You got a real mouth on you. Seeing as you're sixteen, Quinn forgot to mention your other option." The sergeant became more serious. "We could escort you to the army recruitment office. It's the patriotic thing to enlist, go fight the Kaiser's army. I'd see you off myself. You look a little young, but it seems you have no problem lying with a straight face."

"New York is tough enough," Leo said.

"I suppose so. Place of birth?"

"Pittsburgh." Lie number three.

"No parents, aunts or uncles, legal guardians? Any family whatsoever?"

Leo thought back to earlier in the day when Boris said they were all a family. Funny how that had changed. Some family.

"None to speak of," Leo said flatly.

"Place of current residence?"

"New York City."

The sergeant threw down his pen.

"Okay, I think that's enough from you," he said to Leo. "Quinn, you're free to go now."

Quinn mouthed *Bye-bye* to Leo and walked briskly out to the street, holding the tear in his jacket like he had been shot in the arm.

The sergeant signaled to an officer standing nearby. "Hankstrum!" he called. The new cop was enormous. He lumbered like an upright bear and he breathed out heavily with each step. His face was chunky and white like a mound of mashed potatoes, and as he reached the sergeant's desk, Leo could see that he was secretly chewing on something.

"Hank, take this kid's mug shot and then put him in cell 52 on the boys' side."

"Wait," Leo said. "What's the deal here? What's going to happen? How long am I going to be stuck here? What am I even being charged with?"

"Disturbing the peace and loitering and petit larceny. A trio of misdemeanors. That's enough to hold you until you go before the judge. All questions answered?" The sergeant raised his voice. "All right, Hank. Take him away."

"Wait! Go to Eighth Avenue at Thirty-sixth Street! There's a boarded-up building next to Keeley's Saloon. That's where you'll find the cripple. He's a liar and a thief. It's all one big setup!"

"Sure it is. Except you were the one caught red-handed with the gold pocket watch. And even though I don't have it to book as evidence, I'll take Officer Quinn's word over yours any day."

The large policeman positioned Leo in front of a white painted wall with instructions not to move. He handed Leo a card with his false name on it and positioned the camera so that it was level with his face. Without warning he set off the flash, blinding Leo.

"Turn right."

Leo did. The flash went off again. Leo, still seeing stars, was grabbed and pulled to the back of the booking room. The cop threw open a door that led into a small room. The smell hit Leo first. It was damp, sickeningly sweet, metallic like pennies.

Leo was led to a barred door. The cop fiddled with a ring of keys. Finally he found the one he was looking for, unlocked the door and pushed Leo ahead. Before him were tiers of cells stretching up so far Leo couldn't see the top. Around him he could hear people hacking up phlegm, cursing at each other, cups rattling against the bars, moans and above it all a few sad hummed melodies. Leo felt a chill. The jail was easily fifteen degrees cooler than the processing room.

"Hey, kid, this is your lucky day."

Leo looked up at the cop. "What are you talking about?"

"Well, let me put it to you this way. People pay a fortune teller a nickel to find out their future. But you've got it free." The cop made a spooky ghost sound. "Look into the mirror and see your destiny!"

Leo looked to his left. A man with an eye patch and scars crisscrossing his chest spat at Leo through the bars. Leo turned to Hankstrum. "It looks sort of fuzzy, officer. What happens to me next?"

"Don't worry. We'll hold you here for a few weeks. I dunno, maybe six or seven. Depends on how busy the judge is. Once you see him, you're either going to get a little slap on the wrist, or you're going away to a reform school or work farm. Your future—it should be less fuzzy now. Why, in fact, I can see it clearly! It's so bright! It's right there, at the end of the hallway. Keep moving."

Leo stepped into the passage. The cells were packed so tightly that Leo had trouble counting how many people were in each one. Officer Hankstrum jabbed Leo's back with a chubby finger, pushing him on. Leo kept his head down and stared at the brick floor under his feet.

"Relax," said Officer Hankstrum, breathing heavily. "Nothing to be afraid of. These are just the thieves and the drunks down here. We keep the murderers together up top."

At the end of the hall they took a right turn, walked down a short ramp and stopped in front of another large barred door.

A strange calm fell over Leo. It had grown quieter in the halls. He wasn't in Hell. Not yet, anyway. He could hear the smallest sounds—the scrape of the metal key inside the keyhole, the subtle click of the lock releasing.

Officer Hankstrum opened the door. "Boys' wing," he said, and led Leo inside.

The place was like a crypt. It was a lot like the main area of the Tombs but on a smaller scale. There was only one level, covered by a high curved ceiling. A few lightbulbs flickered down the hall. Sounds were muted. Leo could see dark spots the size of a quarter speeding up and down along the walls. One fell off and started racing toward him on the floor. Leo hated roaches, and these were the fastest he'd ever seen.

Hankstrum stopped at a supply closet. "Take it!" he said, tossing a gray wool blanket at Leo.

The cells in the boys' wing were smaller than the ones in the main wing, with only two or three kids in each. No one paid Leo much attention as he walked by. In fact, the boys' wing didn't seem horrific at all—not at all the way the Mayor had described it. Some kids played cards, others read books. Trays of empty bowls with silverware scattered beside them lined the floor. Leo felt huge relief.

Halfway down the wing Officer Hankstrum stopped in front of a cell. A boy about Leo's age with long stringy black hair lay on a cot inside. The boy sat up and watched as Officer Hankstrum opened the cell door and gave a shove. Leo tripped, nearly hitting his head on the frame of the metal cot. The lock clicked and Hankstrum was gone.

Leo lay down on the other cot and wrapped himself in the blanket. The two boys stared at each other in silence. They were about the same weight, the same height, but Leo thought he could take him if he had to.

"What's your name?" the boy finally asked.

"I don't have one," Leo said.

"Coincidence. Neither do I. Give me your blanket."

The boy got up and started toward Leo.

"You take one more step and I'll tear you apart."

The boy stopped. "Take it easy. I was just kidding." He pulled a balled-up piece of paper from his pocket and unfolded it, revealing a small piece of chocolate in the middle. He snapped it in half and tossed a chunk to Leo. "Welcome to the Tombs."

Leo ate the chocolate and mumbled "Thanks," and flipped over on his bed. He played the day's events backward and forward until his eyes became heavy. With his ear pressed against the cot, he could hear the hum of the jail. The drone of the boiler and the shuffle of hundreds of feet were comforting in a way. He curled up in a ball and fell asleep.

CHAPTER 9

His Goose Is Cooked

The only way Leo knew it was the next day was by the faint sunlight trickling in from a high window at the end of the hall. He had no idea what time it was. Apparently he had missed breakfast. There were two empty bowls at the cell door that weren't there the night before. His cellmate had not bothered to wake him for his portion of . . . whatever it was.

Leo stretched and breathed deeply. The dank smell of the Tombs filled his nostrils and clogged his throat. It was everywhere. A family of roaches milled about the empty bowls. Leo felt ill. He ran to the cell door and immediately the contents of his stomach shot out in a thick greenish rope of vomit. He sank to the ground, shivering.

Leo wiped his mouth and went back to his cot. His cellmate stared at him, but did not say anything. The other inmates yelled at him and complained of the stink. Hours passed. Leo kept his head under the blanket for most of the day, only poking it out periodically to see the ball of light at the end of the hall grow dimmer.

Eventually Hankstrum came through. Leo heard his heavy footsteps approach the cell. He sat up and looked at the massive guard through the bars.

"What is this?"

"New kid puked," Leo's cellmate said.

Hankstrum about-faced, returning a few minutes later with a mop, a bucket and some rags. He unlocked the cell and told Leo to step into the hallway. Once Leo was outside the cell, he locked the door again.

"Now clean it up."

Leo took the mop and began to clean up his mess.

"Disgusting," Hankstrum complained. "I can't believe I always get stuck taking care of you little jerks."

His breathing was heavy. He jabbed his fat finger at Leo. "Get the bars, too."

Leo wiped down the bars with the rags. Without looking up, his cellmate called, "Say, when do we get our supper, Hanky Panky? Now that the sick is cleaned up, I'm starving. You didn't bring us any lunch."

"Do I look like a waiter from Delmonico's to you?" Officer Hankstrum said. "When you hear the wheels of the food cart is when you eat. Until then, quit your bellyaching."

"Suck an egg, Hanky Panky."

Officer Hankstrum took out his billy stick and smacked it against the bars, making a crack that echoed through the hall. The boys' wing became silent. Leo stood very still.

"Show some respect!" Officer Hankstrum bellowed. His enormous cheeks flapped as he shouted. "I've had enough of you brats. All you do is complain here!" Officer Hankstrum spun wildly around to each side of the wing, flailing his club all over. "*When do we eat? What time is it? When do we get out? I miss my mommy.* Shut up!" His face grew red. "I hope you all get shipped off to some godforsaken work farm. I'm sick of you. I'm sick of . . . sick of . . ."

His face turned from red to purple, and the veins in his neck bulged. He grimaced. Gurgling sounds came from his drooping mouth. He reached a hand to his chest. As he dropped to his knees, Leo jumped out of the way. With a thump, Officer Hankstrum fell to the ground.

Leo's cellmate walked over to the bars.

"Is he . . ."

"Dead? I don't know." Leo looked down at the body. He had never seen a dead person before. "We need to get help," he said.

"I'm not really in a position to do that," his cellmate replied, grasping the bars. "And I really admire your sympathy, but there's nothing we can do for him now. His goose is cooked. My uncle went the same way."

Leo looked at the door to the boys' wing hanging open. He half expected the sergeant to come bounding through it.

"Also, I hate to break it to you, but this is manslaughter, or maybe even murder," Leo's cellmate said, squinting his eyes.

"What are you talking about?"

"The guys in the uniforms on the other side of these bars ain't exactly our friends. If they found out we caused one of their buddies to pop on the job, there's not a judge in this town that would give any of us a break. The way I see it, there's only one thing to do."

"If anyone made him drop dead it was you!" Leo shouted.

"That's your version of what happened. But look up and down the row of cells. See all these guys? They've been here for weeks, just like me. And we're all itching to bust out. So here is my suggestion: you get the keys, we all make a run for it. Otherwise all these guys will give a full description of you, the new inmate, who killed Officer Hankstrum. Get the picture?"

Leo got it. He knelt down and pried the key ring from Officer Hankstrum's belt. He tried not to touch his body. Leo worked quickly, first unlocking the cell in front of him, then going down the hall letting everyone out. When the entire hall was set free, they huddled in the middle of the wing. Among the twenty or so boys, a troubled mood spread as they shuffled around Officer Hankstrum's body, trying not to look.

"What next?" someone said.

Leo still held the keys. He looked around and saw the excitement and nervousness of all the kids.

"We double back through the adult wing," Leo said. "Then I'll throw the door open and we'll all run for it. If we stay low and run fast there's no way they'll catch us all. Every man for himself. Ready?"

Leo led the group, running past the inmates he had seen on the way in. As the kids streaked by a cheer arose from the inmates urging them on. At the entrance, Leo stopped and looked for the right key. His hands shook and his lungs pushed out air like a full-steam-ahead locomotive. He swiftly tried each key and his body lifted when he finally felt the right one catch in the lock. He felt like Houdini wrestling out of a straitjacket.

Leo pushed the door open and made a mad dash. He could hear police officers shouting confused orders. But Leo stayed focused on the door as he raced past the sergeant and all the other cops. He was less than two feet from the door when he heard someone call, "Keep running!"

With Leo's hand pulling the door open, the cool air outside already smacking his face, he turned his head to see that his cellmate had been nabbed and was being put in handcuffs. A few other kids were also caught, but Leo wasted no time worrying about it. He pushed forward through the doorway and out into the street. Leo didn't stop running until he reached West Thirty-sixth Street and Eighth Avenue.

CHAPTER 10

White Knuckles and Green Dollars

Leo climbed the fire escape on the building across the street from the hideout. He hid behind shirts hanging stiffly on a clothesline, looking around to make sure no cops were on his tail and watching the door of his former home. The bells of St. Clare's Church on West Thirty-sixth Street rang seven times. Leo watched men returning from work at the many slaughterhouses that dotted the neighborhood. The smell of blood wafted through Hell's Kitchen. Funny how it had never really bothered him before. All around him he heard the sounds of families sitting down to dinner. He hadn't noticed his own hunger until then.

At seven thirty, the Mayor and Boris emerged from their building. As they rounded the corner, Leo scurried down the fire escape, across the street and into the tenement.

The apartment door was locked. Leo kicked the knob over and over until finally the metal plate on the lock broke loose. Once inside, Leo peeled off his dirty clothes and scrubbed the filth from his body. The cold water was a shock on his skin. He quickly dried off and dressed. Then he filled a knapsack with the rest of his clothing.

He saw the Mayor's baseball bat lying on the floor. He picked it up and went to the row of mailboxes. He swung at the box for apartment A5, denting the door. He stuck in his fingers and pried it open.

The gun was not there, but Leo didn't care. That was not what he was after. Leo grabbed the strongbox. He put the box on the floor and steadied it with his foot. He lifted the bat above his head and brought it down on the lock, snapping it off. The lock clinked as it flew into the wall.

Leo crouched and went through the box. Inside were the Mayor's ledger, a pencil and eight dollars. Leo pocketed the money. He stood up to leave. The empty box lay by his feet, like some sort of rat trap. He lifted it. It should have felt lighter. Something wasn't right. He slid his fingers around the inside of the box. He tapped a back corner. It sounded hollow. Jabbing his finger down onto that spot forced the bottom up. Leo grabbed the square piece of metal and tossed it to the side. Inside the false bottom were fat stacks of bills kept together with rubber bands, and the wallet.

Leo's rage grew. All the dangerous things he had done, and all that money they could have used to find a *real* home had gone straight into the Mayor's personal piggy bank. Leo stuffed the piles of cash and the wallet into his knapsack. He turned to leave and got about two steps before stopping in his tracks. Someone was coming. He picked up the baseball bat again. His knuckles whitened.

Murph entered the hideout, head down. He hummed quietly to himself. He got within inches of Leo before Leo poked the bat into Murph's stomach.

"That's as far as you come. Got it?"

Murph let out a shriek.

"Geez, Leo. You scared me half to death," he said, gasping for breath. "Where've you been? I've been worried. I thought you'd be back yesterday afternoon for your stuff."

"What are you talking about? You think setting me up for something I didn't do and shipping me off to the Tombs was a joke? Huh?"

"The Tombs? That wasn't part of the plan."

"Not part of the plan?"

"The Mayor said Chinatown was full of crooked cops. So he found a cop and slipped him a ten-spot and said it was from the Dropper, who wanted to teach a kid a lesson. But nobody said nothing about locking you up at the Tombs. The cop was just supposed to cuff you and stick you in the paddy wagon and take you for a ride, then dump you off in the Bronx."

Patrolman Quinn. The Tombs was his idea. All because of his torn jacket. *I'll make you stew*, he'd said.

"And you thought this was funny?"

"I tried to talk him out of it but he never listens to me."

"I guess you didn't try hard enough, did you?"

"Leo, you know how he gets."

"You could have told me about this little plan at any time on the walk to Chinatown. I asked you to come with me when I left. But you're no better than they are. What's happened to you? You sold me out, after everything we've been through."

"I'm really sorry, Leo. But the Mayor said that because of how you messed things up with the Dropper, we'd be stuck in this hole for another winter."

"Take a good look around. Because you'll never escape from here. The Mayor's promises are all lies. Every single word. He's the thief. He's been stealing from us for two years. He used us. He had his own secret pile of cash. Hundreds. Did he tell you he had enough savings already to get out of here?"

"I don't know, Leo. Maybe that's true, maybe it's not. But if it is, maybe there's an explanation. Aren't there two sides to every story? Just like when you hid the wallet."

"Except I was telling the truth. It's not the same thing *at all*. It's the *exact opposite*. Murph, you've just lost the only person in the world who cared about you. And the day is coming, probably pretty soon, when the Mayor and Boris will turn on you, too."

Leo reached into his knapsack for the bundled bills. He waved them in Murph's face. "What do you think now? Who do you believe?"

Murph's eyes widened. "Where did you get that?"

"The Mayor was sitting on it the whole time."

"I don't believe it. Why would he keep us here? Look, Leo, I don't know where you got all that cash. But you gotta beat it," Murph said. "I'm sorry about all this. I promise I won't say nothing."

Leo let the bat drop to his side.

"I don't care what you do."

He pushed past Murph, who stood still in the middle of the parlor. Once Leo was out of the tenement he walked double-time, heading uptown.

CHAPTER 11

Henry Hankstrum Jr. Checks In

Leo was free, truly on his own, without any promises to keep or people to please. He could go anywhere he wanted. Up, down, sideways, in circles. If he chose, he could stand still all day and watch people go by. And he realized he would have to do just that—closely. He still didn't know if the cops were looking for him. But first, Leo had to find a place to sleep. He had plenty of cash and decided to treat himself.

He walked to Forty-fourth Street and looked into the lobbies of all the fancy hotels—the Chatwal, the Royalton, the Mansfield. The Iroquois and the Algonquin were next to each other like opposing Indian warriors. Suddenly a hubbub with flashes from cameras spilled out of the Algonquin lobby onto the sidewalk. A muscular man pushed his way through the tangle of reporters. Once he climbed into a car and sped off, the press vanished.

Stooping in front of the door, a bellboy wearing a red jacket and matching fez filled a dish with milk. Soon a fluffy cat appeared and began lapping up the milk. The bellboy looked up.

"Couldn't feed Mathilda with all those news hawks around," he said.

"Who was that getting his picture taken?" Leo asked.

"Dempsey."

"Jack Dempsey? The fighter?"

"One and the same. Odds are he'll be the next heavyweight champ of the world. He's got some left hook," the bellboy replied.

"Did he forget his cat?"

"No. Mathilda lives here at the hotel, but nobody owns her. She's kind of the boss of everyone. Are you staying with us?"

Leo didn't hesitate.

"Yes."

"Well, welcome."

The bellboy pulled open the door. Leo walked into the lobby. There were leather sofas arranged every few feet, and shiny brass glinted everywhere. Some people sat on plush chairs, talking in hushed tones. Others were eating small snacks or drinking from crystal glasses. A puff of cigar smoke swirled around Leo's head.

Leo took a seat on a couch. After a few minutes a waiter in a white tuxedo came by and asked if he would like anything.

"A ginger ale, please."

"Certainly. May I have your room number?"

"What for?"

"To charge the drink to your account, sir."

"I can do that?"

"Yes, sir."

"Good. Can I also have a steak with my ginger ale?"

"Of course."

"And french fries?"

"Yes, sir."

"With a side of sweet peas?"

"Excellent, sir."

"And a banana split. Three scoops."

"Wonderful choice."

Leo sank into the sofa. He could get used to this kind of living.

"Your room number?"

"Oh. Uh, three-thirty-two. Registered under Hankstrum."

"Thank you, sir."

Leo had enough money to stay the night. He didn't have to lie, but he had. He hadn't even thought twice about it. Conning was second nature to him after living on the streets. Being on the level was going to take some work. But at least for the moment he felt safe. The cops probably would not be looking for a juvenile prison escapee in a swanky hotel lobby. Leo watched the people around him. They were all well dressed and seemed sophisticated. Mathilda came up next to his feet and purred. He reached down and petted the fluff ball. When Leo looked up he saw the waiter standing stiffly in front of him.

"I'm sorry, but we have no record of anyone named Hankstrum staying here. Are you sure you're a guest?"

Leo licked his lips nervously. He'd backed himself into a corner. The straight and narrow was going to have to wait. "Of course I am," he said.

"Come with me, please. The concierge would like to have a word with you. It seems that room three-three-two is occupied by the Burton family."

The waiter motioned toward the front desk. Leo followed.

"I don't know where the mix-up is," Leo said quietly, "but I am starving and I've had a long and difficult day. My father's assistant specifically made the reservation for me. Of course you've heard of him. Henry Hankstrum. President of the United States of America Woodrow Wilson's Secretary of Industrial Commerce, and self-made millionaire with fortunes from steel and railroads?"

Before the concierge could answer, Leo placed his knapsack on the front desk. He opened the flap wide enough for the concierge to see the bundles of bills inside.

"So you see, if you're worried about payment, you needn't be. But you will have something to worry about if you refuse me a room and my dinner. My father will be furious if he finds out that I was turned away."

The concierge frantically flipped through his register book, mumbling apologies to Leo and curses at the waiter. He found an empty suite. The penthouse, in fact. Would that be suitable? Leo said it would, and he signed for it as Henry Hankstrum Jr. The concierge handed him a key. Leo thanked him and slipped him and the waiter each a five-dollar bill.

"And if you don't mind, please bring my food up to my room. I wish to eat in privacy."

Leo walked to the elevator bank past the lobby with his head high. The elevator attendant held the door for him.

"What floor?"

"Penthouse suite."

"You got it. You have the key?"

Leo handed it over. The elevator attendant inserted the key next to a button with a P in the middle, on top of all the other floor buttons, and unlocked it. He handed the key back to Leo and pressed the P button. The elevator lifted quickly and smoothly. Leo felt like he was flying. He imagined what was happening on all the floors he passed, people in their rooms reading or sleeping or getting ready for a night on the town. After a minute, the elevator came to a stop and the doors opened into a room fit for a king.

The first thing Leo noticed was the telephone. It sat on an end table like a small tank. It was some new kind with the receiver and the mouthpiece attached in one piece. He lifted it up and put it to his ear. A woman greeted him. Leo asked about his dinner, and the woman said it was on its way up. He hung up and kicked off his shoes. In the corner of the room he saw a gramophone, just like the one in Macy's window in Herald Square. A horn sprang out of the top of the box like some kind of dangerous tropical flower. Leo read the instructions printed on a piece of paper that was glued to the back of the gramophone. He selected "Alexander's Ragtime Band" from the stack of records in the cabinet, then placed it on the turntable. When he cranked the lever until it stopped, the record began to spin on the turntable. Leo dropped the arm with the needle onto the record, but it screeched and jumped the groove. It took several attempts before Leo mastered placing the arm onto the first groove. Music filled the room. He cracked open the window and looked down at the street. The cars were so small below him they looked like mice racing through a maze.

A minute later the elevator dinged. Leo went to the door and let in a waiter holding a tray of plates with steel domes covering the food. He set it down on the table in the middle of the room and whipped off the domes with a flourish. Steam rose from the steak, but the bowl holding the banana split was on top of a bed of ice so it would stay cold. Leo pulled the table closer to the couch and dug in, not even waiting for the waiter to leave. He devoured everything. He had never eaten so well in his life.

Leo stretched out on the sofa. First he took the cash out from his knapsack. He sorted the bills into piles of ones, fives, tens, and twenties, and he counted it up twice. Three hundred and forty-seven dollars. Leo liked the feel of all that cash.

Next Leo removed the stolen wallet. In the front compartment were a few identical business cards. They read: THE GREAT BARZINI, ILLUSIONIST. 184 EAST 7TH STREET. NYC. Leo burst out laughing. He'd stolen the wallet of a magician! And right under Houdini's nose, too! He wondered what the King of Handcuffs and his *Right Way to Do Wrong* would say about that.

Folded behind the business cards was a scrap of paper with handwritten script. On the top of the paper was written *Advertisement for New York Tribune*. Some of the ink had smudged. But from what Leo could read, this magician Barzini had placed an ad in the newspaper looking for an assistant. It said all applicants should go to Martinka & Co, located at 493 Sixth Avenue. This would be even better than working as an usher at the Palace Theater. Magicians have quick hands and so did Leo. Maybe everybody gets one lucky break in a lifetime. The key was to recognize it when it smacked you in the face. Leo would follow up on the ad first thing in the morning. He put the paper back into the wallet and put the wallet on the table.

He wrapped a blanket over his body and folded his arms behind his head. Leo never got the chance to try out the fancy bed in the other room. He drifted into a deep sleep on the sofa as the needle on the gramophone circled around the center of the record, making a soft hissing sound, and cold night air floated in from the open window.

CHAPTER 12

The World Wants to Be Deceived

Leo awoke to the sound of cars honking. He rolled over on the sofa and looked out the window. The sky was a peachy red. He took the needle off the record, then drew a bath in the claw-foot tub. As he soaked, he thought about his future. For the first time in his life he felt as though he might *have* a future. He'd slept peacefully through the night. No bad dreams, no worry about rats crawling over his chest. And as far as the money, he had no regrets at all about taking it. *He* was the one who'd stolen the lion's share. The way Leo figured, it was small compensation for the gang's betrayal. And realistically, it wasn't as if the money could be returned to the rightful owners. So Leo decided to use it to guarantee he got on the path to a better life. But what about the cops? That could be a serious problem. His cellmate could have told them that Leo was responsible for Hankstrum's death. And to make a deal, he might have told them how Leo masterminded the prison escape. They had his photo and fingerprints. There was probably an all-points bulletin issued for him.

Leo dunked his head under the warm water and held his breath. He let air bubbles slowly leak out of his nose. When he surfaced, he decided to take things one step at a time. He would have to think smart, stay one step ahead and try his hardest to blend in with the five and a half million other people in the city.

Leo got out of the tub and got dressed. Henry Hankstrum Jr. would not be returning to the penthouse at the end of the day. Leo slung his knapsack over his shoulder and impatiently pushed the button for the elevator. He was eager to be on his way.

But he had to start out on the right foot. In the lobby he went to the front desk and asked the same concierge how much was owed for his night's stay.

"Young Mr. Hankstrum," the concierge greeted him. "We are so sorry for the confusion last night. Your stay is on us. Your father still has not checked in. But when you see him next, we would *greatly* appreciate your keeping our little misunderstanding between us."

Leo readily agreed.

Outside, he coursed through the thicket of people on the sidewalk on their way to work. The first order of business was to stop at the corner of Forty-fourth Street and Sixth Avenue to listen to the newsies hawk their papers. From the south corner of the street the hollering was all about the Bolshevik revolution in Russia, but the pitch coming from the north corner made Leo's blood run cold.

"Get your paper, get your paper. Guards unable to stop prison rush."

He envisioned it all there, in black and white. His mug shot plastered across the front page. He wrote the headline himself: LEO HOUDINI, KID PICKPOCKET, RESPONSIBLE FOR DEATH OF A TOMBS GUARD AND ESCAPE OF OTHER INMATES.

Leo fished out a few pennies to pay for the Tribune and yanked the morning edition from the pile tucked under the kid's arm. Leo ran with the newspaper toward the Forty-second Street IRT subway station. His heart was pounding as he went underground and walked through the corridor. He passed the buskers with their violins and barrel organs, and went on to the token booth. On his way down the stairs he noticed a cop leaning against the wall, waiting to nab anyone who tried to jump the turnstile. He dug through his pocket for some change and handed over twenty cents to the man in the kiosk. In return he got four tokens. He opened the paper in front of his face as he passed the cop.

Leo went through the turnstile and onto the downtown platform. Moments later the train came screeching into the station. Leo positioned himself so he would be first on the train, and when he was inside he found a large space on the wicker bench underneath a fan on the ceiling.

Leo held the newspaper high and scanned the first page. The prison story was dead center of the first column: MASKED MILITANTS BREAK PAST GUARDS. Leo didn't know if he was going to laugh or cry in relief. The story was about forty-one suffragist ladies who rushed prison guards to visit one of their leaders in prison. This didn't mean Leo was completely in the clear. It was only the early morning edition. The story *could* appear in the evening paper. To be on the safe side, he would check the newspapers each day for at least a week. And there was also the possibility that no story would appear at all, especially if New York's finest didn't want news of a bunch of kids breaking loose from jail to get out. Maybe he'd get a double dose of good luck. Leo slumped backward in his seat and stretched his legs. At each stop the conductor called out the station, and at Twenty-third Street, Leo stepped off the train and ran up the stairs back into daylight.

The next task of the day was to ditch his old brown cap and buy another. Something big enough to pull down over his forehead. Leo selected a black and white houndstooth wool cap with a wide visor. If he held his head high and didn't act suspicious, maybe he wouldn't give himself away to the cops.

He walked up Sixth Avenue and found number 493. A sign on the wall inside read THE WORLD WANTS TO BE DECEIVED, LET IT BE DECEIVED. There were shelves upon shelves of miniature devices like mechanical monkeys and windmills and mystery boxes. Leo stopped in front of something that looked like a devil's head mounted on a wooden stand. Its face was painted bright red and it had horns, a wide-toothed smile and a pointy goatee.

"I call him Walter."

Leo spun around. A girl with long blond hair and glasses stood behind him. She looked to be a few years older than Leo.

"He's a satyr, a Mephisto, or whatever you choose to call the devil. But I figured since he's been sitting there for years, he ought to have a name. He's not for sale, mind you. He's kind of the store mascot."

Leo nodded dumbly. He hadn't much experience talking to girls, except for the nuns at the House of Providence, and that definitely did not count.

The girl walked behind the counter and took the satyr's head down from the shelf along with a deck of cards. She placed them both on the countertop in front of Leo, and then shuffled the cards.

"Pick three cards, one at a time. Look at them, remember what they are, but don't show me."

Leo followed the girl's instructions. Ten of diamonds, three of spades, jack of clubs. She returned the cards to the deck at random points and then pried open the satyr's mouth with her index finger and inserted the complete deck of cards.

"Now watch," she told Leo.

The satyr's eyes began to move from right to left and its teeth began to chatter. Suddenly it stopped and a single card shot from its mouth. The girl took the card and presented it to Leo.

"Ten of diamonds. Is this one of your cards?" she asked.

"Yes!"

The satyr's eyes began to roll, and from the top of its head shot out two cards.

"And?" the girl inquired, handing the three of spades and the jack of clubs up to Leo for inspection.

"These are the cards I picked."

"I know." The girl extended her hand. "I'm Penelope Martinka."

"I'm Leo," Leo said, and shook her hand.

"Leo what?"

"Just Leo."

"Welcome to the store, Just Leo."

Leo realized he was still shaking her hand. He pulled away and laughed sheepishly.

"So, how did it pick my cards? What's the secret?"

"Ah, secret, you say," Penelope said, leaning closer. "Just Leo, here's the first thing you'll need to learn if you want to become a magician. All magicians keep their secrets private. That's the golden rule."

"What makes you think that I want to be a magician?"

"Well, Just Leo, first of all, you're here, right? This is Martinka & Co., the most famous magic store in all of New York City, maybe even the world. And second, take a look around. How many boys your age do you see in the shop?"

Leo counted at least a dozen other boys peering into glass display cases. Disappointed, he said, "Funny, I really didn't notice them before. Are they all here to apply for the job, too?"

"What job?"

"The magician's assistant job. The one from the ad in the Tribune."

"I don't know anything about that," Penelope said. "You'll have to ask Opa."

"Opa?"

"That's German for grandfather. My Opa and Oma own this store with my Grossonkel Antonio. They started the business in Germany a long time ago. Opa says that hundreds of boys come into the shop every year wanting to be the next Houdini, Thurston or maybe even Herrmann the Great."

"Who is that?" Leo asked. "Does he perform in New York City?"

"He died a long time ago. Opa thinks he was the most talented magician that ever lived, but maybe that's because they were the best of friends."

"What did he do?" Leo asked.

"He caught bullets," Penelope said, her eyes wide. "Opa says that's the most dangerous illusion a magician can perform. If it goes wrong, no magic will save you. But it never went wrong for Herrmann the Great."

"Where is your grandfather? I want to apply for the job before all these other boys beat me to it."

"Opa is in there right now," she said, pointing toward a drawn velvet curtain at the back of the room.

"What's in there? More things for sale?"

"No. Back there is the theater where magicians try out their new acts and the workshops where my Oma builds custom props. My Oma is famous for her fingers."

"Magic fingers?"

"In a way," Penelope said. "Oma designed an extra finger that's painted to look natural and it attaches in between your real fingers. It's hollow, so a magician can hide a silk handkerchief up there." Penelope laughed. "I just told you a secret and I said I wouldn't do that."

"Penelope, I have to tell you a secret too. I don't know anything about performing magic. But I really want this job. Can I go back there and talk to your grandfather?"

Penelope shook her head. "Nobody's allowed back there unless Oma and Opa say it's okay. Not even me."

"All right, then, I'll just wait. But in the meantime, you must have a book here that can teach me how to do tricks," Leo said. "I've got to put something down on the application that'll help me get the job."

"Of course there is," Penelope said. "But Opa always says that a dog learns tricks, a magician creates illusions."

"Oh," Leo said.

"Don't look so glum," Penelope said, tugging Leo's hand. "I'll ask Grossonkel."

Leo followed Penelope to a side room, where a plump old man with spectacles like Penelope's sat reading a paper.

"Grossonkel, this is Leo. He's in a hurry to learn magic. Do you have any advice?"

The old man put the paper down. He inhaled so deeply that his head fell back with the breath. He looked down his nose at Leo.

"He should first find out if he has the gift. Do you have quickness of the hands? Can you pull things out of thin air, young man? Can you make yourself invisible?"

"Yes. I can, actually."

"That's a good start, then. So I will tell you what I tell every young man who walks through our door. Tutelage is the answer! You must learn at the hands of another magician. That's how you'll find out if you have what it takes to be the next great Stupendous So-and-So, or the Fabulous What's-His-Name. That is the one and only way."

"Leo is here for a magician's assistant job," Penelope told her great uncle. "He saw an advertisement in the *Tribune*. It said to apply here."

"I don't know about any ad."

"It was for a magician named Barzini," Leo said.

Grossonkel Antonio put his hand to his chin and puckered his lips. "I don't know if that would be the right job for you. He is a difficult man."

"But is he good?"

"He is an excellent illusionist."

"Leo wants to apply with Opa, like the ad said," Penelope said.

"He won't have to. Barzini is back in the theater right now. I will get him."

"Can I look through a book while I wait?" Leo asked.

"Go on, but you won't understand a word in it. Most of the books are quite technical. A baby can't run before he walks."

Leo walked over to the bookshelf and pulled down a volume titled *A Few of Robinson's Good Ideas*. There was an introduction and a table of contents listing six illusions. Leo thumbed through the pages. "Fire Juggling" and the "Bowl of Water Trick" were illustrated with diagrams and detailed instructions. Penelope's Grossonkel Antonio was right. Leo didn't understand a word. Leo looked at the opening paragraph for illusion number four in the book.

GONE

> *For this very clever illusion, the world of magic is indebted to the fertile brain of* William E. Robinson.

Leo flipped the page. A large diagram showed a woman suspended high in the air, positioned over a chair, with some type of cage built around her. Underneath the diagram was an explanation about stage lighting and how to make the woman disappear.

Leo's concentration snapped when the book was plucked out of his hands. He looked up and saw a man standing in front of him. It was difficult for Leo to determine the man's age. He wore a goatee, in the style of many of the magicians Leo had seen on theater posters. In a way, he resembled Walter, the mechanical satyr.

"This book," he said, slamming it shut, "is far beyond your comprehension, I should think." He gripped it so tightly the hard cover bent.

"It has been brought to my attention that you wish to apply for the assistant's position. Is that correct?"

"Are you Barzini?" Leo asked.

"Signor Barzini," he said. "Mr. Martinka tells me that you saw my advertisement in the newspaper."

"In the *Tribune*," Leo lied. "Please give me a chance. I know I'm the right man for the job."

Barzini squinted as if trying to see through a window into a dark room.

"What is your name?"

"Leo, sir."

"Have you been in a magic act before? Do you have any professional experience?"

"Well, see, the thing is—" Leo began. Barzini put up his hand.

"I understand. The sum total of your experience has been in viewing magic shows from the audience. Am I correct?"

"In a way, I . . . I do have some . . . well, I am not completely unskilled. And I'm a fast study."

Barzini took a card out of his vest and handed it to Leo. It was identical to the ones from the wallet deep in Leo's knapsack.

"Be at this address at six o'clock sharp."

Barzini then tossed the book to the side and left without another word. Penelope picked up the book from the floor and put it back on the shelves. Antonio Martinka put his hand on Leo's shoulder.

"I found something better for you," he said. "Come with me."

He pulled down a thin volume from the far end of the bookshelf and handed it to Leo.

"*100 Simple Magic Tricks for Children's Parties*," Leo read aloud.

"Don't frown. You have to start somewhere," he said.

"Sure."

Leo paid the thirty-five cents for the book. He put it in his knapsack and headed for the door.

"Well, good luck, Just Leo," Penelope called after him. "I hope you get the job!"

CHAPTER 13

Under Contract

After Leo left Martinka's he walked down Twenty-eighth Street. He enjoyed the flower district. Even though it was cold outside, shop windows were brimming with blooming flowers and shrubs and tropical trees. Leo walked east and spent the day wandering around the East River. The farther away from Hell's Kitchen, the safer he felt. But he still scanned the streets looking for the glint of a badge.

He sat on a bench watching the river sluggishly flow, boats bobbing on the surface. The sun was bright but not hot, and everything seemed to move at half speed. People were working out on the piers unloading cargo ships, and a few men with fishing poles lazily flicked their lures into the water.

Leo took out Barzini's card. The address was all the way downtown on the Lower East Side. He decided to walk it. Leo stopped at a street cart selling roasted yams. He bought one and snacked on it as he leisurely made his way downtown. As Leo went south from Kip's Bay he watched the city change. He walked by Bellevue Psychiatric Hospital, a gated complex with half-dead ivy crawling up the brick walls. The building gave off a cold, silent air. He had some time so he took a detour west and circled around Gramercy Park, another gated area, accessible only to the well-off residents who lived around it. He hurried by Union Square, where some sort of strike was going on, with protestors holding signs in several different languages. The farther south he got the more signs he saw in Italian. Black women walked the sidewalks selling hot corn. When Leo curved back east and came to Barzini's neighborhood, he slowed his pace to a shuffle. He didn't know this part of town at all.

Leo entered the vestibule to 184 East Seventh Street. He saw that the magician's apartment was listed as number 3. All the other floors were broken up into several apartments. The first floor alone went from 1A to 1E, but it seemed Barzini had an entire floor to himself. Leo spoke into the flared cone for the voice pipe to apartment 3.

"Hello? H*ello*?"

"No need to shout," answered the voice at the other end of the pipe. "Who is it?"

"Leo, from the magic shop. Is this Signor Barzini?"

"Come on up."

Leo entered the foyer. The tile floor was new and clean, like the rest of the building. Leo took the stairs two at a time. The third floor had only one door. Leo knocked. No answer. He knocked again. There was a low hum in the hallway, the sound of electricity. Again he knocked with no answer. He tried the knob. The door swung open smoothly.

On the other side stood a chocolate-colored poodle, its muzzle flecked with gray. For a moment Leo thought the dog was a statue, it stood so still, until it bounded over to Leo and licked his hand. The dog's toenails clacked on the wooden floor. It moved aside and ushered Leo inside. Barzini's apartment was spotless. A few still-life watercolor paintings hung on the walls of the parlor. The rugs were bright, with complex designs. End tables by the sides of wing chairs were draped with crisp white cloths held in place by lamps. The apartment was rather large, with at least four different rooms. There were no pictures of children or a wife, no signs of a family. Leo was impressed. Barzini must have had some success to be able to afford such a big place all to himself.

"Welcome, Leo. Have a seat," Barzini said, coming from the kitchen.

Leo sat in one of the comfortable wing chairs. The poodle sniffed his right hand, then lay down on the rug by Leo's feet.

"I see you've met Horatio. He seems to like you."

Leo rubbed the dog's head.

"Horatio."

"It's from the play *Hamlet*. Horatio was Hamlet's only true friend. He shared all his secrets with him."

"Oh."

"But you haven't come here to discuss Shakespeare, have you?"

Leo shook his head. Barzini reached into a drawer in the table and pulled out a sheet of paper and a pen. He held the paper facing his chest so Leo could not see what was printed on it.

"I apologize for running out of Martinka's so abruptly. I was in a rush."

"I understand," Leo said.

"But the fact remains that I know absolutely nothing about you," Barzini said, "and I'm afraid I may have acted too hastily."

"Oh," Leo said, feeling dejected. "Well, if you just give me a shot, I know I can be a good assistant."

"That's not what I'm getting at. I already knew you were without experience. I am putting together a demanding act. I need to know if you have other obligations that may conflict with my training."

"No," Leo said. "I'm free."

"You don't go to school?"

"Not anymore. I'm done with all that."

"Good. You will need to be here from early in the morning until late at night most days of the week. Will your parents consent to that? I am assuming since you are here you not only told them about this job, but they have some fondness for show business."

Leo was not quite three years old when he was placed in the House of Providence. His memory of his parents was so distant and fuzzy that he never got very emotional when he spoke about them. There was only a little pang of something in his stomach.

"I don't have any parents. No aunts or uncles. No guardian or gramps. Like I said, I'm free."

Barzini nodded, as if this were something he already knew.

"What is your age? Do you have any other job to support yourself?"

"Technically I'm three and a half, because I was born on a leap day. But add ten to that, because I'm really thirteen, almost fourteen. And at the moment I am between jobs."

"In that case, I propose the following arrangement: since I do not know you, and you do not know me, I think the best course would be to go through a trial period. You may stay here with me. I have an extra room. I will not charge you room and board. If you like being my assistant, and I find you capable, fine. If it doesn't work out, then no hard feelings. However, I will need some assurance that whatever I may tell you in confidence remains secret. So I would like you to sign this."

Barzini handed the paper and pen to Leo. Leo quickly read the sheet. It was a simple contract running only a few sentences. Leo was to keep all of Barzini's tricks, methods and conversations regarding magic confidential, and in return Leo would get to learn them. He read the page to himself three times. With nothing to lose, he signed and handed it back. Barzini looked at it and half smiled.

"If you make it through the trial period, then we will become partners. And if the act is successful, then there will be profits, out of which I will pay you a modest salary. I believe that to be a fair arrangement. Do you agree?"

"Yes, that's fair."

"Good. Now I'll show you to your room. Then you can go and get your belongings from wherever you came from and bring them back here."

Leo patted his knapsack.

"Everything I own is in here."

"Confident, aren't you?"

"I like to be prepared."

Barzini led Leo to a small room with a neatly made bed set against the wall. The wallpaper was a light blue, and the thick drapes blocked out any light from outside. Leo noticed a small trunk at the end of the bed. There was no lock, but it would have to do. When Barzini walked out of the bedroom, Leo removed his clean clothes from the knapsack and stuck it at the bottom of the trunk, piling his clothes on top to hide it.

"I'm going downstairs to get the mail," Barzini said. "I'll be right back."

Once Leo heard the door shut, he popped his head out of the bedroom door and looked both ways. Horatio was snoring softly on the rug. Leo crept down the hall and tried the handle of the room next to his, but it was locked. Then he went the other way and opened the door at the end of the hallway. It was another bedroom. He tiptoed inside and found a setup much the same as his own room—a bed made up with blindingly white sheets, nothing hanging on the walls, a waxed wooden floor.

Leo's heart pattered against his chest as he pushed open a closet. Inside were a few suits hanging next to a few tuxedos, with a row of polished shoes underneath. He pushed the hanging clothes aside but there was nothing else. He rushed back to his bedroom to wait.

A few minutes later he heard the front door open and shut, then a sizzle coming from the kitchen, where he found Barzini at the stove cooking sausages. He took a seat at the table in the kitchen and watched Barzini cook. When he set the platter on the table Leo asked if he could feed a small piece to Horatio.

"No. Horatio has been trained not to beg for table scraps. There's nothing worse than a dog slobbering all over you when you're trying to enjoy a meal. He has to wait for his dinner."

They then ate in silence, and in silence Barzini showed Leo back to his room when dinner was over. Leo asked Barzini if he had an evening edition newspaper. Barzini explained that it was his habit to purchase a daily newspaper, but he'd been in such a rush during the day that he forgot. Instead he offered Leo a magazine, the *Saturday Evening Post*, to read. Leo crawled into bed and flipped through the pages of the magazine. He'd check the newspapers in the morning. All he needed was to get arrested just as his new life began. Steam hissed from the cast-iron radiator. He dozed off, and when he awoke a few hours later, his calm had departed.

He sat up in a panic. Barzini's wallet lay at the bottom of his knapsack next to his cash. Not ditching the wallet was a sloppy mistake. What if Barzini went snooping through his new assistant's possessions? He pulled thirty dollars from the banded bills and put the cash in the wallet. Then he left his room and entered the dark hallway in his bare feet. Leo had to plant it in the apartment, someplace not too obvious. Maybe sticking out of the cushions of a chair, or behind a stack of magazines. That way the magician would think he absentmindedly misplaced it himself.

Leo felt the walls for a light switch. Halfway down the hall a lamp suddenly turned on. Light showered over Barzini's folded hands resting in his lap. His face was in darkness. Leo quickly stuffed the wallet into the back of his pajama pants.

"I see you're having trouble sleeping. Sit with me. Let's talk."

There was a sweet sharp scent of alcohol in the air. Leo walked over and sat in a chair across from Barzini. His heart was racing. His throat was dry. Barzini's face was hidden in the shadows.

"You are probably a little curious about me. Don't be. But I am curious about you, Leo. You remind me of someone from long ago. An orphan, just like you. I envy you that, Leo, if you can believe it, because you can choose who you are. Who are you, Leo? Are you a German Leopold? An Italian Leonardo? A Russian Leon? An English Lionel? Maybe you could be Leo the Magnificent. I don't know yet."

He unfolded his hands and brought them to his face. He leaned forward into the light with his palms covering his eyes. "Sometimes I look into a person's eyes and they are just dead. Nothing there. But other times I see someone like you, someone who I could make into something."

He uncovered his eyes. "Go to sleep. Now."

Leo got up and moved toward his bedroom.

"Wait. One thing first."

Leo turned.

"Leave my wallet on the kitchen table."

"I didn't . . ." Leo started.

"I don't tolerate lying."

"But how?"

"That ad was never placed. You and I are the only two people who could have possibly known about it."

It took a moment for Leo to process the information.

"Then why am I here? Why would you hire me when you knew I was a thief?"

"A good question."

"Are you going to kick me out?" Leo asked.

"No. But you're free to leave if that's what you want," Barzini said. "You're here because you picked my pocket in broad daylight without my feeling a thing and without anybody noticing. *That* is a talent. So I am offering you the opportunity to develop that talent in a legal way. A magician must be dishonest, deceptive, manipulative with his audience. These are qualities you already possess."

"Thanks . . . I guess," Leo said. "I do want to stay. Please."

"One last thing. If you are not sincere in your desire to turn your life around, to become someone of importance and respect, then it will soon become evident and things will not work out between us. You cannot hide that from me. I will know what's squirming in your dirty little heart and the thoughts that toss in your indecent head. And if you try to steal from me again—it could be a penny or an extra lump of sugar—I will send you into a world of misery that you cannot imagine. I do not tolerate theft. It is the worst possible crime."

Barzini turned the lamp off.

"Sleep well, Leo. Your lessons will begin early."

Leo left the wallet on the kitchen table and went to his room. On his bed, he stared at the ceiling. Seconds turned into minutes, minutes turned into hours, and still his chest was tight. What had he gotten himself into?

CHAPTER 14

The First Lesson

In a dream Leo saw Chung Ling Soo. He stood behind the counter of the shop in Chinatown. He held out the golden lion trinkets to Leo. When Leo grabbed for them the lions turned into crickets. They chirped and jumped off Chung Ling Soo's hand in an infinite parade.

"Wake up."

Barzini thrust open the curtains. The bright morning light made Leo squint. Barzini was fully dressed, wearing a starched shirt with cuff links made from jagged blue stones. He held a small white porcelain cup in his hand and casually sipped.

"What time is it?" Leo asked. He blinked and wiped away crust from the corners of his eyes.

"An irrelevant question. In a few days' time I expect you to rise on your own. Now get up and make your bed. Then wash thoroughly. Everything you need is in the bathroom, including a new toothbrush and a towel for your personal use. Then come to the kitchen."

Leo started for the bathroom, but about-faced and made the bed. He tucked the corners in tightly. After washing, he joined Barzini at the kitchen table. Barzini set a roll and a mug of coffee before him. Leo didn't like coffee, but he lowered his head and sipped the hot liquid anyway. It was bitter. Leo spat it out on the table. Barzini reached behind for a towel draped on the oven and wiped up the coffee spill with circular motions.

"There's sugar on the table and milk in the icebox."

"Sorry."

Leo took three sugar cubes from the dish in the middle of the table and stirred them in. They helped the taste a little. Even though he only took small sips he could feel the coffee shoot to his head.

"I am a man of manners," Barzini said. "A man of high moral standards in my personal life, and also in my professional life. When I perform, I give the audience my best. I am neither vulgar in speech nor in performance. People trust me. This is the first and most important lesson I will teach you, and it is something that you either naturally grasp or don't.

"Each time I misdirect my audience, I am earning a bit of their trust. In the moments before the show begins, they tell themselves that they are smarter than me, that they can figure out my secrets."

Barzini paused, a smile spreading across his face. "Lookers-on feel most delight who least perceive the conjuror's sleight, and still the less they understand, the more they admire his sleight of hand."

"Did you write that poem?" Leo asked.

"Oh no, it is a well-known ditty among magicians. But as I was saying, the audience can't figure out my secrets because when I wave my right hand, I am hiding an object with my left. I hold on to it and place it on my servante or in my profonde and then it's gone and no one has any idea what just happened."

"What's a servante?"

Barzini banged his hand on the table, splashing coffee. Leo's ears turned hot.

"The definition of servante is *not* the lesson. The lesson is to never be nervous. Always be in control. Look at me, Leo. It's okay, look at me."

Leo raised his eyes.

"Let me start over. You look at me when I speak. Try to think of any other way to control a room, without having all eyes on you. There is none. Now notice everything else about me. My posture, my clothes, my demeanor. It is all intended to command attention. I prefer to wear a tuxedo, but you can also command attention by wearing a clown suit.

The difference is style. Think of the famous magicians. Herrmann had style, Thurston has style. Chung Ling Soo"—Barzini shook his head—"is someone to gawk at."

"I saw a newsreel about him."

Barzini waved his hand in a dismissive manner.

"What about Houdini?"

Barzini paused.

"Houdini is somewhere in between."

"So then what makes a good magician?" Leo asked.

"A good question. Ingenuity? Yes. But more so, humility. A good magician is humble. He is neither too showy nor too funny. He is only a vessel for the illusion. If you are a thirsty traveler, and someone offers you a jug full of water, do you care how beautiful the jug is? No, you care about the water. And then, once you have drunk your fill, you notice how nicely ornamented the jug is. Such is how a magician should be. Always second to the illusion."

Seemingly from nowhere, Barzini produced a pack of cards. He fanned them out in front of his face.

"Since you are the assistant, your job is much more devious than mine, in fact. You will be doing my dirty work, and you must be invisible while you are doing it. You will be my second set of unseen hands. The act I am envisioning is elaborate and technical, but some of it relies on basic sleight of hand. Stand up."

Leo stood and faced Barzini across the table. By now the city was beginning to come alive outside. A mourning dove cooed on the windowsill in the kitchen and Leo could hear pushcart vendors setting up below.

"Pick a card."

Leo pulled the queen of diamonds.

"Now put it back anywhere in the deck."

Leo slid it in at a random spot. Barzini proceeded to quickly shuffle the deck, and found Leo's card. He then went on to shuffle the deck and find Leo's card three more times. *Some elaborate act,* Leo thought. "That's the oldest trick in the book," he said.

"It is a very simple trick, yes, but can *you* do it?"

He pulled out the ace of spades from the deck and showed Leo. Then he put it on the bottom of the pack. "If you can figure out how to get the ace to the top without me noticing, we can stop for the day. To be fair, I'll give you a hint. There are at least two ways to do this."

Barzini handed the deck to Leo. Leo fixed his eyes on the red and blue design on the back of the cards and flicked the edges. He tried to remember any movements that Barzini had made, but it had happened so quickly, and he realized that he hadn't even really been paying attention to what Barzini's hands were doing at all. He was too busy focusing on the deck. Lesson number one.

Leo tried shuffling the deck as Barzini had. He started slowly, but after a few tries he speeded up the shuffle. It was useless. Each time he did it the ace landed somewhere in the middle.

"Do you enjoy banging your head against brick walls? Try something else." Barzini got up and sat in the other room. Leo could hear him snapping the pages of the morning paper open. The sound taunted him.

Leo flipped the deck over and looked at the faces of the cards. With the deck in his left hand he took the ace and moved it back and forth from top to bottom. Then he fanned out the cards as Barzini had done. At about the middle of the deck, he cut the cards into two piles. He knew the ace was on the bottom of the left pile. If he just shuffled now, it would be the same as before and the ace would wind up in the middle.

But if he quickly picked up the left pile, dropped the bottom card onto the top of the right pile and shuffled again, making sure the ace stayed on top, that would do it!

"I got it!" he called out.

Barzini walked to his side. His newspaper crinkled as he folded it and tucked it under his arm.

"Go on," he said.

Leo cut the deck, but he fumbled trying to get the ace to drop before he shuffled. Barzini smacked the cards out of his hand.

"The task was to get the ace to the top without me noticing. You failed. Now that you have alerted me to your method you must find another one."

Barzini left the room again to read his paper. Leo sat down at the table and sulked. He stared at the cards strewn across the wood floor.

He'd been proud of himself for figuring out the trick. But now he felt like an idiot.

"Looking at the cards on the floor won't help you understand the trick," Barzini called out.

Leo got down and picked up the cards and sorted them. He sat on the floor and counted the cards to make sure they were all there. There were only fifty-one. One card was missing. He scanned the room, underneath the table, beneath the stove, along the walls. But it was nowhere to be found, it had disappeared, simply vanished. He looked down. It was stuck to his forearm.

He pulled the card off his sweaty arm and looked at it. Then he gave his right palm a lick. He placed his hand, palm down, on the top of the deck and lifted it. The top card came with his hand. Arching his hand kept the card in place.

For the next few hours he practiced on the floor with his back to Barzini. He would sneak the ace from the bottom of the deck and hold it in place with his palm while he shuffled the cards, then drop the ace back on top. He did it over and over again until the motions became fluid. When noon bells rang he stopped. His stomach was gurgling and the room was stuffy. He felt he was ready to show his new skill.

He called Barzini over and sat him at the table. He showed the ace on the bottom of the deck. As seamlessly as he could, he kept the card tucked in his palm as he shuffled, and dropped it on top of the deck. Then, with a huge grin, he let Barzini turn the card over. Barzini flipped the ace over and kept it in place on the table with his finger.

"You palmed it."

Leo felt like a popped balloon. His smile melted and his shoulders slumped.

"Don't worry, you did it well enough. But why did you also shuffle the deck?

"I thought it would make it look better."

"Well done."

Barzini took the deck and put the ace back on the bottom.

"Of course, you could always simply force the shuffle, the way you first attempted."

Barzini quickly cut the deck a few times and then gave it a proper shuffle. When he was done, the ace was on top. "I'll show you the method one more time. Slowly."

This time, Leo could see that as Barzini cut the deck, he gripped the ace between his thumb and index finger. After letting chunks of the deck fall from one hand to the other, he dropped the ace on top and shuffled the deck card by card, making sure the ace landed last. He did it slowly again, and then sped up to as fast as before. Barzini was so quick the sound of the deck being shuffled was like a zipper being ripped.

"But there is one more way." He led Leo behind the table and rapped on the side with his knuckles. A hidden shelf dropped down from the table. Barzini reached into a slot, a sort of drawer in the table, and pulled out a stack of cards. They were all aces.

"You can always discreetly take one from the servante. And there is your first secret. See? I am a man of my word. Any card cheat knows how to force a shuffle. Only magicians know how to use the servante. Are you hungry?"

Barzini grabbed a loaf of bread and an aged salami from the cupboard and put them on a cutting board on the table. He opened the icebox and pulled out a wedge of cheese.

"The ice man has been cheating everyone between Avenue A and Avenue D, with a thousand excuses for his price," Barzini said as he sliced up the food. "It's been too warm and the river hasn't frozen yet, demand is up, there are shortages, there's a war on, so on and so on. I asked him how he plans to ship the ice to the doughboys. Of course he has no answer. That man is a crook. I should get rid of the icebox altogether."

"Don't do that," Leo said. He had never lived in a place with an icebox.

"When you pay for the ice, you can give me your opinion."

"Oh," Leo said, copying Barzini's soft accent, "you mean that when we start earning from performances my share of the ice will be deducted from my pay?"

The unflattering impersonation did not go unnoticed. In a split second, Barzini's entire demeanor changed. "Listen to me, you little street rat. If it weren't for me you'd still be elbow deep in the working man's pockets and depriving his children of their supper. So watch your mouth."

"It was just a joke . . . and I don't do that anymore," Leo protested.

"As of when? Last night when I confronted you?"

"I was trying to return the wallet, I swear," Leo said.

"Maybe you were." Barzini said. "But until you prove yourself to me, I have no way of knowing that the itch for theft is out of your blood. I remind you once more that you are in the trial phase only. Your talent, if you can call it that, will only take you so far. If you are going to pass my test, you will need to give up your thieving ways completely and submit to my teaching."

"What test? You didn't say anything about a test."

"Don't upset yourself over it. If you take my lessons to heart, you will have no problem passing."

Barzini handed Leo a knife and gestured to the bread and salami. "Slice some more, please," he said.

The salami was greasy and difficult to chew. It gave Leo indigestion, and the only way to relieve the discomfort was to force a belch.

"Are you ill or merely a pig? Which is it?" Barzini demanded.

"I'm sorry."

"That kind of crude behavior belongs to bumpkins, slatterns and ignoramuses," Barzini said. "Not the assistant to the Great Barzini."

Barzini told Leo to leave the kitchen and to practice until it got dark, going back on his word about ending practice for the day. Barzini was letting himself into the locked room when he called out to Leo, asking him if he had a clean change of clothes.

"Yes. Why?"

Leo's answer was the door slamming shut and the click of the lock.

What a cagey man, what a strange first day, Leo reflected. He took up a pack of cards and let his thumb strum the deck. The cards smacked loudly as Leo thought about Barzini. He already knew enough about him to understand that like a palmed ace, he would always find a way to be on top. In an argument or anything else. *Thwack thwack thwack.* Leo's first instinct was to lash out, but he realized that was futile. *Thwack thwack thwack.* He didn't want to run anymore, either. And Barzini was offering him a fair deal. *Thwack thwack thwack.* The only option left was to become a great magician.

CHAPTER 15

There Have Only Been Four

When evening fell, Leo put the cards back into their pack and sat at the table, waiting for Barzini to come out of his workroom. Then he tiptoed to the locked room and put his ear to the door.

Faint voices squeaked inside. Leo had seen only Barzini enter the room, but it sounded as though there were other people in there. Leo lifted his hand and knocked on the door. The sounds stopped. After a moment he heard footsteps. Then the lock clicked. The door cracked open. Barzini poked his head out.

"Yes?"

"It's dark. You told me to practice until it got dark."

"And?"

"Is there someone in there with you?"

"Nobody."

"I thought I heard voices."

"You heard nothing." Barzini's eyes narrowed. Leo craned his neck to try to get a look inside. On the back wall a picture of roses in a vase hung at an odd angle. Barzini stepped in front of Leo to block his view. As soon as Barzini stepped outside the room and locked the door behind him, Leo realized the picture hid a wall safe. Leo felt a bite of remorse. Barzini didn't want Leo to know where he kept the valuables.

"That room is off limits."

"Sorry," Leo said.

"You said you have a change of clothes. Do you have something to wear to dinner?"

"I have a white shirt."

"No tie? Then I will loan you one of mine. Go scrub yourself and get dressed."

"But I already washed today."

"And yet you still stink like a cow. We are going to an important man's house tonight. Try not to behave like an animal. And do not speak unless you have something intelligent to add to the conversation."

Leo went to the bathroom and splashed water on his face. He smelled his armpits. They didn't stink, but he threw some talcum powder into them anyway. Then he went to his room and got dressed. When he came back out, Barzini was waiting for him with a row of bow ties draped on his arm. He held his arm up to Leo's neck.

"Black? No, you'd look like a waiter. Red? No, you'd look like a clown. Blue will work."

He took all the ties except for the blue one and put them on the table. Then he took Leo's collar and flipped it up. He quickly tied the bow tie. When he finished he took a step back.

"Now you look like a person."

They took the el to Grand Central Station, then transferred to the IRT line. Barzini seemed tense, and shushed Leo whenever he tried to speak. At 110th Street Barzini led Leo to the street. Carriages clopped through Central Park. People were out walking their dogs in crisp night air. On the corner, Barzini hailed a checkered taxicab. Leo refused to get in.

"Where are you taking me? We ride the subway for half an hour to get into a cab?"

"It's not much farther."

"Then let's walk."

"Just get in the car."

Reluctantly, Leo crawled into the back of the cab. The driver turned to them. "Where to?"

"Two-seventy-eight West 113th Street."

"That's only three blocks away. I'm going to have to charge you the full fifty-cent fee for the first mile."

"That's fine."

The driver drove off, and after a brief ride stopped in front of a brownstone with a terrace on the second story. At the door Barzini paused and straightened his jacket. He clanked the knocker three times.

The door opened. A maid stood in the frame.

"Mr. Barzini, we have been expecting you."

They trailed the maid to a beautifully decorated parlor. Leo plopped down on one of the chairs, and in another, Barzini sat crossing and uncrossing his legs and smoothing the pleats in his trousers. As the maid left, she said, "Mr. Houdini will be in shortly."

Leo gaped at Barzini. "*We're in Harry Houdini's house?*" he squealed. Leo's mind reeled. *Who, really, is this guy Barzini?*

A woman with short dark hair entered the room. Barzini got up to greet her. He kissed her on the cheek. "Bess, so good to see you. You'll be joining us tonight?"

"You know I don't like to talk business, Franco. I see you brought along a friend."

"Where are your manners, Leo? Stand up."

Leo stood and wiped his clammy hands on his pants. "Hello, ma'am."

"He's not much of a showman yet. I am trying to make something out of him."

A new voice was heard from the adjoining hall. "Don't sell him short."

Houdini bounced into the room with a quick step. This was really happening! Houdini looked friendly and without that scowl Leo had seen when he was hanging upside down in Times Square. He grabbed Barzini by the arm and shook his hand. He pointed at Leo.

"An assistant, Franco?"

"Yes, sir," Leo said. "The name is Leo. It's an honor to meet you."

"The pleasure is all mine. Everyone sit, relax, get comfortable."

As Bess Houdini bid them a good evening and left, the maid reappeared with a tray of drinks and hors d'oeuvres.

"So," Houdini said, taking a sip from his glass. "I was so pleased when you telephoned yesterday. It's been far too long since we last saw each other. What have you been doing with yourself? Still doing private engagements?"

"I have actually taken a break from working, recently. I needed to rest my name. I am planning a shift in my path. Leo is part of this process."

Houdini leaned toward Leo. He spoke in a hushed voice, as if to take Leo into his confidence. "I remember the old days. Dime museums, touring with the circus. We would do five shows a day. Barely any pay, but at least we got our cakes."

"They paid you in sweets?" Leo asked.

Houdini laughed. "Wouldn't that be nice? No, 'cakes' is a circus term for meals included."

"Oh," Leo said.

"We learned so much from the circus performers," Houdini said. "How to bend over backward and pick up a pin with your teeth."

"And remember Lutes?" Barzini turned to Leo. "This poor soul was armless, but that didn't stop him from doing the most amazing tricks with his feet. How do you think Harry learned to hide keys and pick locks while his arms were shackled?"

"Remember Evatima Tardo?" Houdini said.

"That woman felt no pain, so her act was letting a rattlesnake bite her on the shoulder," Barzini said.

Leo's eyes widened. "But how could she do that and not die?"

"Milk. When she drank milk it neutralized the venom in her bloodstream. But only for her. Others have tried it and died," Barzini said.

"Our act was more hocus pocus and acts of mystification," Houdini said. "The crowds would pack in to see the three of us. They loved us."

"Three?" Leo asked.

"Of course. Me, Franco and Billy. Don't tell me Franco hasn't entertained you yet with stories from back then. Best times of our lives."

"Leo is a recent arrival," Barzini said.

Houdini nodded. "Well, let me tell you. One summer we traveled from small town to small town. Billy would go to the local café and listen to people talking about their business, gossiping. He'd write everything down in a notepad. We'd hold a séance, and Franco would rig up automatic table knockers, gauze on a stick for a ghost, and floating hands and faces painted on balloons. Then the spirits would spill all the gossip we'd collected. People fell for it every time."

"Oh yes, people fell for it every time until the day one farmer chased us out of town with a loaded shotgun," Barzini told Leo. "Billy was listening a little too hard and the ghost broke the bad news that the farmer's wife had a boyfriend on the side."

"Franco, do you remember Walla Walla?"

Barzini grinned slyly.

"We were touring with the Welch Brothers Circus," Houdini continued. "We all had to do our share. One day your mentor here filled in for the wild-child attraction. They put him in a cage and he stripped down to his bare chest, rolled in the dirt, gnawed at meat, spat at the crowd. The usual stuff. He was a natural. At the end of the day, they forgot to unlock the cage. He was stuck there all night. We found him the next morning trying to push his head through the bars."

"Alas, I am not as skilled as you at escape," Barzini said.

"No, but maybe braver. For revenge, the next night he went and unlocked all the animal cages. Elephants stomping down tents, lions roaring into the night. It was incredible. How did you ever get the tiger to wear that tutu?"

"I asked politely."

"No one ever found out who did it," Houdini said. "Billy and I kept our mouths shut."

"That must have been rather difficult for him," Barzini said.

A quiet fell over the room. It was obvious that Barzini didn't like this Billy, whoever he was. But Leo wanted to jump into the conversation and ask Houdini questions. Did he really understand the criminal mind? Leo had read *The Right Way to Do Wrong* so many times that he wondered if Houdini himself had a shady past.

"Everyone must make peace with his own actions," Houdini said finally.

"If that were true," Barzini countered, "then there would be no need for laws or police. Even our own Society of Magicians is based on the idea that there must be a standard of ethics among us. 'Unity,

Brotherhood, and Originality.' No stealing illusions, no imitation. Allowing an environment where everyone can earn. No stomping on someone to get ahead. It is all written down, and each member signs it. As current president, you know this, and should intervene when the code is broken. You have to be an example."

"That is where I disagree," Houdini said. "The Society of Magicians is not a police force, and the code is voluntary. One can decide to not join."

"But there must be consequences for those members who choose to disregard the rules. Regardless of their fame."

"Franco, of course I agree. But you cannot change the past. It was so long ago."

"Only for you."

"Sometimes it is better to let sleeping dogs lie," Houdini said. "And besides, we don't want to give poor Leo the wrong impression of our guild. I hope one day to count him as a fellow member." Houdini raised a glass toward Leo and grinned.

Barzini smoothed out his trousers. "Well, then, enough reminiscing. I have to admit, I didn't come here only to entertain Leo with stories."

"I thought not."

"I have an idea for a new act. A stage show."

"That's fantastic."

Leo couldn't tell if Houdini was being sincere, or just polite to an old friend.

"I always wondered why someone with your talents never went for the big time. Better late than never."

"This is a completely new program," Barzini continued, "with an improved bullet catch for the finale."

Houdini choked on his drink.

"After your speech about ethics and not stealing tricks? This is your new act?"

"It is not like what you think. You must hear me out first."

"Franco, why do a bullet catch? It doesn't make sense. Billy has cornered the market on that trick."

Barzini's lip curled with disgust. "Billy is a disgrace onstage in those Chinese clothes and that fake name. Chung Ling Soo? How can people be so ignorant? Can't they see that Billy, Will, Mr. Robinson, whatever he wants to be called privately these days, is a white man?"

Leo's mouth dropped.

"Wait a minute! Your friend Billy is Chung Ling Soo and he's not really Chinese?"

"A well-kept secret in our business," Houdini said. "Promise you'll keep it."

"Leo is a liar and a thief. But trusting him to keep Chung Ling Soo's secret will be nothing compared to what I will require of him onstage. Leo is going to kill me," Barzini said. "He will shoot me onstage and I will die in front of the audience. My ghost will appear above my body and hand Leo the bullet. And then young Leo will revive me."

"Ah! So it's not actually a bullet catch at all. It's a stickup, a bloody spectacle. Very intriguing."

Leo was speechless. He assumed his part in the act would involve card tricks and secret tables.

"Call him a healer. Say you found him on a farm somewhere in the Midwest, where he was known for bringing prized farm animals back to life. Play up the *boy* aspect."

"But I need a theater," Barzini said. "There are complicated aspects to the trick, more than the regular bullet catch that Billy does. Black art, a modified Pepper's ghost setup, and so forth."

"I'm happy to provide any help once you give up the gun idea." Houdini turned to Leo and held out his left hand. "Look right here," he said, pointing to the fleshy part between the ring and middle fingers. "There's a bullet in there. Been carrying it around for over twenty years."

Leo's eyes widened.

"Harry, you were shot by a robber," Barzini said. "It's not the same thing."

"True, true," Houdini said, nodding gently. "Franco, I have to admit, this act sounds terrific. Really first rate. I can tell you put a lot of thought into it. So if this is the course you want to set, then I will help you find a theater."

"Then why do I hear hesitation in your voice?"

"Because I just got a letter from Billy. He's planning to come back to America finally. Sometime this spring."

Leo straightened up. He already knew that from the newsreel in the Palace Theater: *Chung Ling Soo Will Triumphantly Return to America Soon*. Strange how in less than one week he was now connected to the news story.

"The reality is that this sort of trick, whether you catch the bullet or it catches you, is Billy's signature illusion. How will you compete with him?"

"My act will be so spectacular people will remember it for years to come. They'll be talking about how the Great Barzini was killed onstage every night and how his charmed young assistant brought him back to life. I guarantee you theater-goers will be saying, 'Chung Ling Who?' "

"I appreciate how enthusiastic you are, Franco."

"I have been planning this for years. All I need is a space to show it."

Houdini nodded. "Let me ask some theaters, then. I think it would be best to start at Coney Island."

"Coney Island?" Barzini pursed his lips. "I think we are suited for a larger space. A better space."

"That may be, Franco, but you know how the game is played. You have been around for a long time, but as far as what you're planning now, you're the new kid on the block."

As the seconds passed in silence, Leo gripped the velvet armrest tighter. Half of him wanted Barzini to refuse, so the bullet-catch talk would go no further. But Barzini finally nodded. "All right," he said. "We can make that work. Thank you."

"It's nothing."

"So tell me, Harry, will you be touring abroad this spring or staying at home?"

"I've got some things in the pipeline. A new stage show. The details aren't firmed up yet, so I'd rather not say too much. I would like to think that, like your new illusion, mine will be something the world will never forget either. But enough of that for now. Let's have dinner."

The evening continued pleasantly after the business talk was finished. Barzini and Houdini told more stories. Leo sat quietly. The idea of holding a gun again turned in his head. There was nothing about it he liked. At the end of the evening, Houdini bid them farewell and promised to call in some favors.

"I'll be in touch shortly," Houdini said at the door. "It was so good seeing you, Franco. And Leo, it was very nice to make your acquaintance. Listen to this man. You can learn a lot from him."

The street was empty. Leo and Barzini stood alone on the curb.

"Are we going to wait for a cab or walk to 110th Street?" Leo asked.

"Cabs cost money. Walk."

They waited in silence on the el platform. Barzini paced back and forth, deep in thought. Leo paced too. He couldn't figure out Barzini at all. One moment he was telling Leo he had been a successful performer with New York society, and the next he was pinching pennies and telling Leo to walk because cabs cost money. One moment he was even-tempered, and the next he was in a fury. So who was Barzini?

A train heading in the opposite direction screeched to a stop. Leo waited to speak until it pulled away from the station.

"Listen, I'm having second thoughts," Leo said. "I'm not the right assistant for you."

"But you are under contract."

"This shooting ghost thing is too dangerous. This isn't what I expected when I signed on. I hate guns. Believe it or not, I've held one before, and I didn't like the feeling. What if something goes wrong and I . . . you know."

"What? Kill me?"

"Yes! That's exactly what I mean. I don't want to go to jail."

Leo almost finished the sentence with "again" but caught himself.

"Nothing to worry about."

"But I just heard what Houdini said. The bullet catch is dangerous."

"Whose assistant are you, Houdini's or mine? It is an *illusion*, Leo. I just told you that nothing will go wrong. What happened to your bravado? We both know you've done more brazen things in broad daylight."

"But what if it does go wrong? Has anyone ever died doing this trick? Be honest with me. I need to know."

"Yes, some have died. But if it's any comfort to you, it has never been the assistant."

"Very funny. It's still my skin if you get shot. Tell me what happened."

Barzini exhaled deeply.

"I only know of four. The first to die was a magician named Coulen, more than three hundred years ago. His routine was to catch the bullets in his bare hands. But that's not what killed him. His assistant beat him to death with his own prop gun. Then there was Madame de Linsky. Her act was to be executed by a firing squad of six soldiers, who were all shills. They always bit the lead bullets off of the cartridges before loading the rifles. But when one of the shooters forgot to do that, Madame de Linsky and her unborn child died. That was a hundred years ago. Then there was Arnold Buck. His misfortune was to select a crazy volunteer from the audience to load the weapon. The bullet was a blank but the volunteer thought it would be humorous to also load the gun with nails."

Leo grimaced.

"And the last was an illusionist named Professor Adam Epstein. About fifty years ago he foolishly used his magic wand to ram the ammunition into the gun barrel. He thought nothing of it when it broke inside the barrel. He faced the shooter and died when pieces from his wand pierced his forehead. Feel better now?"

"No! I'm still not convinced this is safe," Leo said.

"Don't worry about a thing, Leo. You'll make a fine murderer."

CHAPTER 16

A More Respectable Look

They tried pennies, buttons, marbles, bottle caps, a rubber ball, a small ladies pocket watch, the cap to Barzini's cologne, cherry pits and a cork from a wine bottle. When none of those worked, they moved on to matchbooks, round stones from the park, a tooth that Barzini had left over from an old trick, pistachios and Barzini's gold ring. After four days of practice, they agreed there was a problem. Leo's fingers were nimble, but his hands weren't strong enough to palm anything for more than a few seconds.

Barzini propped up a mirror so Leo could view what the audience would see when he was hiding something in his hand. In the mirror, when Leo finally managed to hold something in place, his hand looked like he was cupping water. There was nothing subtle about it. Barzini sat with him and patiently demonstrated over and over how to palm, conceal and move small objects from hand to hand to pocket to anywhere he needed them to be. But when it was Leo's turn, he quickly realized that taking something out of a person's pocket and immediately dropping it into his own was one thing. Taking something and holding it in his hand in a way that looked natural and keeping the thing invisible was quite another. He grew frustrated. Barzini remained calm.

"I know what can help," Barzini said. "We need to go to Chinatown."

The word alone made Leo panic. He could still smell the rancid odor of the Tombs, and the image of Patrolman Quinn's face was etched in his memory. Other than the excursion to Houdini's house, Leo hadn't left Barzini's apartment since his arrival. It was, in fact, exactly one week since his escape from the Tombs. Leo scanned Barzini's newspapers daily, and even though he hadn't found an article about the prison break, that still was no guarantee that he wasn't wanted.

Leo got up and went to the bathroom and locked the door. He folded down the back of the toilet seat and sat with his head in his hands. Minutes passed as he tried to think of excuses why he couldn't go to Chinatown. The past few days had been stressful enough, wondering how he was going to handle the bullet catch.

"I don't like to be kept waiting," Barzini said as he knocked on the door.

"You go without me," Leo said. "I feel sick."

Barzini banged on the door.

"You're not sick. Open up."

Leo slowly opened the door. There was no good excuse. He decided to come clean.

"I can't go to Chinatown," he said. "There might be people looking for me."

"Police?"

"And some others. You see, what happened—"

Barzini waved his hand.

"You don't understand."

"I don't really want to understand. If there is any trouble I'll say you're my nephew and it must be a case of mistaken identity."

"That's the dumbest thing I ever heard. Who's going to believe that? We look nothing alike."

Barzini turned. Leo watched him spring down the hall to the workroom. After a few moments Barzini reappeared holding a puck-shaped canister.

"We'll dye your hair black," he said, coming back to the bathroom.

Leo sighed. He didn't think a new hair color would he enough to fool the cops. But it was better than nothing. Barzini pushed Leo's head into the sink and worked the paste into his hair. They let it sit until it started to burn Leo's scalp, and then they washed it out. The dye left a trail of black leading to the drain.

"Very good," Barzini said.

Leo dried his hair and looked into the mirror. He thought the black hair made him look mysterious. He nodded approvingly.

"The audience expects a certain appearance of a magician," Barzini said.

"So you dye your hair?" Leo asked.

"For some time. I'm not as young as I seem, perhaps."

"Oh. I didn't mean to embarrass you."

Barzini patted Leo on the shoulder. "Not at all. Now before we go, let me give you a trim to complete the transformation."

A few snips and Leo's forehead was clear and the straggly ends trellising down his neck were gone. "Much better," Barzini said. "You're a completely new person."

Leo grabbed his large cap to wear as well. An added measure of disguise wouldn't hurt. Barzini called Horatio and attached a leash to his collar.

"Here. You walk Horatio. It'll give you a more respectable look."

Horatio licked Leo's hand. As they went downtown, Horatio stayed by Leo's side, keeping pace with his steps. Leo walked slower than Barzini. He couldn't shake his nervousness about going back to Chinatown so soon.

The neighborhood was already bustling. Produce men were breaking open wooden crates of vegetables and fruits to display. Shopkeepers poured buckets of water on the patches of sidewalk in front of their shops to wash away the filth from the previous day. When Barzini led Leo to the corner of Mott and Pell, Leo's stomach flopped. The Hip Sing Tong members eyed him suspiciously. Maybe they recognized him from the ruckus of the smoke bombs and the police chase. Thoughts raced through his head. Is this a trap? Some kind of sick joke—revenge for the stolen wallet? Why was Barzini being so nice all of a sudden? Did the Mayor get to him?

"Where are we going?" Leo asked.

"To a friend's store," Barzini said.

Leo's eyes darted left and right, looking for anyone who might recognize him. Fortunately, the Chinese undercover cop was not sipping his tea by the front window of the teahouse.

But Patrolman Quinn was still on the beat. He was walking down Pell Street heading toward Barzini and Leo. Leo shrank, certain that Quinn would remember him. Barzini took one look at Leo's terrified face. "You know this one?" he asked while pretending to adjust his pocket watch.

"*He* knows *me*," Leo said out of the corner of his mouth. He couldn't take his eyes off Quinn as he dawdled nearer.

"No, he does not. Smile, and tip your hat at the nice policeman."

Leo looked at Barzini, who reassured him with a great grin.

"You're just a kid. He'll see your hat, not your face. Go ahead. Steal his trust."

Quinn was mere feet in front of them. They started walking again.

"*Buon giorno*," Barzini said. Leo tipped his hat as told. Quinn looked straight through him.

"In America we say 'good morning,' " Quinn said as he walked passed.

Barzini turned.

"*Mi scusi?*" he said loudly and curtly.

Leo was frozen stiff. They had gotten away. What was Barzini doing now?

Quinn did an about-face. He squinted at the two of them.

"It's 'good morning,' " he said. "It's ENGLISH."

"Ah, yes, of course. Thank you, officer, for the lesson in, how do you say? English. Gooooood mooooorniiiing!"

Quinn nodded and continued on his beat.

Leo walked forward, focusing on the thumps of his feet on the concrete. After a minute passed he allowed himself to breathe. He turned his head ever so slightly and saw Quinn harassing a street vendor.

"Why did you do that?"

"In part, to demonstrate lesson number one. But maybe also because this officer Quinn made my blood boil."

They had stopped in front of the shop where Leo purchased the firecrackers and smoke bombs. "Here's our destination," Barzini said.

"The old Chinese guy with the white hair is your friend?" Leo asked.

"So you've been here before. That man has a name. Bo Shen. He is a magician who carries certain articles that even Antonio Martinka would love to get his hands on."

"Like what?"

"Herbs, tinctures, special gunpowders. Other items related to Chinese magic and alchemy. Be sure to show respect to him. He is a great man."

The bells tinkled as Barzini shut the door behind him. The shop was dark, only early morning streaks of light brightening the room. Barzini took the leash from Leo and unhooked Horatio. He immediately set to exploring the shop, sniffing at all the corners of the room. Leo walked in behind Barzini and tried to remain in his shadow.

"Good morning, Mr. Shen."

The man came out from behind the counter and put an arm around Barzini, pushing him to the side and revealing Leo.

"Ah, *baozhu*," Mr. Shen said, wagging his finger at Leo.

"Leo, what were you doing with firecrackers?"

"How do you know Chinese?" Leo asked, trying to avoid the question.

"I know it because I learned it. But you still didn't answer my question," Barzini said.

"I guess my disguise didn't work as well as you thought."

"Nothing escapes Mr. Shen, unlike your average New York City policeman. And I suppose setting off firecrackers in Chinatown has something to do with what you were trying to tell me before. Never mind, then. Mr. Shen, I need a set of *baoding* meditation balls."

"New assistant?"

"I'm trying him out," Barzini answered.

Mr. Shen took down a small red box covered with silk. Inside were two shiny silver orbs. They chimed as he took them out of the box and handed them to Barzini.

"Now watch," Barzini said.

Barzini placed the balls in the palm of his hand and slowly rotated them around each other in an even, constant orbit. They seemed to fly around in his palm with very little finger movement. Suddenly he stopped and moved them in the other direction. He turned his palm downward, but the *baoding* didn't fall. Then he dropped the balls into Leo's hand.

"You try."

The balls rolled around clumsily in Leo's hand. One fell to the floor.

"What's the point of this?" Leo grumbled.

"This technique will build muscles in your hand you didn't know were there. You will be able to hold a bullet between the folds in your palm when you've mastered it. Now take the *baoding* and sit over there while I discuss a few things with Mr. Shen."

Leo sulked while he sat again on the big dusty oversized chair. Horatio came to his side and dropped his head in Leo's lap. He closed his eyes and let his tongue roll to one side as Leo scratched behind his ears. Barzini leaned over the counter and spoke to Mr. Shen in Chinese. The old man pulled away for a moment. He seemed confused. Barzini kept talking, drawing a little diagram in the air with his finger, speaking more passionately. Mr. Shen shook his head. Leo pretended to fiddle with the balls, but he watched the whole thing from his seat. After a while, Mr. Shen nodded. He looked slightly troubled, but eventually they stopped talking and bowed to each other. Barzini motioned for Leo to get up.

Mr. Shen clapped his hands and Horatio ran to the counter, tail wagging. He ate what Mr. Shen offered from his fingertips.

Leo looked down through the glass case. The golden lions were still displayed on a satin pouch. Mr. Shen took them out and set them on the countertop.

"Do you want to buy the lions today?" he asked.

"They are quite beautiful," Barzini said.

"They're nice and all, but I was just curious," Leo said.

Leo picked up Horatio's leash, and they left the shop and walked down Pell Street. "How did you learn Chinese?" Leo asked.

"I have many interests," Barzini said. "In my life I've known a number of Chinese illusionists. Mr. Shen, for example. In his youth he was a famous magician in Canton province, in southern China. I learned a lot from him, including his language. Mr. Shen is like a father to me. And years ago I spent time in Hong Kong."

"If Mr. Shen speaks English, then why did you talk to him in Chinese? Was it a secret?"

"You think you're very clever, but have you considered that Mr. Shen might prefer to speak in his native language?"

Leo didn't answer Barzini. He was fixated on the Hip Sing Tong members still standing on the corner of Mott Street. Only now they were huddled around a man Leo recognized as the customer with the diamond ring in Mr. Shen's shop when he bought the firecrackers.

"That's Mock Duck," Barzini whispered to Leo. "He's the boss. He runs Chinatown."

Leo looked over his shoulder. Mock Duck had long fingernails and a sly smile. Gold jewelery shone from every possible place. As he unbuttoned his jacket, Leo saw a gun tucked into the waistband of his trousers. Leo turned away and pulled Horatio to make him move quicker.

Back at Barzini's apartment, Leo received his simple practice instructions.

"Start with your right hand."

Barzini went to his workroom and turned the key to unlock the door. "Horatio, come!"

Horatio followed his master, and Leo was left alone. He opened the red box, placed the silver orbs in his right hand and attempted to rotate them in his palm. It seemed so easy in his mind, but the movements were intricate and slow. He stared intently at his hand. Every so often he thought he had the hang of it, but then they'd drop to the floor again. Leo practiced for over an hour, until his head hurt more than his sore hand. But by then the balls were swirling past each other in his palm like boxers squaring off.

CHAPTER 17

Let Go of Reality

Horatio curled up across Leo's bare feet, keeping them warm as Leo polished his shoes. Barzini had locked himself in the workroom, but left a string quartet spinning out soothing adagios on the gramophone. Leo was taking a break from practice. He'd been working nearly non-stop with the *baoding* balls for days. That morning he'd woken up with aches in his knuckles and decided to let his hands rest.

The shoe-polish vapor stung his eyes. He looked down at Horatio. The dog looked up at him. Leo sighed and tossed his shoes aside.

Barzini came out of the workroom and locked it. "I am going to Martinka's for a while."

Leo nodded.

"You can change the record if you want. But make sure not to scratch it."

"Mhmm."

"I'm sorry, but you cannot come with me. I've arranged a meeting with the heads of the Magician's Society," he said with a bit of pride in his voice. "They do not allow non-members to sit in on the proceedings."

"Okay."

In the short time Leo had known Barzini, he had already learned better than to dig for more details about strange statements. When

Barzini wanted to share, then, and only then, he would. Until then, there would only be hints and little tiny pieces of a story. The thought crossed Leo's mind that Barzini enjoyed this game.

At the door, Barzini put his hand on the knob. He hesitated.

"This does somewhat involve you," Barzini began. "It has to do with what I was alluding to at Houdini's house. Many years ago, Robinson, before he became Chung Ling Soo, broke our code of conduct in the Magician's Society in a most egregious manner. His violations were never properly addressed. If the society means anything at all it should recognize this fact. Even if he is world famous, he is still a member of the society. Perhaps I can make his homecoming more difficult for him than he is expecting."

"Good luck."

Barzini opened the door and abruptly took a step back into the apartment. Leo could not see who was in the hall.

"Is Leo here?"

The voice was familiar, but he couldn't quite place it. Barzini glanced over his shoulder at Leo.

"You have a visitor."

Leo moved his feet and Horatio got up. Leo went to the door. Penelope was there, smiling.

"Hi."

"Hi."

Penelope let out a little laugh.

"Hi."

Barzini looked at the two.

"Leo, why don't you get some shoes on and walk Horatio. And have Penelope join you."

Leo slipped his shoes on and returned to the door. While Penelope waited for them near the stairs, Barzini dug into his pocket and produced some change. As he sifted through the coins, Leo caught his eye. Over the past weeks, Leo had noticed the denominations of Barzini's bills getting smaller and smaller. He realized that Barzini now had another mouth to feed. Leo didn't want to take anything extra from him.

"You don't need to give me anything," Leo said.

"No, I insist. Not another word."

Barzini gave Leo some change, and few moments later they were all at street level. Barzini went one way and Leo and Penelope the other. They strolled along for a few blocks. Leo gripped Horatio's leash tightly, his palm clammy. He wanted to say something, but everything that popped into his head sounded unbelievably dumb. He looked at the dog for inspiration.

"So," he said, "is this your first time meeting Horatio?"

She reached down to scratch the dog's head.

"Nope. We're old friends. He comes to the shop sometimes."

A gust of wind blew her hair into her face. She swept it aside. They both hugged their coats tighter around them.

"I wanted to make sure you were doing all right," she said.

"Oh."

"I had half a thought that Barzini might have driven you crazy already. He came in the other day and mentioned to Oma he had hired you. We all feared for your sanity." She waved her index finger in front of Leo's eyes. "But you seem all there."

They both smiled.

"There's something different about you," Penelope said.

Leo laughed.

"You mean this," he said, running his hand through his hair.

"Yes, that's it! Why the change?"

"Barzini thought it might give me a more theatrical look," Leo said.

"I like it. So, what have you learned about magic so far?"

"Not much. I mean, I guess a few card tricks. Barzini wants me to become a master at sleight of hand before I learn anything else."

"Well, you can't just start off with levitation, you know."

"Yeah, I know. More than anything I'm sort of watching. It seems like everything Barzini does has two reasons. The one he wants you to know about and the secret one that he keeps to himself. But I guess that's what makes him so good, right?"

"Maybe. But Barzini eats and sleeps magic. Magic is his entire life. What is it that you like so much about magic, Leo?"

Leo thought about it. He knew there was nothing really supernatural about the floating water jugs, the twigs that miraculously grew into orange trees or the levitating bodies that he had seen onstage. They were only illusions. But if the man onstage could make him believe what he was seeing was real, while he *knew* it was fake, then that was truly amazing.

"I guess I just kind of like being able to let go of reality."

Penelope looked stunned.

"That's a really good answer."

Suddenly a flash of shyness burned through Leo. He realized how cute Penelope was. He also realized Horatio was relieving himself by her feet.

"Hey, is that Wally Pipp?"

"Where?"

Penelope spun around. He yanked Horatio's leash and shot him a dirty look.

"Nah, must've been someone else. Anyway, do you want to get something warm to drink? Hot chocolate. On me."

"Yeah! That'd be nice."

They ducked into a nearby tearoom and got a table by the door. The owner did not want to seat them with Horatio, but Leo convinced him, showing how well-behaved and placid the dog was. The hot chocolate arrived in large glass mugs with enormous marshmallows on top, slowly melting into the steaming liquid.

"So, do you work in the shop all the time?"

"No. I also go to school. Well, home school. Everyone kind of teaches me. Oma, Opa, Grossonkel. What about you?"

Leo wasn't sure what to say. "I, uh, I wasn't much of a bookworm. I went through sixth grade only, like lots of other boys in my school. Where I came from, things were done a little differently."

"And where was that?" Penelope asked.

"Upstate."

"Ah, a country boy."

"Well, sort of. I've been in the city for a while."

"With family?"

The conversation was getting complicated. He didn't want to lie to Penelope. A twisted bit of truth would have to fit instead. "I had brothers. But they're gone now."

"In the war? That's so sad."

"Not really. It was like Cinderella, except with boys. They didn't take good care of me. I'm in a much better situation now with Barzini. We both want our arrangement to work. I'm paying better attention to his lessons than I ever did in school. And we're starting to get along just fine. It's gotten easier. At first I wasn't too sure, but I guess it's like anything else. It takes time to get adjusted to something new."

They talked and talked, long after they had finished their hot chocolates. When Penelope said she had to be getting back, Leo paid the tab and they walked together to the apartment on East Seventh. At the door, Leo stopped.

"Well, I guess this is good-bye," he said.

"For now. Do you want to come with me to a magic show sometime?"

"Yes! Sure! That'd be fun."

"Good. I have an extra ticket for Harry Blackstone's show next Thursday. I'll see you then, okay?"

"Okay. Where should we meet?"

"Here," Penelope said. "I'll come by for you at three o'clock."

Leo skipped up the two flights of stairs. Horatio panted by his side. In the apartment he found Barzini hanging up his coat.

"Just getting back?" Barzini asked.

"We got hot chocolates."

"I will give you some advice. Keep her out of your head. Don't let a girl distract you from your progress. Of course you won't listen to me."

Leo couldn't tell if Barzini was teasing him or not. "We're just friends. How did the meeting go?"

"I was heard out."

"And? Are they going to do anything? He broke the rules, right?"

"They decided it was in the best interest of the community to let the past stay in the past."

He reached into his vest and pulled out a new pack of cards. "I noticed you skipped your morning practice." Barzini tossed the pack to Leo.

"Thanks," Leo said, and sat down in a chair in the parlor. Horatio followed and curled up again across his feet. "I mean for the money. You know, you really didn't have to give me anything."

Barzini put up his hand. "You do not have to keep thanking me. Once was enough. A little diversion is good for you. You've earned it and I am happy to be able to provide it. Believe it or not, I remember what it was like to be your age. Now practice your shuffles until I come back out. I can hear the cards when I'm in there," he said, gesturing to the workroom. "I will know if you're slacking."

Barzini retreated to the workroom. The customary sound of the lock clicking set Leo at ease. He took some comfort in Barzini's odd ways as they became more familiar. He knew that the rug could get pulled out from under his feet at any second. Leo didn't want to delude himself into thinking that Barzini's apartment was his home or that Horatio was his dog. But it was getting harder not to.

He tore away the stamp sealing the deck of cards and began to shuffle them. He looked down to Horatio. "Pick a card."

Horatio seemed to consider the offer, but then dropped his head to the floor and left Leo to his practice.

CHAPTER 18

The Same Trick Twice

The next morning Barzini announced that they were going downtown.

"Where downtown?"

"Mr. Shen's shop, among other places," Barzini said.

Outside, the wind was picking up and sticking needles in Leo's face. He pulled his cap down low over his forehead and turned up the collar of his coat. After stopping at the grocer for espresso beans, they continued toward the subway. Barzini set a lively pace.

Leo considered Barzini carefully. As far as Leo had observed, Barzini kept his interactions with the world to a minimum. The telephone rarely rang, nobody paid an afternoon social call, he never went out to the corner saloon. Barzini had told Leo that he'd lived in the same neighborhood for years. But Leo noticed that he made little conversation with the barber, the grocer or the woman in the hand laundry who washed and starched his white shirts. And yet he appeared to be happy in his solitude. Leo thought how being a loner with an assistant on your heels all day didn't exactly add up for someone like Barzini. But the slow steps they'd been taking with each other so far seemed to be working out.

"Can I ask you something?"

"You just did," Barzini said.

Leo clenched both fists with the thumbs extended upright.

"Do my thumbs look peculiar to you?" Leo asked.

Barzini furrowed his brow.

"Why do you ask?"

"I've been wondering if I have the thumbs of a criminal."

"Is this your attempt at a joke?"

"In Houdini's book, *The Right Way to Do Wrong*, he says that a criminal's hand is very different from a regular hand, and that you can always tell a criminal because of his plump thumbs."

"That's ridiculous."

"Yeah, I thought so too," Leo said, giving his thumbs a quick once-over. "How come Houdini knows so much about criminals?"

"From his younger days. He'd go to the police station in every city he visited and asked to get handcuffed and locked in a cell, from which he'd escape. He made friends with police chiefs, and even with John E. Wilkie, who was the head of the Secret Service as well as an amateur magician. Houdini likes to boast that he trained Wilkie and his agents in the arts of mind reading, for interrogation, and sleight of hand techniques."

"Really?" Leo said.

"I suppose it's all true. With Houdini you can never be completely sure."

"I was wondering . . ." Leo said.

"What?"

"I just wondered why you never spend time with your friends."

"People fill their lives with things they don't need. It's wasteful."

"Friends are wasteful?"

To Leo, that sounded like one of the most awful things a person could say. He thought of Murph. Leo missed him. Or maybe he just missed the friendship they once had. Life was good with Barzini, but their relationship was not like having a best pal your own age.

"No, that's not exactly what I mean. I am just careful who I share my life with."

On the subway platform, Leo looked over his shoulder to the right and then to the left. It had remained a habit even though he saw no posters advertising a reward for his arrest, nor any mention of the jailbreak at the Tombs in the newspapers. He breathed easy now, he was relaxed, but only when he was out with Barzini. When he was by himself in a public place, he could not completely shake his jitters.

Leo lightly elbowed Barzini as he caught sight of a man with a full beard carrying a beat-up satchel. To Leo, something about the forward momentum of his walk and the way his eyes flitted around was immediately familiar. The man weaved in and out of groups of people on the platform. When he chose a spot next to a well-dressed businessman, Leo knew he'd been right. The businessman had an alligator-skin briefcase on the platform by his foot.

"See that man, the one with the satchel over there?" Leo whispered to Barzini.

"What about him?" Barzini asked.

"Well, you know how you told me that being a magician is like being a thief? I think that guy over there is about to do some magic."

Leo led Barzini closer, within earshot of the two men.

"Old Man Winter has arrived, wouldn't you say?" the satchel man said to the businessman. When he didn't get a reply, he pressed on, chattering fast about the outgoing mayor, the weather and the vexing delays of IRT trains, until he landed upon a subject that stuck.

"Excuse me, sir," he said, "but you seem like a churchgoing man."

The businessman cleared his throat.

"I observe the Lord's Sabbath, if that's what you mean," he said.

"Wait until I tell the missus tonight. She says I have a knack for picking out customers. See, my line is selling Bibles." He reached into his satchel and took one out. He held it up dead center in front of the businessman's nose. "Take a good look! In front of you, sir, is the finest Bible in print today. The King James Version, translated from the original tongues. Genuine kid leather covers and gilt edges. The Lord's words in red. Gutenberg himself would be delighted. With Christmas coming up, it would make a fine gift for your wife."

"No, thank you."

"Well then, how about for your dear mother?"

"She is deceased."

"Rest her soul. Well then, perhaps for a neighbor? Or employees? These Bibles are a real deal. Only three dollars apiece. I'll tell you what. Two dollars apiece if you buy more than one."

Leo whispered to Barzini out of the corner of his mouth, "How's that for patter?"

The businessman took a deep, annoyed breath and took a few steps backward. From inside the tunnel, the horn of an approaching train sounded. The Bible salesman continued with his blabber, and kept the book in front of the businessman's face.

"Allow me to recite my favorite passage," he said. "*For the love of money is the root of all evil: which while some coveted after, they have erred from the faith and pierced themselves with many sorrows.*" As he spoke he squeezed the handle of the satchel, opening up a false bottom, and dropped the satchel over the businessman's briefcase. At the same moment, the businessman craned his neck toward the first glimpse of headlights in the tunnel. He didn't seem to notice that the preaching had stopped, the Bible salesmen had left and his briefcase was gone. The thief walked quickly in Leo's direction, trying to get to the exit.

As the fake Bible salesmen passed, and the train came to a stop in the station, Leo stuck out his leg. The thief tripped, and squeezed the handle of the satchel looking for support. The alligator briefcase tumbled out the bottom. Leo scooped it up and told the thief to get lost.

Leo flagged down the businessman and, handing him his briefcase, said, "Mister, I think this belongs to you. That guy selling Bibles stole it. You can't trust anyone in this city."

"Thank you, young man!" the businessman said. He reached into his breast pocket for his wallet. "I would like to reward you. You are quite right about trust, and such integrity should be noticed."

He pulled out a bill.

"Put it back. I don't want a reward."

"And such modesty! There is hope."

"Oh yes," Barzini said in a mocking tone. "That's the word."

The train doors opened and Barzini led Leo inside. They settled far away from the businessman, and Leo explained the setup.

"The beard was fake," he said. "And at the next train station he'll probably have on a fake moustache, or maybe a wig, or glasses. And if you looked closely at his coat, you could tell it was reversible with a checked pattern. He could switch himself inside out and be somebody different all day. It's like what we're doing. The man with the briefcase *trusted* him completely."

"I disagree," Barzini said. "You stick that man on a stage, he would be lost. He would feel naked in front of an audience. It is not the same."

"He didn't look like he felt naked on the subway platform. He was comfortable performing in front of dozens of people."

Barzini shook his head but remained silent.

"Would it kill you to give me a little compliment?" Leo said. "You know, I've been trying to prove myself to you, working nonstop. I'm getting really good."

"Don't exaggerate. Although you have shown improvement, that is true. Let's say that you are no longer a worm," Barzini said.

Leo smiled.

"I'll take it. So, you must be happy you chose me."

Barzini turned to face Leo. His lighthearted expression turned serious.

"You have a gift, Leo. Magicians practice for years hoping to have that kind of invisibility, but for you it comes naturally. Of course, that first night I was not sure if it would work out, but I think we can both agree we're on the same course."

Barzini stuck his hand out to shake. But when Leo grasped it, he felt an object there. It was a small Mexican lime held in the crease between his ring and middle fingers.

"What's that for?"

"This is your test."

"Right, the mysterious test. I thought you had just made that up to keep me in line."

"No, the test is real."

Barzini swiveled his wrist to show off the fruit, and then carved an X into the skin with a fingernail. Then he let it drop into his sleeve.

"Do you remember the first rule I told you?"

"To always be confident?"

"Yes. However, I made a mistake. Please forgive me, I am new at teaching. The first rule in magic is to never perform the same trick twice for an audience. If you can get the lime without me noticing by tomorrow, then you can consider the contract fully executed and your position as assistant final."

This was not at all what Leo expected. Barzini had already admitted that Leo had invisible hands when it came to picking pockets. So what was he testing for? Sometimes with Barzini it seemed like one step forward, two steps backward.

The train came to their stop. They got up, and as they followed everyone out to the street, Leo became uneasy. When picking a pocket, the mark should under no circumstances have any inkling he is about to get robbed. Worse, Leo had no idea where the lime was hidden in Barzini's clothes. A smoky aroma of burning incense met Leo's nose as they entered Mr. Shen's shop. Mr. Shen was praying in front of a jade Buddha statue, Leo tried to gauge any little bumps in the fabric of Barzini's clothes. He'd seen the lime slip down Barzini's jacket sleeve, but by now it could be anywhere.

Mr. Shen got up and greeted them. In English, Barzini said that they wouldn't be staying long, and then he started to speak in Chinese. Then Barzini turned to Leo. "I need to do my errands now. You stay here and keep Mr. Shen company. Show him your progress. I will be back soon."

"Why can't I come?"

"I don't think you would want to. I'm going to the dentist for a toothache."

"You have a toothache? You didn't say anything."

"It's just a minor problem, but I'd like the dentist to look at it," Barzini said. He buttoned his coat and left.

"Barzini said you have something to show me," Mr. Shen said.

Leo took the silver *baoding* balls from his pocket and spun them clockwise and counterclockwise in both his right and left hands. The balls never banged into each other, nor did they slip from Leo's hands.

"Well?" Leo asked.

"Not bad," Mr. Shen said.

Leo took a seat on the cushy chair and rested his head against the wall while Mr. Shen organized items in his display case. Mr. Shen pressed his index finger to his lips for complete silence while he counted the money in his cash register.

A few minutes passed. Leo settled back in the chair and slipped into excruciating boredom. "I'm going to get something to eat," he said. "Where's the dentist's office?"

"Half a block down on Mott toward Bayard."

Leo left the shop and walked toward Mott. In the distance, over the tops of a few buildings, he could see the gray roof of the Tombs. He wondered if the kid with the black hair was still inside, and felt a knock of sadness. He walked slowly and deliberately, looking for anyone in uniform or anyone out of place who might be a plainclothes cop. When he got to Mott, he looked for a dentist's office and easily found it by the picture of a molar hanging in the window.

He peered in. A Chinese man in a white smock sat idly reading a newspaper. The dentist's chair in the middle of the room was empty. Leo was about to go when he noticed something on the ground by his foot. The lime. He knelt down and picked it up. It was the same one, with the X marking. Just then the door to the dentist's office swung open, knocking Leo to the side. The dentist made a gesture of apology and walked off, leaving his office empty.

Leo looked around. Barzini was nowhere in sight. Leo put the lime in his pocket and was about to move on when he spotted something out of the corner of his eye. A red door at the back of the dentist's office slid open, and a man dressed in rumpled clothing shuffled out. He breezed past Leo like a sleepwalker and slunk down the street. The red door closed on its own.

Leo entered the office and examined the red door. There was no knob. He pressed his hand against it and moved it to the side, revealing a short hallway with red and gold silk tapestries on the walls. Leo went in. The door slid shut behind him. At the end of the hall there was a bead curtain. He pushed his way through and found himself in a large room with dozens of people lounging on cushions, smoking from long pipes. Women dressed in traditional Chinese garb attended to the patrons. There was some muted laughter, some people speaking in low voices. He had stumbled into an opium den. Leo stayed close to the wall and tried to not catch anybody's notice.

The people lying on the floor were pathetic. They had sunken eyes, and skin the color of soapy water. Some of them did not have on their shirts, and Leo saw how thin they were. Their ribs jutted out and their shoulder blades were sharp. Leo crouched low and scanned the room for Barzini, even though he really did not expect to find him there. Leo figured that if Barzini had an opium addiction he would look as sickly as the people in the room. Leo didn't linger, but made his way back to the hallway. As he swept aside the bead curtain, he ran into three men whose slippers gave them away as members of the Hip Sing Tong.

They regarded Leo as if he were a fish in the middle of a desert. Leo prepared himself for a blow to the head, or for one of them to grab him and toss him out. But they simply walked around him. Behind him, he heard one of the men barking out some orders in Chinese. Leo looked over his shoulder and saw a girl rush out to them. She handed over a wad of money and bowed as she backed into the opium den through the bead curtain. The tong members began counting the cash.

Leo left them behind. He emerged back into the dentist's office, which was still empty. When he reached the street, he saw Barzini down the block, strolling next to Mock Duck. Very strange. Leo trailed behind, keeping most of the block between himself and the two men. At the end of the block they stopped, made slight bows to each other and parted. Perhaps from Barzini spending so much time at Mr. Shen's shop, they had become acquaintances.

Leo ran to catch up. Near Mr. Shen's shop he stopped by the fishmonger who sold the frogs that Boris and Murph had had a good laugh at. The man had gotten smarter since then. Instead of keeping the frogs in a barrel, he tied them back-to-back so that none of them could jump away. Leo bought one and held it in his hand. He went into Mr. Shen's shop, where Barzini was at the counter deep in conversation with Mr. Shen.

"I'll just sit here and wait," he called out to Barzini.

Barzini nodded but did not turn around. He resumed his conversation with Mr. Shen. Leo crept up behind Barzini, carefully placed the frog on his shoulder, and then tapped next to it. Barzini turned, got an eyeful of the amphibian and let out a yawp. The frog hopped off onto the glass display case. Mr. Shen grabbed for it, but the frog was too terrified to stick around. It jumped to the floor. Leo held open the door and let the frog out onto the sidewalk.

He tossed the lime to Barzini.

Barzini patted down his coat pockets. Then his sleeves and pants. He even felt underneath his shirt.

"Interesting touch," Barzini said shakily, "using the frog for distraction."

"Thank you."

Leo bowed deeply. Mr. Shen shook his head in disapproval.

"Allow me to examine the lime to make sure it's mine," Barzini said, once he had his wits back.

"Go ahead. But it is," Leo said. "You'll see the X on the outside."

"You could have gotten a lime and marked it yourself."

Barzini ripped open the skin of the lime and pulled out a small tack.

"But you wouldn't have known about this."

Leo turned to Barzini. "I didn't pick that lime off of you. The frog was too much to pass up, but I found the lime on the ground near the dentist's office."

"Did you?"

"Yeah. I'm not going to lie to you. What's the point? I came looking for you but you weren't there," Leo said. "Instead, I found the lime."

Barzini nodded.

"So I guess you'll have to hide another lime," Leo said. "Or pick something else."

"There's no need for that, Leo. I hoped that you'd come looking for me. I actually planned it that way. If you hadn't found the lime in front of the dentist's office, you would have found it on the seat next to you during lunch, or perhaps in front of our apartment later. The test was never about your skill. It was about trust."

"So I passed?"

"In spades," Barzini said.

He clapped Leo on the shoulder and grinned. A smile grew on Leo's face as well. Barzini trusted him! He rolled the word "assistant" around in his head. It had a nice ring. It sounded official. Before he was only a trainee, but now he had a position. He had a place. He and the magician were a team.

CHAPTER 19

A Tight Squeeze

Barzini pulled out a thick roll of bills and placed ten dollars in Leo's hand. Leo wondered what had happened to make Barzini flush with cash again.

"There is a saying in this country. You have to spend money to make money. Take this deposit to Bellini's tailor shop on the corner of Prince and Elizabeth. He needs to take your measurements for two tuxedos and two sets of farm clothes for our grand finale. I know it's months away, but it'll be one less detail to worry about."

"Okay," Leo said.

"I called him yesterday with all the details," Barzini said. "And don't let Bellini talk you into getting only one profonde. He's lazy, but he has been doing my costumes for years and he knows we need secret profonde pockets in both coattails."

"Got it."

"And if he has any questions, tell him to call me before he cuts the cloth. While you are out I will be at Martinka's. We need to reserve the back theater."

Leo played it cool, but inside he was electric. If Barzini was reserving the theater, that meant Leo he was going to learn the bullet catch soon. He felt ready to start practicing the other acts they'd do onstage and he was happy Barzini saw that as well. But he still had grave concerns over the illusion.

Outside, a fine dusting of snow covered everything. Footprints dragged through the thin layer, revealing streaks of concrete and pavement. The molded steel of fire hydrants looked like enormous French pastries with sugar sprinkled on top.

As Leo passed a storefront window, he paused to study his reflection. He liked what he saw. His hair was long enough now to slick back like Barzini's. His breath frosted the window, making the image of himself ghostly.

He moved along, crisscrossing blocks as he headed west toward the intersection of Prince and Elizabeth. When he entered the tailor shop he hung his coat on a rack.

"Can we help you?" The tailor was hunched over a sewing machine working the foot pedal. Behind him were rolls of fabric piled high and bins filled with buttons stacked in order of size. The tailor's wife, working next to him, looked up and nodded in greeting, a row of straight pins clamped between her lips.

"Gianfranco Barzini sent me," Leo said, hoping that would explain everything.

The tailor nodded.

"I remember. The tuxedos to his specifications but in your size. And the overalls with small pochette pocket at the hips plus white work shirts. I quoted Signor Barzini ten dollars as a down payment for all the work together. Then I realized, with the extra pockets, the price I gave was too little. I meant to call back but I got busy and forgot. I'll need at least fifteen upfront to start the project, with the rest due at the end."

Leo approached the husband and wife. He laid the ten-dollar bill on the sewing machine.

"This is all I have."

"But it is not enough."

"Ten was what was quoted."

The tailor pushed the bill back toward Leo.

"But fifteen is what it costs."

Leo took the bill.

"Tomaselli's is only a few blocks away. He makes costumes for Broadway shows. I'm sure he will be able to handle this," Leo said, turning to go. He heard a sigh behind him.

"Wait." The tailor grabbed Leo and directed him to an elevated platform in front of a full-length mirror.

"So, your tuxedo is just like Barzini's?" the tailor repeated.

"Just like he told you, with two profondes, six inches deep. On *both* sides."

"Yes, all right."

The tailor removed the tape measure from around his neck and wrapped it around Leo's waist. "Now let your arms relax, and stop balling up your hands. I need to know exactly where your knuckles fall by your side. Otherwise everyone in the audience will see how you hide things in your pockets. How many inches left in the seams?"

"What do you mean?"

"It's good to leave something to let out."

"I don't know. I want it to fit perfect, like a glove. But Barzini said to call him with any questions."

Leo put the ten-dollar bill in the tailor's palm while his wife wrote a receipt. He left the store. Salt on the sidewalk crunched under his feet. He went back to the apartment and spent the early afternoon going through his clothes, trying on every combination of outfit he could find and posing in front of the bathroom mirror. He wanted to look dashing when he met with Penelope. He wished his tuxedo were ready. Then he could really impress her.

He settled on the best he had, a clean white shirt tucked into slacks with a sweater over top. Then he spent a long while pacing around the apartment, opening cabinets for no reason, fiddling with his collar, with Horatio trailing him. He waited until nearly four o'clock, and then he could pace no more. Maybe Penelope had forgotten about their date. Leo got his coat.

All the snow had melted, leaving the streets dark and wet. Leo hopped onto the train, and sooner than he could scrape the dirt off his shoes, he was back on the street in front of Martinka's. He peered inside. The coast seemed clear of Barzini. He walked in past Walter the satyr and looked around. The end-of-the-day business was slow. He didn't see Penelope anywhere, but Grossonkel Antonio was sitting in his chair, reading as usual. Leo went to him.

"Hello," Leo said.

Grossonkel Antonio tilted his paper down.

"Ah, Barzini's assistant. You just missed him."

"That's all right. Is Penelope around?"

"Penelope? Why do you want to see Penelope?"

"Uh, she told me she had a book she wanted me to see."

"I can help you with that."

"Thanks, but I forgot the title. Maybe if I talked to her I could get it."

"I'm afraid that's not possible."

"No?"

"No. She is being punished. And not taking visitors."

"Oh. Well, can she at least come out to tell me which book it was?"

"Not possible. Right now she is helping her *oma* with chores in the back. Young man, I suggest you come back in a few days if she truly is the only person that can help you find the book you need. Otherwise, I can suggest many books of interest."

"I guess I will come back, then. Tell her I stopped by, please."

Grossonkel Antonio nodded and flicked the newspaper back into place.

As Leo left the store, he spotted a hatch that led into the basement of the building for deliveries. It was secured with a padlock. He had an idea. He ran to a nearby shop and bought some hairpins. At the hatch he kneeled and got to work on the lock, acting natural, as if someone had put him to the task. Passersby came and went from both directions, but no one paid him any attention.

Leo was never a great lock-picker, but after some fiddling he finally gave the lock a jerk and it released. He lifted the hatch and descended the stairs to the basement, guiding the hatch down so it would not clank. Balancing himself on the steps, he took off his shoe and propped the hatch open so that he would not be in total darkness.

As his eyes adjusted, he saw the stairs at the other end of the basement and made his way toward them, careful not to step on anything or knock something over. He climbed the stairs and put his ear to the door. He could hear Oma talking sternly, and Penelope trying to interrupt, and then Oma's voice rising. Then a door slammed and feet stomped down a hall. Leo waited a few moments, and when he felt the coast was clear he opened the door and entered the back of the shop.

He came to the nearest door and gave a faint knock.

"*What?*"

"It's me. Leo. Open up."

The door opened. Penelope looked confused.

"What are you doing here?"

"I snuck in. They told me you couldn't come out."

"Leo, you can't do that. You're not allowed back here. You can't just sneak in like some kind of burglar."

"I'm *not* a burglar. We had a . . . a . . . we were going to see the show together today. Blackstone. I waited for you but you never showed up."

Penelope's glare softened.

"I know. I'm sorry. I'll make it up to you. I'm just being punished for a few days. Oma and Opa are stuck in the old country, and they don't understand how things are in America sometimes. You wouldn't get it."

"What did you do that was so bad?"

"When I came to see you they thought I was at my violin lesson. But I called my teacher and told him I was sick. Later, my teacher called the shop to find out how I was feeling, and they caught me lying. I hate the violin. I just wanted to have a little fun. I don't know what all the fuss is. It's not like we're in love or anything."

A splash of heat hit Leo's face. He suddenly became extremely aware that he had only one shoe on.

"No, of course not."

"Anyway, you better go. Can you get out without being seen?"

"Don't worry about me, I've already learned how to disappear."

CHAPTER 20

The Healing Child

He practiced every waking moment. Magic was on his mind when he ate, when he walked Horatio, when he did his laundry, and it was what kept him from falling asleep right away every night. When Leo mastered one movement, Barzini threw another at him. He welcomed each new challenge. Barzini watched, and commented only when his student needed correction. The less he talked, the happier Leo was. One night after dinner, after he finished cleaning the dishes, Barzini called Leo into the workroom.

What Leo noticed at first was the junk strewn everywhere. It was nothing like the rest of the pristine apartment. Metal gears and springs and jars filled with liquids and half-finished machines were lying on a workbench. A trunk overflowing with clothes was pushed to one corner. Stacked in another corner were metal birdcages and a black iron soup kettle with a lid and a handle. A huge object that looked like a giant oyster shell was positioned on a raised platform. Books and papers littered every surface. A round table took up most of the middle of the room. The center of the table was hollowed out, with a mirror resting inside.

Leo reached for a large wooden box on the workbench. "What do these cranks and dials do?" he asked.

Barzini quickly slapped Leo's hand.

"Every good illusion is the same illusion. You take something unbelievable and make it believable. Say I cut off my own head and toss it between my hands. The audience gasps, *Ah, that's impossible, how did he do that?* But a truly great illusion creates the unbelievable, something people cannot understand. These . . . cranks and dials, as you put it, are the skeletons of illusions of the future."

"How does it work?" Leo asked.

"I have a countryman, a genius from Bologna, where I grew up. His name is Guglielmo Marconi. Have you ever heard of him?"

Leo shook his head.

"He is not quite as famous as our own Thomas Edison. But he is a brilliant man. He invented a way to allow the voice to travel through the air without any wires."

"My voice already does that. What's so special?"

"With the right equipment, a person could speak into a box in one room and another person could listen in another room twenty miles away. No telephones, no wires, no dots and dashes. That is what's so special."

Leo remembered the voices he heard through the door.

"But that is not for today," Barzini said.

Barzini gestured to the chair next to his. He unfurled a scroll of paper. The sheet was so long the ends flopped over the edges of the table. He smoothed the scroll down flat. The drawings were like a little play, similar to what Leo had seen in Robinson's book. The stage was drawn in, and two people were sketched in different positions, with markings and notes all along the sides. At the top in big block letters were the words RESURRECTION BY THE HEALING CHILD.

Leo clearly saw a stick figure, meant to be himself, holding a gun. He saw the moment he palmed the bullet and then the moment he shot the gun. But after that the schematics became unclear. There were scrawled notes, lines breaking into the stage, little icons that looked like lightbulbs.

"That's you and me, right?" Leo asked, pointing to the first scene on the scroll. Barzini nodded.

"What else do you see?"

Leo pointed to the fourth frame down. "This is where the gun goes off."

"Yes. And then?"

"And then I can't read it anymore."

"That day you first saw me, when Houdini hung in Times Square. What else did you do?"

"I went to a magic show after."

"And what did you see?"

"The *Black Magic Mysteries of the Yogi*. At least, most of it."

"The techniques used in that illusion make up two-thirds of this bullet-catch trick."

Barzini scanned the scroll with a satisfied smile, as if he were looking at a particularly beautiful sunset or finishing a great meal. "Here is how it is done," he said, and then described how he and Leo would walk onstage. Leo would produce a revolver and have an audience member inspect it. The gun would be genuine. Then Leo would find another audience member, and have him use a pin to scratch his intials on the bullets. Keeping the bullet and the gun high in the air, he would walk back to the stage. All the while, Barzini would be making chatter. He would relay Leo's phony history as a boy wonder charmed with a unique gift, plucked from a farm somewhere in Kansas, and would urge the audience to remain calm.

When Leo was back on stage, he and Barzini would square off. Leo would make a show of loading the revolver. But in reality he would palm the bullet and replace it with a blank. Leo could tell them apart by feel alone. The real bullet, the one marked by an audience member, had a fake metal cap over the projectile. It was smooth and rounded. The blank had a crimped tip with a paper wad inside.

Across the stage, Barzini would hold aloft a white sheet. Then he would say his prayers and close his eyes. Leo would shoot. There would be a bang, a puff of smoke, a flash of fire. The real bullet would be safely inside Leo's pocket.

Barzini would yank the sheet, making it seem as if the bullet had just passed through it. He would then fall through a trapdoor, dropping the sheet as he fell and grabbing a black cloth that was covering a life-size wax dummy of himself. As the sheet settled by the dummy, the audience would be shocked. Women would faint, men would howl in outrage. Leo would have to calm them. But his tiny voice could in no way overpower a hundred people crying out in horror. During the commotion, Leo would pull off the marked cap from the live round and place it over a dislodged projectile. This would make it look like the bullet had actually been shot. Below the stage, as the uproar reached its peak, Barzini would run up a set of stairs to an area behind the curtain. A spotlight would turn on and be aimed directly at him. No one would notice the light, as it was all hidden behind the thick black curtains.

On stage, just as the crowd was about the rise up and haul Leo to the police, Barzini's image would be reflected in a large sheet of glass that had been there the whole time. The glass would be positioned to place Barzini's ghostly image hovering above the wax dummy. The glass would be angled in such a way that Barzini could appear to reach down to the dummy, pull out a bullet, walk over to Leo and place it in his hand. Leo would display the marked bullet that had been in his pocket. The spotlight would switch off and the ghost would vanish.

Leo would place the bullet in a handkerchief that had been stained red, and present it to the man who had marked it. The man would confirm the bullet was his.

Then for dramatic effect, Leo would place the bullet in his mouth and pretend to swallow, but really keeping the bullet underneath his tongue. He would place the white sheet over the dummy, hold his hands over its form and perform a solemn rite. Meanwhile, Barzini would rush back to the trapdoor, climb up through it and toss the dummy down. As he wriggled into the sheet, it would appear that he was coming back to life. He would throw the sheet off and bound up. Then Leo would "regurgitate" the bullet and present it to the man who'd marked it. Barzini would shake Leo's hand. They would bow for the audience, and the lights would go black.

"Are you still frightened of the illusion?" Barzini asked.

"Yes."

"But you see everything here. It's crystal clear. The bullet will never come close to the chamber."

"What if I mix up the blank for the real one?"

"You won't."

"How do you know?"

"Because if you make a mistake there will be no second half of the trick." Barzini laughed. "Because," he said, "by that time you will be a professional. You will make a diversion. Or something. You will be able to do the trick blindfolded. I will see to that."

"I'll be a professional," Leo repeated.

"Yes. You'll be an inventor, not a mechanic. An artist, not a scribbler. You have that untapped potential within you. I am trying to chisel it out. What you don't realize is that even before I met you, you had the ability to do the things you worry about. What would you have done with a stolen wallet in your hand and a cop's grip around your neck? You would have done . . . *something*, right?"

Leo nodded. He understood. He straightened out the diagram in front of him and started from the beginning.

CHAPTER 21

As Good as Gold

The concrete-sky month of December went on with only two types of days: those when Leo did not leave the apartment, and those when, the morning still dark and gray, he trailed Barzini to the subway going to Martinka's. By the end of the month, the walls in the theater at Martinka's were beginning to close in on Leo. They'd practiced the basics of the illusion—palming the bullet, making the exchanges, yelling bang! over and over again until his head pounded. And it didn't help that Barzini nitpicked everything about Leo's performance. The way he held the gun was not dramatic enough, and the way he examined the bullet was too quizzical. He wanted Leo to look natural, like he'd done this a thousand times before. But not *too* natural, as though the trick had no drama, as though he were not about to shoot Barzini dead in a few seconds.

One day in the middle of the month, when they had been in the theater since sunrise, Leo became exasperated. He was hungry and tired and sick of Barzini's voice. When Barzini started the act over for the eighteenth time, holding his hands out to the imaginary crowd and urgently incanting, "And now, you will witness an illusion which is greatest among the great, one that is unequalled, unrivaled, unparalleled, one that has thrilled and mystified the sultan of Turkey, the rajahs in India, the dowager empress of China, all audiences from the desert plains of Arabia to—" Leo snapped.

"Enough!" he yelled.

Barzini turned to him.

"Yes?

"That introduction is the corniest, cheesiest thing on the planet! And another thing. The way I hold the gun and the way I show the bullet is just fine. I'm only the assistant. My sleeves are *rolled up*. No one is going to think I'm up to any funny business. So can we please move on?"

Barzini fell quiet. He sat down on the edge of the stage and put his hands over his eyes. Leo sat next to him.

"I'm sorry. I didn't mean to yell," Leo said.

"Cheesy? Really?" Barzini asked.

"And old-fashioned, too. I think you need to be sincere, honest, like you're letting the audience in on the biggest secret they've ever heard," Leo said. "I mean, you call the act 'Resurrection by the Healing Child,' so tell the audience something about the Healing Child. Make the audience feel mystified, like they're under a spell of some kind," Leo said. "All the best shows I've seen have done that."

Leo expected a temper tantrum to follow. Or an outright dismissal. The air seemed to be getting thick as Barzini maintained silence. Leo hopped off the stage.

"Yes," Barzini said finally. "Your part is more important for this illusion. For the rest of my show, you are my assistant. You wheel in the props I need and take away the things I want to hide. You set the tone without making too much fuss or calling too much attention to yourself. But our roles are switched for the bullet catch, the grand finale. The audience has their eyes on *you*. I am just a thing that dies onstage. People will be concerned, they will want me to come back to life. But they will be begging *you* to do it. For the bullet catch, you become the magician and I become the assistant. That's why this is so important."

He got up and walked to the back of the theater where the exit was, not waiting for Leo to follow. He pushed the doors open and light flooded into the theater. Leo rushed after him. At the front of the store, Penelope was adjusting some things on a shelf. Leo saw her watching him. They had not spoken since he'd snuck in through the basement. But he had missed her.

Barzini asked her where her grandmother was. The crucial prop needed for Barzini's new bullet-catch illusion was a lifelike dummy of himself. Barzini had told Leo that the only person skilled enough to construct the dummy was Mrs. Martinka.

"She should be back any minute, Signor Barzini."

"Thank you."

Barzini gave Leo a nudge with his elbow.

"Hi, Penelope," he murmured.

"Hi, Leo. Nice to see you."

Penelope smiled sweetly and Leo's head felt prickly. He turned away from her so she wouldn't see him blush.

Just then, Mrs. Martinka entered the shop holding a small bucket and a stack of newspapers. She led Leo and Barzini to her workroom. Set upon a table were a mortar and pestle, a jug of water, a spatula and some other tools. She opened the bucket, which had a fine white powder inside, and poured the water in, making some of the powder fly into the air. Then she stirred it until it became a paste.

"The wax replicas will be very lifelike. Nobody will be able to tell the difference," Mrs. Martinka said. "I will use beeswax. It looks like skin and it takes pigment well. Once I have the papier-mâché mold, I pour in the wax. Once the wax hardens, then I make it look real. The hands will look like your hands, down to the very wrinkles and life lines. I can capture any facial expression you want."

"The mask of death is what we need for this illusion," Barzini said.

Mrs. Martinka squinted at Barzini's face. "Then that is what you'll get."

Leo pulled up a stool and sat at one end of the table while Barzini sat at the other. Mrs. Martinka began by soaking cotton balls with mineral oil. She rubbed the oil all over Barzini's face and neck. Then she shredded the newspaper into long strips, moistened them and crisscrossed them going one way and then the other over Barzini's face. With a penknife she cut slits below the nostrils large enough for Barzini to breathe. Working quickly, she covered the latticework of newspaper on Barzini's face with the paste from the bucket.

"Now we wait," Mrs. Martinka said as she wiped her hands on her apron.

A few minutes passed. Mrs. Martinka felt the edges of the mask, from the forehead to the ears to the chin. "It's ready," she said.

She took a small chisel and gently tapped along the edges. Then she grasped the mask on the sides and began to wriggle it away from Barzini's face. The mold pulled away in one piece. Mrs. Martinka handed Barzini a towel to wipe away any residual oil and plaster. He cleaned out his beard, but it still had white flakes in it.

"What about his goatee?" Leo asked. "And his hair? You can't just paint that. No one will believe it's real."

Mrs. Martinka pulled out a scissors from a drawer on the bench, and snipped a lock from Barzini's head.

"From the hundreds of barber shops in this city, I will be able to find enough hair to match this color."

Mrs. Martinka then made molds for each of Barzini's hands using the same method. After they had dried, she pried them off and carried them away. There was a knock on the door. A familiar head popped in. Leo jumped up.

"Mr. Houdini, come on in," he said, throwing the door open.

"Leo, right?"

Leo nodded.

"Good to see you again. Franco . . ."

Barzini had fragments of plaster all over him. Leo could imagine how uncomfortable he must feel. Barzini never had so much as a speck of dirt on him.

"Excuse my appearance."

"Don't worry about it," Houdini said. "I've got good news. I managed to secure a booking for you. The Eden Musée. No strings needed pulling, no favors called in."

Barzini turned to Leo. "Leave us."

Leo went out and closed the door. He heard Houdini's muffled voice.

"That's wonderful! But, the act is nowhere near ready," Barzini said. "Not for Coney Island. Not even for the theater in the back of the shop. The props haven't even been made yet."

"That's all right. Coney Island can wait. I've got something else. A private party."

"I told you I was done with those." Barzini's voice rose. "I'm not a two-bit rabbit-out-of-the-hat man. I have spent *years* planning this while entertaining overfed rich ladies and their sleepy husbands. But you wouldn't know anything about that because you and Billy were off touring and raking in millions. I do not want to do any more private bookings. Not now. Not when I'm so close."

"I'm sorry to hear that, Franco," Houdini said. "But for once in your life stop being a hothead and just hear me out."

Leo could hear footsteps come toward him, then stop.

"These people aren't just rich," Houdini said. "They are filthy rich. The Whitfields. Have you heard of them? They're patrons of the arts who happen to appreciate magic. I really wish you would reconsider. Did I mention that Arthur Conan Doyle will be there? He's rich *and* famous."

"Arthur Conan Doyle? He's a spiritualist! You want me to get involved with those people? It's too easy, it wouldn't be right. No, thank you, Harry."

"I'm trying to help you, Franco. I'm sure you need the money. And besides, your version of the bullet catch is not so far from Spiritualism, anyway. You could try out some of the other tricks. It would be great practice for your young assistant. Why not ask for his opinion?"

"*Leo!*" Barzini yelled.

Leo jumped.

"Get in here now."

Leo opened the door. Houdini was a few feet in front of him.

"Mr. Houdini has a proposition for us," Barzini said.

"I told Franco that I know some important people, wealthy people. They personally asked me to recommend a magician, and so naturally I thought of you."

"Well, what's the problem with Spiritualists? I could hear you talking. You were pretty loud."

"They believe they can communicate with the dead," Barzini said. "It's absurd."

"Would we do a séance?"

"Absolutely not," Barzini answered. "The tricks employed in a séance have been exposed over and over again. I am shocked people still believe in that nonsense. If any one of these Spiritualists walked into Martinka's, they'd see that all the tools of the medium's trade are sitting there in plain sight on the shelves. It's beneath me."

"What difference does it make to you what they believe?" Houdini said. "They just want some after-dinner entertainment, but more along the lines of supernatural illusions."

"Who's Arthur Doyle?" Leo asked.

"Sir Arthur Conan Doyle?" Houdini said. "Sherlock Holmes?"

"Wow! I saw that movie."

"Yes, well, he wrote the books."

"Do these Spiritualist people live in a mansion?" Leo asked Houdini.

"Indeed they do. On Long Island."

Famous writers, ghosts from beyond, a mansion and people paying him to do all the stuff he'd been practicing for free! "I say we do it," Leo said. "Sounds like fun."

"That's the spirit," Houdini said. "Franco, listen to your assistant. I can't even imagine the sort of money you are spending to mount this act. You need to think of the Whitfields as potential investors."

Barzini sighed. He stuck out his hand to Houdini. "All right. Thank you, Harry."

"Good," Houdini said. "The recommendation from me is as good as gold, but if you can really impress them with what they want, then the gold is all yours."

"How much time do we have to prepare?"

"Weeks. The party isn't until the end of January. I'll ring you with the details as soon as I have them."

Houdini offered to take them to lunch nearby, and Leo and Barzini accepted.

"Do you think we could do any of those tricks you talked about from the old days?" Leo asked Barzini.

"Not exactly," Barzini said. "Performing for the Whitfields with the same tricks used to con Iowa farmers doesn't seem appropriate."

"I'm sure that whatever you finalize will suit their pleasure and be tasteful at the same time," Houdini said.

Near the front of the store, Leo raised his voice.

"So, Harry," he said, "did I ever tell you about the time I . . ."

He wanted to impress Penelope, to show her he was getting chummy with the most famous magician in the world. But her back was turned and she was busily attending to some malfunctioning prop. As he passed her, Leo called out, "Oh, there you are, Penelope. Good-bye."

"So long," she said, but she did not look up.

Houdini put his arm around Leo's shoulder and ushered him north on Sixth Avenue. A few minutes later they were sitting in Keen's Chophouse.

The air in the room was thick with smoke. People were puffing long, thin clay pipes, talking fast and loud. Leo recognized some actors from the moving pictures standing by the tap. The room was dim. Soft orange light glowed from a few bulbs. Christmas wreaths on the walls, and candles on sills and at the ends of the bar, made the place feel festive.

When they were seated, Houdini asked to have the pipe they stored for him brought to the table. Even Barzini loosened up and ordered a pint of lager, and in the buzz and smoke of the room, amid the talk of show business, somehow Penelope Martinka slipped from Leo's mind.

CHAPTER 22

Guardians of the Forbidden City

The windows of apartments flanking Tompkins Square Park glowed with candlelight. Harmonies of neighborhood Christmas carolers floated through the third-floor apartment. Leo was shocked to hear Barzini hum along.

Barzini hung a fresh evergreen wreath with a red bow over the fireplace in the parlor. Leo displayed the few Christmas cards that came in the mail on the mantel. There was one from Martinka & Co., one from a magician by the name of Professor W. E. Floyd, as well as an ornate card with gilded printing from Bess and Harry Houdini. Inside the Houdinis' card was a personal note inviting both Leo and Barzini to their annual New Year's Eve party. *Black tie, regrets only*, it read.

"Have you ever put up a Christmas tree?" Leo asked as they settled in the parlor.

"Never. I consider it an extravagance for just one person."

Leo pictured Barzini sitting alone on Christmas Eves past. Just him and Horatio in the parlor listening to some tragic opera spinning on the gramophone.

"Did you want one? Is that your custom?"

"No. I was just wondering, that's all," Leo said.

At Christmastime at the House of Providence, the nuns hung a few wreaths around the halls, but it did little to brighten up the cracked plaster of the walls. The year that Murph arrived at the orphanage, Mother Superior set up a small tree outside her office. At the very top was perched an angel. Draped over the branches were decorations of strung popcorn. Underneath the tree were a dozen or more wrapped boxes. Leo and Murph thought they were intended for the best-behaved children at the orphanage, so they came up with a plan. All December they volunteered to help the nuns by sweeping, taking out the trash, reading to the younger children. Anything to get a gift. Murph got the idea to peek inside the packages, so that if they were given a choice, they'd know which box to pick. But they discovered that the boxes were empty, only for show. Leo later grabbed all of the strung popcorn and one of the smaller boxes. He carefully unwrapped the box and stuffed it with the popcorn. He gave it to Murph as a Christmas gift. They had a good laugh about it. Leo wondered what Murph was doing this Christmas.

Leo had been nervous all evening. This Christmas marked the first time in his memory that he was in a real home. It was his first *good* Christmas. But beyond that, in looking back on the past months of apprenticeship, Leo had realized he was in the middle of his first good *year.* He'd wanted to show his gratitude. He'd thought about what to get for his teacher, and quickly decided anything related to magic would fall flat. An article of clothing? Too chancy—Barzini had very strict tastes. Any small trinket would be just as risky. Barzini was not the sort of man to cherish a cheap toy. One day while shopping with Barzini at the Italian grocer, Leo had spotted a display of boxes of fancy chocolates with cherry and caramel fillings. He'd gone back alone and purchased a box with his own money.

When the carolers had moved on to the next block, Leo retrieved the box from under his bed and rejoined Barzini in the parlor.

"Merry Christmas," Leo said. "I thought you'd like them. They come from Italy."

Barzini took the box from Leo. He looked surprised.

"Ah, yes. I remember this brand! Very expensive, even in Italy. I'm sure it cost you a treasure. How did you afford them?"

"I had a little money saved," Leo said. "From before."

"Well, then," Barzini said, "I thank you. That was very generous of you."

Barzini placed the box of candy on the coffee table and told Leo to help himself. Barzini went to his workroom for a moment, and while he was gone, Leo popped two truffles into his mouth.

"How are they?" Barzini asked.

"Guh," Leo said with his mouth full.

They both laughed. Barzini sat down. He had brought back his bottle of anisette liqueur and a tumbler. He filled the tumbler halfway and splashed in some water. As the water mixed with the clear liqueur, it turned a milky white color.

"I like the smell of that stuff. It reminds me of licorice from the penny candy store."

"Both the candy and the liqueur are derived from the anise seed. I like it not only for the taste. It connects me to the past."

"Did your dad drink it or something?"

"No, no. It has an old history with our profession. Magicians used the anise seed to train dogs."

Leo used his thumb and forefinger to wipe chocolate from the corners of his mouth.

"How'd they do that?" he asked.

"For a while, it was popular in Europe for magicians to use dogs in their acts. Not for big theater shows, but for small gatherings, salon or parlor performances. The magician would lay the cards down on the floor and spread them around in a wide circle. Then he would pose a problem to the dog. He might say, 'Find me the card with the answer to five plus five,' for example. The dog would then take his cue and walk around the circle of the cards once or twice, with his head hanging down, as though he were reading the cards. Then he would turn back and select the correct card, either by picking it up with his mouth or scratching it. The trick was, when the magician spread out the cards, he pressed the answer card with an anise seed he had secured under a long fingernail. The dog had been trained to respond to that scent."

"But what if somebody in the crowd smelled the seed and accused the magician of fixing the cards?"

"Simple. The magician would scratch his neck and say that the scent was from his cologne. One must never admit he is guilty of fakery onstage."

"Did you ever try to do that with Horatio?"

Leo knew that Horatio could respond to four hand signals: come, sit, stay and shake. He also knew to howl, but only if you scratched under his throat.

"No, I never did. In all honesty, it is a simple trick. In fact, I was never very happy with animal tricks. Except I do remember seeing one spectacular illusion when I was studying in Canton, China. I had just recently arrived, and didn't know a soul. I was lost and wandered down an alley. I came across a man folding two pieces of paper into the shape of butterflies. He then fanned them to bring them aloft. He could control them with excellent precision, landing them on someone's shoulder or making them hover in place. The butterflies were never more than an inch or so apart, and moved in complete unison like perfect twins. After he flew them for a while, he called them back to his palm and turned them into real butterflies. That is one I will never forget."

Leo could see it in his head. It was much more poetic than a dove from the sleeve.

"Who was the magician who did it?"

"You've met him."

"Mr. Shen?"

Barzini nodded and knocked back a gulp from his tumbler.

"I remember a good one," Leo said. "A while back, we all went to Coney Island. I saw a guy eat sawdust and spit out fire. I think that's what did it for me. That was the moment I realized I loved magic. It was just so real. And in my head, I can go back anytime and sit in the theater, just like how I was then. It never left me. I want to be able to do that for someone else one day."

"That is an excellent motivation," Barzini said. "A very pure inspiration. But I have a question. Who is 'we all'?"

"Oh. No one," Leo said. "Some people I used to know. Anyway, what about you? Was meeting Mr. Shen the moment you knew you wanted to be a magician, or was there something before that?"

"My introduction to the world of magic is a story for another day. I have a Christmas gift for you as well."

Barzini went into his workroom again and came out with a red silk box. He handed it to Leo and settled back in his chair. Leo opened the box to find the golden lions from Mr. Shen's shop. He was stunned.

"Thank you," he finally said.

"You're welcome. Perhaps you will find some good use for them in an illusion. Or you can just keep them for good luck."

Leo examined the lions. They were highly detailed. Each tooth was individually carved and sharp. The little red crystals for eyes glinted. Just by holding them, Leo felt as if he were halfway to some far-off land. He hoped one day he would make it to Canton, like Barzini did, and learn something mysterious, a secret, a bit of magic.

They sat in the parlor for some time. Barzini had another glass of his liqueur and a few chocolates. They did not say anything else to each other, and as far as Leo was concerned, nothing more needed to be said.

CHAPTER 23

A Pointy Bargain

A few days after Christmas they went to Kaminsky's Dry Goods on Orchard Street to order four bolts of black velvet fabric, and then to a glass shop on Houston to arrange for a large pane cut to Barzini's specifications. Leo enjoyed the errands. Using everyday materials from ordinary stores, they were making something special.

They arrived at the tailor shop shortly before noon and tied Horatio to a streetlamp. Bellini looked up from tacking on the sleeves to a black and white pin-striped suit being worn by a headless mannequin. The tailor's wife was at the ironing board. Steam billowed as she glided the iron along the pants. She brushed a damp lock of hair out of her eyes.

"The boy's trousers," she said, gesturing to her handiwork. "So, Signor Barzini. Is today the day?"

Barzini forced a smile. "Perhaps."

"You say that every time. I'm getting old waiting for you to make up your mind." Leo shot Barzini a puzzled look. In response Barzini did something remarkable. He rolled his eyes.

"About twenty-five years ago she saw a needle-swallowing bit at a dime museum," Barzini explained to Leo quietly. "She has been asking me to do it ever since."

The tailor wiped his hands clean of the chalk he used to mark the suit seams. While he presented Barzini with the final bill, his wife folded Leo's tuxedos. Then one last time she smoothed everything out with her hands. She boxed the tuxedos together with Leo's bullet-catch costume, carefully separating the outfits with tissue paper. Leo took the box from her.

Barzini studied the tailor's bill. He tapped the paper with an index finger. "Signor Bellini, I have just one question. Before I pay, I'd like to know: how many extra inches did you leave at the seams? At these prices I expect you allowed at least three. The boy is growing faster than the weeds in Tompkins Square Park."

The tailor pushed his pince-nez glasses back up his nose.

"I left nothing. I asked the boy and he said to measure exact, so that's how I cut the fabric."

Barzini shook his head.

"Not acceptable," he bawled. "What does a twelve-year-old boy know about custom tailoring?"

"I'm not twelve," Leo protested.

"Be quiet. No one is talking to you."

"I am sorry if there's been a misunderstanding, Signor Barzini," the tailor said. "But the work is complete. The final sum of twenty-eight dollars and forty cents is due."

"No misunderstanding, Signor Bellini. I cannot pay this sum. It would not be right. I feel dishonored after all my years of loyal patronage to your shop. You must take some responsibility in this matter. A simple telephone call would have straightened everything out."

The tailor looked back and forth between Barzini and Leo, who had the box of clothing firmly secured under his arm. Mrs. Bellini spoke to her husband in rapid Italian. She clasped her hands together and raised them to her chest.

"Listen to your wife," Barzini said. "She's right. You didn't use common sense when making the suits."

The tailor threw his hands up in defeat.

"Fine, fine. I'll make a bargain with you. Five dollars from the bill," the tailor said, "if you perform the trick my wife has been waiting for."

Leo looked at Barzini. He didn't know how the needle swallowing trick was done. Barzini grinned.

"Thank you, that's only fair," Barzini said. "Signora Bellini, if you wouldn't mind, I'd like you to select twenty size-ten sewing needles. And please bring me a spool of white thread and a small cup of water."

Barzini broke off a piece of thread almost two feet long. "Now, signora, the first thing I want you to do is inspect my mouth. Do you see anything hidden inside?"

Barzini used his two index fingers to pull his cheeks wide apart. The tailor's wife giggled.

"I just see your tongue and teeth," she said.

"Signora, you are certain that I have nothing hidden in my mouth?"

"Yes."

"If you would be so kind, please hand me the needles, one at a time."

Barzini swallowed the needles in rapid succession. He stared at the tailor with each swallow. Next he rolled up the length of thread into a ball and swallowed that as well. Barzini then sipped the water and tilted his head backward just slightly. He stuck his right index finger and thumb deep into his mouth. Slowly he tugged, and inch by inch out came all twenty sewing needles, with the thread straight through the eyes. The needles swayed back and forth as he held the line tightly for display.

"*Magnifico!*"

While the tailor's wife babbled to her husband about the marvel she'd just witnessed, Barzini passed the cup of water to Leo.

"Untie Horatio and ditch the cup outside. Wait for me across the street," he whispered.

Leo did as told. Through the window he saw Barzini press the balance of the adjusted bill into the tailor's palm.

"*Arrivederci*, Signor Bellini, Signora Bellini," Barzini said as he walked out of the store.

"I don't want your business anymore," the tailor shouted after him. "Go become Tomaselli's headache!"

Barzini tipped his hat and let the door close behind him. He crossed the street and took Horatio's leash from Leo.

"Good riddance. I had a feeling this was how it would play out. A good tailor would without question leave extra room for someone your age. However, someone who is looking to make a new suit in a few months might not do the same. Every single penny counts with this production."

"Forget about that. I saw what was in the cup," Leo said.

"You didn't actually expect me to swallow needles, did you?"

"That would be crazy."

"More dangerous than the bullet catch?"

"Different."

"But you saw me put the needles in my mouth, didn't you?"

"Yes, that was real. But you only pretended to swallow them. You hid them under your tongue, right? Then you spat them out in the cup when you took a sip of water."

"Very good. Now for the hard question. How did I get the threaded needles in my mouth?"

"They had to have already been in your mouth, unless they were in your pocket and you palmed them in when nobody was looking," Leo said.

"When we left the apartment this morning, the pre-threaded needles were wound up carefully and placed between my cheek and gums. When the tailor's wife inspected my mouth she saw nothing, because my index finger was covering them."

"But how did you know you would have to do the trick today?" Leo asked.

"I didn't. I always go to Bellini's shop ready to do it. Today just seemed the right time."

CHAPTER 24

Sending a Message

When they reached the third floor they both froze. Scratches and gouges marked the brass plate behind the handle of the door. The keyhole was mangled. The door hung ajar. Barzini ran ahead. But Leo could not force himself to move.

"It's safe!" Barzini called from inside.

Leo peered inside the apartment and encountered a scene of complete destruction. He tied Horatio to the door handle to keep him from walking over the shattered glass and wood fragments. Leo walked around the overturned furniture and the smashed lamp and looked into the kitchen. Coffee grounds had been scattered on the floor, dishes and cups thrown against the walls. He walked on to his room.

Leo found the knapsack where he'd put the money on top of his bed. It was slashed to shreds. The trunk where the knapsack had been hidden was bashed in and splintered.

Barzini appeared at Leo's bedroom door. His eyes darted from side to side and he shifted his weight back and forth. "Look at this!" Barzini said, pointing to the trunk. "What kind of an animal would do this? I'll tell you. A jealous, vain man who'll stop at nothing. Well, for once the last laugh is on him. I locked the schematics away in the safe behind the painting, which he did not find. But when he couldn't find what he was looking for, he decided to cause destruction." Barzini spoke fast, shaking his head side to side. He wiped saliva from the corners of his mouth with the back of his hand.

"I don't understand," Leo said. "Who are you talking about? Houdini?"

"It's as plain as day who did this. It was him. Robinson."

"What? You think Chung Ling Soo did this? That's impossible. He's in England."

"Don't be a fool. He had somebody do it for him."

"I don't see how he could have. How would he have even known about your bullet catch?"

"Houdini always had a big mouth."

"Houdini wouldn't do that. He's your friend. He's trying to help us."

"Yes, he is a friend, but he's also a gossip. He's never been able to keep his nose out of everyone's business. I should have known better."

"But are you sure? Maybe you should just ask Houdini if he told Billy."

Barzini rubbed his brow and slid his hand down the side of his face. He gathered up his goatee in his hand and tugged it to a point.

"No. I can't accuse him. We need his help now. I'm going out to get a locksmith. We need a more secure lock. You get the broom and dustpan," Barzini said. "And Leo, I forbid you to be upset over this. Practice begins again tomorrow morning at Martinka's."

"I'll take care of the cleanup," Leo said. "And you're right. I won't let this upset me. We'll have the best bullet catch the world has ever seen. We'll bury him, put him right out of business."

Leo put Horatio in Barzini's bedroom, then found the broom and got to work. He didn't know what to make of what had just happened. Barzini was convinced this was all the doing of Billy Robinson. And if the robber sent by Robinson couldn't find what he was sent to find, then taking a large sum of cash would be a consolation prize. And if the break-in was a random robbery, then it was logical that the apartment would be searched for cash and it wouldn't be unusual to knock things over. But what about his shredded knapsack? That seemed such an angry, vicious thing to do, the act of someone looking for something very specific tucked away in that knapsack. Had the Mayor found him?

Leo's nervousness over being recognized by the police had faded. But now he had something new to worry about. His money was gone, and he feared his past was catching up to him.

CHAPTER 25

How to Learn Wisdom

Sleet tapped on Leo's window. It was well past the time he usually got up, but Barzini had told him the night before that he could sleep in, since they'd be out late that night at Houdini's New Year's party. Leo had talked about little else for days.

Leo stretched in bed and cracked his joints, enjoying the last few moments of warmth underneath his blankets. A new year, a new life. In the kitchen he could hear Barzini preparing breakfast. The tea kettle whistled. Leo carefully made his bed, then joined Barzini.

The overcast weather outside matched Barzini's mood. He had been on edge and depressed since the break-in. The pressure to perfect the show before Chung Ling Soo's return showed in everything he did. And on top of that, tonight he would have to make banter and appear jovial with Houdini. His hand trembled as he drank his coffee.

"So," Leo said. "Expect to see anyone at the party tonight?"

Barzini set down the cup.

"Yes, Leo. I don't think Houdini would throw a New Year's Eve party for just you and me. I do expect to see people there."

"Well, like who?"

"The usual lot."

"Do you think Penelope will be there?"

"So she's still on your mind. Take every piece of my advice except that one—"

"I'm just curious. It's going to be all old people. It would be fun if someone my age was there."

"Oh, of course. Well, I doubt she will be there. Not all guardians are as lenient as I. Harry's parties can get quite lively." Barzini finished his coffee. "Harry is graciously sending a car for us. It will be here at seven. Make sure you're ready."

He left the kitchen and disappeared into the workroom.

Leo spent the rest of the day practicing palming bullets. After five he quit, got dressed in his tux and went to the workroom and knocked. Barzini opened the door. He had ink smudges all around his face and he gripped a fountain pen.

"New illusion?" Leo asked. "Something with invisible ink?" Barzini touched his face and looked at his fingertips.

"What time is it?"

"Five forty-five."

"Then I'll need to get ready shortly." Just then he noticed Leo's attire. "Bellini did a fine job. Take your jacket off now, though. You don't want to crease it."

Leo pulled out a chair and carefully laid his tuxedo jacket across the arms.

"I worked on my introduction to the bullet catch today," Barzini said. "That's why I've been in here. I needed quiet. I tried to make it more . . . modern, more unique . . . as you suggested. But it's not there yet."

Barzini cleared his throat. "First, imagine the setup. The crowd is in front of you. You are silent, the lights dim, but there is a spotlight on you. I make sure the crowd is settled. Once I'm sure I have their undivided attention, I begin.

"*Some facts in the world are so small that no one pays any attention to them at all. Fact: there is only one moon. Fact: men cannot catch bullets from thin air.*"

"Stop," Leo said. "No one came for a lecture. Why don't you point at someone in the audience and say '*You, sir, have you ever seen two moons?*' or '*You, sir, have you ever caught a bullet from thin air?*' Something like that. See, that way it's like you're talking to them directly. Like you want to get a hold on them."

"Good, I like that," Barzini said, making notes on his paper.

"Right," Leo said. "Now I'd add something about dead men staying dead forever. Once you talk about bringing back the dead, I bet you'll have them hooked."

"I was unsure about that. Do you think it will detract from when my ghost appears?"

"No! They'll be dying to see it. You have to let them know it's coming."

Barzini wrote faster. He muttered as he scribbled on his pad. "*Fact: dead men can never come back to life. How strange it is that no one spends the time to think over these facts. Maybe they are afraid of what they may find. A touch of the divine, a flicker of magic.*"

He refocused on Leo.

"Now I begin to raise my voice.

"*Maybe you disagree. Maybe you are the curious sort, the sort who wonders . . .*"

"I'm not sure about that," Leo said. "Maybe take it out."

Barzini gave a short nod.

"*There are stories, wild, incredible stories, that can singe your ears just listening to them. I overheard one such story while traveling through* Nicodemus, Kansas.

"Here, I gesture and walk a little toward you.

"*It was about a boy who was delivered stillborn. The mother and father wept and the funeral party was gathered. A sad day indeed. As they were lowering the baby into the ground, the priest saying words of comfort, there was a noise, a moan coming from the coffin.*"

"Cry, not moan."

"Yes, crying.

"*They all stopped. At first they were not sure what they were hearing.*

"*They quickly raised the tiny coffin from the ground. The baby, very much alive, was wailing from the casket.*

"*Years later that same boy watched his father shoot his favorite pig between the eyes. He cried and cried and placed his hands on the dead hog.*"

"That's supposed to be me. Can't you make it something better? Something so incredible, so shocking, that every person in the audience will gasp," Leo said. "Like, breathe into his snout or something."

Sweat broke out on Barzini's forehead. His head bobbed up and down as he wrote faster and crossed out whole passages.

"The boy leaned forward and breathed the breath of life itself into the animal's snout. A moment later, the pig opened its eyes. It got up, shook itself, and ran off into the field. The boy was marked with a special talent. Whether it was a gift from the devil or from the angels, I will let you, the audience, decide.

"And that's it."

"You left out the most important part."

"No. I don't think so. I've got everything there."

"You forgot me!" Leo said. "You just described me, now make me real. Introduce me to them as flesh and blood."

Barzini went back to his pad.

"The boy's name was Leo. And through the years he has demonstrated this unique gift over and over again. And in a few moments, Leo, the Healing Child, will shoot me down and bring me back to life for your amazement."

Barzini put down his pen. He smiled and let out a short laugh.

"That's good. Very good. Thank you."

An hour later, two honks sounded from the street. Leo looked out the window and saw a black Winton Six limousine waiting, gray puffs of exhaust spouting into the twilight.

"You gotta see this!"

Barzini rushed to the window. He shook his head.

"A leopard can't change his spots."

Out on the street passersby stared at Barzini and Leo, striding in their tuxes. The driver scrambled to open the doors for them and shut them after they were inside. Leo loved the attention. He felt like a big shot.

The driver slowly pulled into the street. The bad weather had continued through the day, and the slush squished under the tires. The driver headed west, then north. The city was all lit up like a big gem rising out of the black streets. Leo's heart felt full. Barzini had asked for his opinion, his help. It made what they were planning so much more real for Leo. He felt like he could really put himself into the shoes of the character, become Leo, the Healing Child. He was truly part of the team, a real partner.

They rounded Columbus Circle and drove along Central Park West. A dense fog blanketed the park. Leo couldn't believe how much his life had turned around. Just a year ago he was hovering over a hot plate, eating sardines out of a can. Tonight he was invited to the party of a famous magician, and on the way to becoming famous himself. He had never really thought about fate. Maybe Leo was just lucky. He owed Barzini an enormous debt of gratitude for everything he'd offered him. And because of that he would try to never let him down.

The car pulled up to Houdini's house. The sleet had turned into snow and the sidewalk was slick with ice. Muffled music came from inside. Barzini knocked on the door. The maid answered and showed them in. A five-piece jazz band was set up in the living room, wailing an upbeat tune. There were dozens of people milling about, all drinking champagne, dressed in tuxedos or sparkling dresses hemmed at the knee.

Leo was the youngest person there. He felt a little out of place. He couldn't see Houdini anywhere.

Bess came over and greeted the two of them.

"Hi, Bess," Barzini said. "Happy New Year! Where's Harry hiding?"

She rolled her eyes.

"Waiting to make his big entrance."

"Always the showman," Barzini said.

Bess grabbed two champagne flutes from a waiter. She handed one to Barzini and one to Leo, with a wink.

"Don't tell your mother," she said, and walked off, waving at some people who had just walked in.

Leo sniffed the champagne. It smelled like grapes and sweat. He took a little sip of the bitter, fizzy drink, then gulped it down. He sat on a sofa and pulled a deck of cards from his trouser pocket. He shuffled and practiced his "jog," allowing one card to protrude just enough from the deck so only he could see it. Leo looked back and forth at Barzini as he mingled with the guests. His earlier nerves seemed to vanish as he chatted with a man who looked like a taller version of Houdini. Leo worked on a flourish next, fanning the cards into a ribbon spread, until Barzini tapped his foot.

"Leo, you're being rude just sitting there like a stone. If you're going to do a trick at least gather some people around. But put that deck away for the moment. Let me introduce you to some people. Who knows? In years to come people might say that at Harry Houdini's 1917 New Year's Eve party, they met Leo the Healing Child."

"Who was that man you were talking to?"

"That was Dash, Harry's brother, also known as Hardeen. Between you and me, he's got the better pair of hands in the family. Years ago they worked together at Coney Island as the Brothers Houdini. Would you like to meet him?"

Leo didn't answer, because sneaking up right behind Barzini was a woman who looked like she's been dusted with chalk from head to toe. She didn't have wrinkles, but she had the faded white hair of an old lady. She put an index finger to her mouth, telling Leo to hush. Suddenly she threw her arms around Barzini's waist. He looked down at the translucent hands.

"Princess Lillian!" he exclaimed as he spun around. "It's been years."

"Franco, word is you're going for the big time. Is that true?"

"Indeed."

"Princess Pee Wee heard the news. She said everyone in the Lilliput Village has been talking about it."

"Franco!" a voice bellowed from across the room.

A man with tattoos covering every inch of visible skin was waving at Barzini. Even the palms of his hands were tattooed. He was standing between two women. One wore a dress and sported a grizzled beard. The other woman stood on four legs.

"Captain Copp! Nanette! Myrtle!" Barzini shouted back. He left Leo sitting on the sofa while he scooted across the room to talk to a congregation of people, who Leo could only assume were part of the freak show at the Dreamland Circus Sideshow.

"So much for introducing me around," Leo muttered as he stood up and stretched his legs. But he quickly softened. These were Barzini's old friends. The people he never bumped into on East Seventh street, or saw at the bank or at the Italian grocer. The people he had drifted away from a long time ago. Leo wandered off and let Barzini enjoy getting reacquainted with his past.

Some rooms in the mansion were decorated with posters from Houdini's tours, and a few props. People were talking or doing little magic tricks for each other—a disappearing watch here, a goldfish coming out of someone's nose there. No one took much notice of Leo.

Leo walked up the staircase to the second floor. Emboldened by the champagne, Leo went from room to room. There was a tiled room with ceiling-to-floor mirrors and a tub so large it must have been used for practicing water submersion escapes. In the library, a room lined with glass-encased bookshelves that stretched to the ceiling, Leo leaned against the single wall that did not have any books on it. He noticed something round. It was a knob. He turned it. He heard a click and pushed open the hidden door, and disappeared from the room.

At first Leo thought he was in a closet. Then he found a light switch. In front of him appeared a workroom, similar to the one in Barzini's apartment, except larger and more orderly. There were trunks and cages and mirrors arranged at particular angles. Leo went to the writing desk in the middle of the room. On it he found drawings with the title *The Vanishing Elephant* scrawled at the top. The first drawing showed a man with an elephant above him on its hind legs. The next page had a design for the special chamber where the elephant would disappear. He could see that Houdini would lead the elephant into a large cabinet. The cabinet was raised off the ground so that no one would suspect a trapdoor. The top had bars that the audience could see through—or so they thought. Assistants closed curtains on the large cabinet. Then someone inside would quickly put up mirrors that reflected at forty-five-degree angles, which also hid the elephant. When the curtain came down, the crowd would just be seeing reflections. It was a simple trick. But Leo could imagine the impact on a theater audience of watching an enormous elephant disappear right in front of them. This was Houdini's next big act. The one he hinted at when they went to his house for dinner.

Underneath the drawings he saw a handwritten note. The stationery had an image of Chung Ling Soo on the top next to the address of his office in London. Leo couldn't resist. He had to read it.

December 4, 1917

Dear Harry,

I read with interest your letter detailing Franco's "comeback." I found it to be a strange choice of words for someone who has never been in the limelight his entire career. But I do like the ghost and resurrection bit. "Defying the Bullets" could use some sprucing up after twelve years. What do you think about this? Chung Ling Soo dies onstage during the trick and a young Oriental girl with mystical healing powers brings him back to life. I think American audiences will lap it up. You know how they love anything exotic from the Far East. My contract at the Wood Green Empire ends March 31. If all goes according to plan, I'll sail into New York City by April 26. I hope to talk business with you then. My manager thinks that a co-billed act at the Hippodrome with the Great Harry Houdini and the Mysterious Chung Ling Soo will be a sure-fire box-office success.

Cannot attend your New Year's bash for obvious reasons, which is probably for the best, anyway. I am assuming that Franco will be there, considering your newly rekindled friendship? A reunion with Franco is not in the cards.

All good wishes for our prosperous New Year!

Sincerely,
Billy

Leo felt sick to his stomach. Barzini was right. Maybe Houdini hadn't meant to stab Barzini in the back with his gossip, but that was exactly what he'd done. All the while Houdini was giving Barzini advice, he already had plans to share the bill at the Hippodrome with Chung Ling Soo. And what made matters worse was that Houdini had given him the specifics of Barzini's act. Leo folded the note in half and dropped it one of his profondes.

Someone was turning the doorknob. Leo dived under the desk and stayed very still. He could hear footsteps coming closer. He held his breath.

"Hello?"

It was Bess Houdini. She came closer. "Harry, are you in here?"

She walked to the desk. Leo heard papers being shuffled and tapped. Then the footsteps retreated. Bess muttered something about being careless with secrets, and then the room got dark. Leo heard the sounds of the party get louder as she opened the door. Then they were muffled again, and then he heard the door being locked.

He stayed balled underneath the desk for a few minutes, unsure if this was a trap or not. Eventually he worked up the courage to pop his head above the desk. He was alone. He couldn't risk turning the lights on again. Leo put his ear to the door. The library seemed pretty quiet. He twisted the knob, which unlocked the door, and, as quickly as he could, slipped out and closed it. Once downstairs, he searched through the rooms for Barzini. He found him leaning next to a piano, talking to a pretty lady.

"I have to tell you something."

"It can wait, Leo, my young pupil," he said, not looking.

"It's important."

"Not now, Leo. We'll talk after the party."

Barzini resumed his conversation with the lady.

"Why don't you request a song from the band. Anything Mrs. . . ."

"Miss," the lady he was talking to said, and blushed. "Miss Fisher. See if they know 'Skeleton Jangle' by the Original Dixieland Jazz Band."

"A foxtrot," Barzini said. "My favorite."

He held out his hand and took Miss Fisher to the other room to dance.

Leo sulked. A bit after eleven o'clock the music stopped. At the top of the stairs there was a small explosion, and gray smoke floated down the steps. Everyone watched, expecting Houdini to appear. Five seconds went by. More. A strange quiet fell over the party. People started shuffling around. Then the front door slammed. A voice called out, "What's everyone gawking at?"

They turned. Houdini stood in the doorway. He popped a bottle of champagne and everyone cheered and clapped. The music struck up again and people began to dance.

At ten seconds to midnight, Houdini led the countdown. Ten, nine, eight. People began rattling their noisemakers. Seven, six, five. People held on to each other, waiting for a New Year's kiss. Four, three, two. Everyone chanted louder. ONE! The party broke into singing and cheering.

A bang on the door interrupted them. Someone from the back of the room said if it was the police they should be offered a glass of champagne. Houdini laughed and opened the door. A telegraph boy in his double-breasted blue uniform and blue cap handed a slip of paper to Houdini.

Leo and Barzini gathered around with the rest of the party. "Who is it from, Harry?"

Houdini read the message over a few times.

"It's from Chung Ling Soo."

Leo went to stand beside Barzini.

"What does it say, what does it say?"

People crowded around.

"*By three methods we may learn wisdom: first, by reflection, which is noblest; second, by imitation, which is easiest; third, by experience, which is most bitter.*"

Houdini looked at Leo and Barzini.

"What does *that* mean?" someone in the group asked.

"It's a quote from Confucius," Barzini said. "Perhaps our host can explain its meaning."

"Sorry to disappoint you all, but I haven't the foggiest notion what this means," Houdini said.

Some guests shrugged and migrated out into the other rooms to continue the party. Others remained and chatted with Houdini. Barzini grabbed Leo and pushed his way through the entourage of guests to speak to Houdini face-to-face.

"*What did you tell him?*" Barzini hissed. Perhaps it was the champagne, or maybe it was the taunting nature of the quote, but Leo saw fury in Barzini's face.

"I didn't mean any harm."

"He knows, Harry. You told him about my act, didn't you? *Didn't you?*"

"I might have mentioned something in passing. No harm was intended," Houdini said, avoiding eye contact. "I merely told Billy that after all these years you had a bold new plan. Look, you're both my friends. I'm helping you, aren't I? The Long Island performance is coming up. Your comeback is just bad timing."

"And I suppose your grand career and Billy's fortune are just . . . good timing. How very perceptive of you, Harry. But it is more than bad timing when we are being threatened."

"I don't think he means anything harmful. . . ."

"You have absolutely no idea what he's capable of," Barzini said with his jaw clenched. He leaned forward. Leo thought Barzini was ready to shove Houdini, but then he relaxed.

"Thank you for the hospitality and for the limousine and for everything else you have done for us. But we need to practice early tomorrow."

Barzini and Leo walked out into the cold. The snow had stopped. They walked toward the limo.

"There's room enough for both of you!" Houdini called after them.

Barzini waved off Houdini behind his back. Leo got into the limo and wrestled the letter out of the profonde. He handed it to Barzini. Barzini read it, turned it over to look at the back and read it again. His head slumped to his chest.

As they floated down the empty avenues back toward the Lower East Side, Barzini rolled down his window. Leo watched him crumple the letter into a ball and throw it into a puddle. Leo wanted to tell him that everything would be all right in the end. But he didn't know if that was true. Leo felt Barzini's pain and humiliation. It wasn't fair. Leo understood that what Barzini needed right then was the comfort of silence, not words.

CHAPTER 26

An Illuminating Discussion

Leo's head pounded. He went to the bathroom and filled the sink with cold water and dunked his head. Barzini's snores from the next room were muffled by the water. As Leo dried off, he felt refreshed, wide awake. But he was unsure where they now stood. Would Houdini still help them? Was it even wise to take his help? What about the upcoming performance for the Whitfields on Long Island? They hadn't even begun to prepare. Leo wasn't so sure it would be necessary anymore. Houdini had arranged the job and could just as easily cancel it.

He heard Horatio pacing outside the bathroom. Leo opened the door and Horatio began to whine. He went to get the leash, with Horatio trailing him. He checked the time. It was very early and still dark.

Outside, the air was warmer than Leo expected. The first day of 1918 was beautiful. The city streets were blanketed with a layer of snow still unspoiled by cars or dirty shoes. Rays of rosy sunlight appeared suddenly, making the snow glisten like rubies. The only sounds seemed far away.

A thin path had been shoveled on the sidewalk. Horatio stopped suddenly and stared into the shadows of Tompkins Square Park.

"C'mon, boy."

Leo tugged the leash, but Horatio didn't move. The dog began barking. Leo had never seen him act like this before.

"Settle down!"

Leo squinted, trying to see what Horatio was barking at. But in the early morning light, everything blended together. He tugged the leash harder and snapped Horatio out of it. They hurried back to the building.

Murph was waiting for them on the stoop.

Leo's stomach and neck instinctively tightened up. He looked around to see if he was about to get jumped. But they were alone on the block. Murph walked toward him.

"How did you find me?" Leo demanded.

"You want to go somewhere?" Murph said. "Get some breakfast?"

"With you? Are you nuts? Just answer my question!"

"Boris and the Mayor spent weeks looking for you. They'd wait by the Palace Theater on Saturdays figuring you'd show up for a magic show. But you never did. Then they'd wait by Horn & Hardart and some of your other haunts, but you never showed up there either. They figured you skipped town. Then a few weeks ago Boris thought he saw you with some guy going into Grand Central Station. He said you looked a little different, but he was pretty sure it was you. So he waited for hours to see if you came back. And you did. He followed you all the way back here.

"I've come to apologize. It's been eating me up, how everything happened. It's all I think about. I'm sorry, Leo. I wish I'd left with you right after the job for the Dropper. I'm sick over what happened in Chinatown. I shoulda had more backbone."

Murph stuck out his hand. Leo remembered Murph looking at his feet while the paddy wagon hauled Leo to the Tombs. He had always underestimated what a good liar Murph was. And how weak. Leo let Murph's hand hang in the air. "I don't care if you grow a new backbone, three heads, a sixth finger and some extra teeth. Just leave me alone. I'm gone, understand? I've got a new life now without any of you."

"Yeah, sure, I can understand that. I came to say what I had to say and I said it. I miss you, Leo. I really do. You were the best friend I ever had and I wrecked that."

"Just go."

"I will. But you should know that the Mayor is really mad about the money. That's why they wanted to find you in the first place. And just so you know, I never told him that I saw you back in the tenement. I swear I never told him you busted open his lockbox and took the cash. At first he figured somebody had been watching us come in and out of the hideout. Maybe even one of the Dropper's guys. But when he saw your dirty clothes on the floor and all your clean ones missing, he knew it was you."

Leo shook his head and turned to go into the apartment building.

"Wait. One more thing. I didn't just come to apologize. I also came to warn you. The Mayor is steaming about not finding the money. When they broke into your apartment they smashed things up because they couldn't find the money anywhere. I didn't go with them. I didn't want to have nothing to do with it. I stood up for myself, Leo. I stood up for you."

Leo opened the front door. His back was to Murph.

"He'll be back, Leo. He says he's not done with you. I needed to warn you."

Leo turned around.

"And you believed him when he said he didn't find any money?"

"No, Leo, I don't believe anything he says anymore. I wish things were different. I'm just gonna keep hoping that someday we can be friends again."

Leo climbed the stairs to the third floor very slowly, with Horatio beside him. Seeing Murph brought back memories of good times together. Murph seemed genuinely sorry. Leo realized how much he'd missed his old friend. But he didn't know why Murph would come to him with half-truths. They all knew the Mayor took the cash. So why try to make it sound like the Mayor was mad there was no money? Maybe Murph was trying to fool him, or maybe he was confused.

Inside the apartment, Barzini sat at the kitchen table drinking his usual espresso. He drummed his fingers and sipped from his small cup. Before Leo could tell him the truth behind the break-in, Barzini spoke.

"Today," Barzini said, "is the end of your sleight of hand training. You do not need to work with the *baoding* balls anymore, and you can put away your practice decks of cards. You are far enough along that your hands have their own brain, and you are free to use the one in your skull for more complicated diversions. We do not have much time before we must appear before the Whitfields."

"But what about last night?"

"Last night has nothing to do with the fact that the appearance has been booked. I feel as though I am in a delicate spot as far as Houdini is concerned. What he did to me was unconscionable, and yes, I am guilty of making a minor scene. If it were anybody else under different circumstances I would sever all ties. But as far as apologizing, he will do just that. I've known the man a long time. All *we* can do is present a superior version of Robinson's bullet catch. Don't forget that Billy failed in stealing the designs during the break-in, so the secret to our version is still safe."

"Look, about the break-in," Leo said. "There's something I have to tell you. It wasn't Billy."

"What are you talking about? The house ruined, nothing stolen, the taunting telegram? It's obvious, Leo."

"I know it seemed that way, and I believed that at first because it all fit. But now I know it was some people from my past looking for me."

Leo felt out of breath.

"How do you know for sure?"

"Trust me, I know."

"No, you *think*. Leo, I know this man, William Ellsworth Robinson. I know how insidious he is. He wants to ruin my life. Let's not discuss this anymore. What's done is done."

Leo began to explain but stopped himself. Barzini knew he was a pickpocket, but he had no idea about Leo's hidden savings stolen from his comrades. And like Barzini said, what's done is done. Leo would have to keep an eye out for them. But there would be no sense for them to break is again.

Barzini got up from the table and went to the workroom. Leo followed him. The clutter was somewhat more orderly, and a space on the table in the middle had been cleared. On it were a few candles in holders, a glass of water, a can of turpentine, a very thin wire, tweezers and a small glass vial with a square of some white substance sitting in a clear liquid.

"I have thought it over," Barzini said, "and I see no reason why the Whitfield performance should be completely different from our stage performance. We can do the candelabra illusion for both, and some mind-reading tricks would work for both a small and a larger audience. The only illusion that can't be performed at the Whitfields, for obvious technical reasons, is the bullet catch."

Barzini lit a candle and then snuffed it out with his fingers. A wispy trail of smoke lingered in the air as he moved the candle toward the water. He dipped the candle into the glass of water, and in an instant the candle started to burn again. He put the lit candle into a holder and then, with his thumb and index finger touching at the tips, as if he were still clamping down on the wick, he motioned to the unlit candles on the table. As he pointed to each one, it, too, burst into flame.

Barzini took up the vial. "This is phosphorus. It is a very dangerous element. It burns just by being exposed to air, or once it's gotten very hot. However, it can remain stable if you keep it in water or turpentine or under candle wax."

He put the vial down.

"So, the first candle?" Barzini asked.

Leo thought about it.

"There's nothing in it. It's a real candle."

"That's right. I snuff out the flame, and the wick is still hot. And on the rim of the glass is a small bit of phosphorus kept in place by candle wax. Once the wick touches it, it lights again. Now, the other candles?"

"It's the wire!"

"Exactly so. Between my fingers is the nearly invisible wire. I heat it up in the candle flame. Each other candle has phosphorus in the wick, kept safe under turpentine until I touch it with the hot wire. This is how we will begin, both for the private party and for Coney Island."

Leo was charged with excitement. He could *see* this happening. The dark theater, the candles lit out of thin air. This wasn't shuffling cards or tucking a cherry pit up his sleeve. This was real and powerful.

CHAPTER 27

History Repeats Itself

Barzini was correct. The show was still on. Houdini apologized profusely, berating himself for his loose tongue. Since the Whitfields had not offered to send a car to pick up Barzini and Leo, Houdini insisted that they use his—a Pierce-Arrow with leather seats—for the drive out to Sands Point, Long Island. Leo helped Barzini pack up, and they were on the road by three in the afternoon. Barzini navigated through the Lower East Side to the Williamsburg Bridge, the car sputtering and jerking at every corner.

"Do you know how to drive?" Leo asked.

"Of course."

For close to an hour they rode like this. Finally they made it through Brooklyn and Queens to the Long Island Motor Parkway, where the traffic lightened. By the time they exited the parkway for the back roads, Barzini's driving had improved.

Leo was enjoying the frosted scenery when Barzini broke the silence. "Tell me about your parents."

Leo blinked.

"Why?"

"I don't know. Curiosity. It's a long drive."

"I can't really remember anything before the House of Providence."

"And where was that awful-sounding place?"

"Upstate."

"And you were never told about your family origins, or how you came to be at the House of Providence?"

"I asked once or twice. But the nuns never gave me many details. Just that my parents died and there were no relatives to take me in."

The mood in the car sank. Barzini tried again. "I have something to confess. I was a difficult child," Barzini said proudly. "A thief. Just like you."

Leo turned to face him.

"Remember that first night when I confronted you over my wallet? I told you that you reminded me of someone."

"You meant yourself?" Leo asked.

"Yes. But I left that life behind a long time ago. When I was ten years old, I was caught stealing money from the church charity box. The priest asked why I would commit such a crime. I told him it was because we were poor. My mother was a widow and had seven mouths to feed."

"Really?"

"Yes. My mother *was* a widow with seven mouths to feed, and we *were* poor. The priest knew that, so he forgave me. He even gave me some money, trusting that I would use it to feed the family. But in truth, I wanted a slingshot. And while perfecting my shooting skills, I blew out the only stained-glass window of the church. The priest dragged me by the ear all the way home. He told my mother that if she didn't find guidance for me promptly, I'd be destined for a life of crime and an eternity in hell."

Barzini started laughing. Leo couldn't believe what he was hearing. Barzini usually spoke only in vague descriptions—*my time in Hong Kong, when Houdini and I were touring,* and so on.

"What happened to you?"

"There were no reform schools in Bologna, where I lived. My mother wrote a letter to my uncle in Rome. She begged him to take me for the sake of his dead brother. He agreed. When the train arrived in Rome, I tugged my cap down low and darted in and out among the people stepping off the train. I was so sure of my getaway. Then I felt somebody's hands under my armpits, lifting me into the air.

"Think of me. A skinny boy younger than you. The man put me down. I turned and realized it was my uncle. I said, 'Uncle Vittorio, I was looking for you everywhere!'

"He smacked the side of my head and dragged me to two policemen nearby."

Barzini deepened his voice to imitate his uncle. "Excuse me, officers. This young man is my nephew, and he's rotten to the bone. He lies, steals, causes grief for his mother, honors nothing and disrespects the church. Take a good look at him. If you see him wandering about, arrest him. Feed him to the rats that live in your jails. Let them chew on his tender flesh."

"What did you do?" Leo asked.

"Nothing. The policemen smacked me on the side of the head as well. They assured my uncle that they would not forget my face.

"So there we were, in front of the train station. He said that since I liked to escape so much, he'd make me a deal. From that moment on I was not to address him as Vittorio or Uncle. I was to only call him Cosimo the Conjuror . . . the most famous illusionist in all of Europe."

"Wow! Did he know Herrmann?"

"It would be stretching the truth threadbare to say he was the most famous magician Europe had ever seen. But he was a magician and he was well-known, until the drink got the better of him.

"Anyway, he said I must prove my loyalty to him. That meant I would be his steward and carry his trunks for him, and if I behaved, he would teach me all the secrets the universe had to offer. From then on, I went with him everywhere. I was a master of sleight of hand by the time I was your age. Then I learned the illusions in Cosimo's act. 'Levitation', the 'Heavy and Light Chest', the 'Vanishing Birdcage.' I became my uncle's assistant.

"And then on a stopover in Milan I discovered a tiny theater featuring a magician. I caught the act. It was the type of show I told you about, using a dog. I went backstage to introduce myself to the magician, one Signor Fucelli. While he sat at his vanity, waxing his moustache in front of a mirror, his poodle, Munito, lay near.

"'Excuse me, signor,' I said. 'I am the Young Barzini, an illusionist such as yourself. Perhaps you have heard of me?'

"'I am sorry, but I have not,' Fucelli said.

"'Perhaps, then, you have heard of my uncle, the famous Cosimo the Conjurer?'

"'Ah, yes. The hack performing at the Piazza Magia?' he replied.

"A rage boiled inside of me. How dare he insult us? When he turned to attend to his moustache, Munito came to me and sat by my foot. He looked up at me, and I saw how thin and scraggly he looked. He was not being well taken care of, and that made me even angrier. So I scooped up Munito and ran off with him.

"I rushed back to the hotel with Munito, my head filled with dreams of fame and fortune touring America with my reading dog. All I needed was a head start. So while my uncle lay in a drunken stupor, I stole his wallet and took a train to Genoa. Since my uncle squandered most of his money on drink, there wasn't enough to buy a ticket for a steamer passage. I had to pay off a deckhand to share his cramped quarters on the journey to New York."

"And that's it? That's how you started out? You trained Munito to do parlor tricks?"

"I wish it had been that simple. That's not what happened. The dog could not bear the heat in the lower decks of the ship. He died during the passage. Maybe the dog was already sick, or maybe I was just young and irresponsible. I truly don't know. But I felt terrible. There was nothing to do but bury the dog at sea. I had great affection for Munito, and since that time, I've been partial to the breed. They are surprisingly intelligent dogs, and a charm to train. Horatio is my third poodle.

"Anyway, no. That was not my start. I had a problem when I arrived at Ellis Island. I had no form of identification and only the clothes on my back. So I took a seaman's cap from the deckhand whose cabin I shared and posed as a cargo hauler. I managed to get past immigration officials. I also spoke no English, except for 'hello,' 'mister', and 'please.' A beggar's three favorite words. Lower Manhattan was filled with immigrants, so I listened for my native tongue. Soon enough I found my way. Being skilled as a magician already, all I had to do was improve my English. After that, getting work at the dime museums was no problem."

There Barzini ended his story. Leo settled into his seat and looked out the window. There were no other cars ahead or behind. Barzini turned onto another road, which ran parallel to Long Island Sound. Far off there were mansions sitting in the middle of vast fields blanketed in rime. Leo saw a few horses nuzzling the guard in search of grass.

"So what happened between you and Robinson?"

Barzini stared silently at the empty road ahead. Then he pulled off to the side and stopped the car.

"I was going to wait until later to give this to you."

Barzini reached into the glove box, pulled out something wrapped in brown paper and handed it to Leo.

"What is it?" Leo asked.

"Consider it a reward for practicing so hard for this show. You have earned this."

Leo tore off the wrapping to find a well-worn copy of *A Few of Robinson's Good Ideas*. Some of the pages were bent at the corners and others were stained. As Leo flipped through the pages, the book gave off the faint licorice odor of Barzini's favorite late-night drink. He turned to the instructions for "Gone" and put the book on his lap.

"This is my personal copy," Barzini said. "I want you to have it."

"I don't understand. If you don't like the guy, why do you have his book? It looks like you've read it a million times."

"Robinson was my partner after Houdini went off on his own. This was long before he became Chung Ling Soo. You have to understand, Billy has no stage presence naturally. His teeth are stained and he mumbles when he speaks. That's the whole reason he has assumed his Chinese character. It allows him to stay silent and adds mystery where there is none. So, even though Billy was talented in other ways, when we struck out together I thought it was best for him to remain in the background as he had when we toured with Houdini. But he wanted the spotlight. As a friend, I agreed to give him equal billing and equal time onstage. Our show was a flop. At the end of our run we had a falling-out and I fired him.

"The book states that the world of magic is indebted to the fertile brain of William E. Robinson, but that is not correct. Most of his illusions were stolen. As you have seen firsthand, Billy is not above theft."

Leo looked at the diagram for "Gone." Now that he had some knowledge, he could understand how the trick worked. A lady was strapped into a chair, which was connected to a crank by ropes. Assistants then elevated her above the stage. Now high in the air, she was positioned in front of a large pane of glass, imperceptible to the audience. When the illusionist shot his pistol, a bright light was shone onto the glass. The glass acted as a mirror and reflected the scenery stretched above it, which was identical in design to the curtain behind the lady. At the same moment, the ropes were released and an empty chair fell to the ground. The lady, now invisible behind the pane of glass, would be sitting safely on a hidden platform. The similarities between "Gone" and their own bullet catch did not escape Leo.

"So all of these illusions are yours?" Leo asked.

"Yes. By publishing this book, Billy spoiled any chance of me performing my own illusions. He violated the Magician's Code of Ethics and our friendship."

"But I still don't understand," Leo said. "You could have re-created the illusions, or changed them."

"The illusions in the book were then in the open. Any magician in New York City could pick up a copy and perform them. Even if I dressed them up, by the time they hit the stage the audience would have seen them five times before. I would have been seen as a hack magician, a second-rate imitator. Billy took what was mine and became famous from it, especially when he moved to Europe. And there was nobody to stop him. I might very well be the last man of integrity in magic."

A short while later Barzini approached a private driveway with pillars and a sign that read HEMPSTEAD HOUSE. He turned in and drove down the twisty lane to the mansion. Barzini pulled off his driving gloves and smoothed his hair. He turned to Leo.

"Ready?"

CHAPTER 28

The Here and Now

The stable hands unloaded the two heavy boxes of props from the car and placed them onto a cart. They rolled it toward the service entrance at the back of the mansion and Leo and Barzini followed. As Leo passed the stable he heard horses stamping, and something else. A low grunting noise, like some sort of monster clearing its throat.

"What are you keeping in there?"

The two stable hands stopped rolling the cart and gave each other a look.

"Might as well show you."

They led Leo and Barzini into the stable and past the rows of strong Arabian horses in their stalls to an enormous cage. Inside was a black form. It was so dark at the end of the stable that Leo couldn't make out more than just a large mound of fur. As he approached, the grunting began again, and he saw the animal's face and its bloodshot eyes. The gorilla picked up a bunch of leaves and began to chew.

"Mr. Whitfield went on safari and brought her back as a gift for his wife," one of the stable hands said.

Leo gave Barzini a nudge. "Now, *that's* rich," he whispered.

When they presented themselves at the servants' door, a butler was waiting. He rattled off instructions before they were allowed to enter the mansion. They were to scrape any muck off their shoes, use only the bathroom to the right of the drawing room, and under no circumstances wander about the mansion on their own. The butler led them to the drawing room and explained that the sandwiches, fruit and coffee on a side table had been left there for their enjoyment.

"Some enjoyment, huh?" Leo grumbled as he inspected the tray of crustless tomato sandwiches with mayonnaise. "This seems kind of crummy for rich people."

"Just eat it, Leo. You'll be hungry later if you don't. But yes, it is a bit crummy, as you put it."

Leo took a bite and a greasy tomato slipped out from between the pieces of bread onto the floor. He scooped it up with his napkin.

"I think I'll stick with the fruit," Leo said. He picked up a bunch of grapes and popped one into his mouth. "So, these Spiritualist people, do you think there's anything to it? Maybe they know something we don't know."

"I believe in the here and now. I believe in getting paid for tonight's performance. I believe in convincing Mrs. Whitfield to produce my theatrical endeavor."

Barzini dropped a partially eaten sandwich onto the tray. His eyes flashed desperation. "There's something I have been avoiding telling you. I'm flat broke. I've spent every penny of my savings staging this new act. The costs are great and expenses are ongoing. I owe a stack of bills. Martinka's for the wax props, the glass cutter, the printer for posters, not to mention the possibility of new costumes at the rate you're growing."

Leo self-consciously tugged at the sleeves. Every time he bent his elbows the sleeves of his tuxedo pulled up, exposing the white cuffs of his shirt.

"Tonight's payment will at least cover this month's expenses."

"Why didn't you say something to me?"

"What could you have possibly done to change the situation?"

"But we're partners," Leo said, thinking about his missing fortune. Barzini walked to the bay window and stared out.

"You're right. I'm sorry. Let's focus on the performance. Ready for your début?"

"I'm fine. Not nervous at all."

Barzini adjusted Leo's bow tie and smoothed down the shoulders of his jacket.

"Good. So you know exactly what to do?"

"If there's dirt, I'll quickly set up box one. If not, it's box two."

Even though Houdini had told them to do an act based on Spiritualism, they had no guarantee they would be able to get enough private information out of their hosts to turn in a convincing performance. So they had come prepared with props for two different presentations. If they overheard choice tidbits in the conversations between the Whitfields with their guests, then Leo would unload the set containing a spirit lamp, a wooden box with a telegraph key, slates for spirit writing, sponges, chemicals and other things needed for a show channeling spirits. If the chatter was empty, they would perform some standard fare such as linking rings, vanishing coins, silk handkerchief knot tricks and others to which Barzini would put a Spiritualistic spin with his banter. The only prop to be used in both scenarios was the candelabra for the magic candles.

As Leo pretended to be busy opening boxes in the hallway outside the drawing room, he heard a booming voice declare, "My companies are investing in the development of more reliable aircraft engines for the military. And I've made many personal recommendations to the aviation commission for once the war is over—and it will be soon, I feel. Aviation will become a bona fide public utility, a service to business."

"Must be Mr. Whitfield," Barzini whispered to Leo.

"I understand there's talk of passenger flights between London and Paris once the war is over. Which I hope is soon. I am a pacifist by nature. And yet I have on a personal note suffered greatly," another man said as the guests spilled into the drawing room.

Leo could see his profile out of the corner of his eye. He was a walrus of a man with long whiskers.

"Yes, may your son's soul rest in peace. Kingsley will always be lovingly remembered in this house. Such a brave boy. His death is hard to make sense of. To have survived the Battle of the Somme only to succumb to pneumonia," Mrs. Whitfield said, clicking her tongue.

"Indeed, it has been hard for me to reconcile that."

Barzini answered Leo's raised eyebrows, saying, "One." Leo opened the Spiritualism box and began to set it up on the table.

Mr. Whitfield cleared his throat. "Sir Arthur, I forgot to mention that I just finished reading your newest story, 'His Last Bow.' Very clever of you to make Holmes an undercover agent. And his code name, Altamont—is that an Irish name?"

"Indeed it is. The middle name of my father," Doyle answered.

A maid circulated around the room carrying a tray with a decanter of sherry and small glasses. Mrs. Whitfield passed one to her husband and then took a glass for herself. The handful of other guests took glasses and talked in hushed tones, surrounding Doyle.

"Sir Arthur, an after-dinner cordial, perhaps?"

"I'm ashamed to say that my own father was an alcoholic who squandered our family's fortune on drink. He ended up quite mad, spent his last days in an asylum. That's why I'm a teetotaler. I appreciate your hospitality, Mr. Whitfield. But it seems tragedy shadows me wherever I go."

Mrs. Whitfield patted Doyle on the arm sympathetically. She turned around and looked at Barzini and Leo, who had finished setting up their props and were standing still as gargoyles behind the table.

"Hello there, Mr. Barzini," Mrs. Whitfield said from across the room.

She walked toward them. Her high heels clicked on the marble floor and echoed back down from the high ceiling.

"Mrs. Whitfield, it is a pleasure to meet you," Barzini answered, extending his hand. She motioned to her husband and Doyle to join her.

"You must be the magician fellow," Mr. Whitfield said. "Harry's chum."

"Gianfranco Barzini. And this is Leo, my assistant."

"Do you study hard in school, young man?" Mr. Whitfield asked Leo.

"Yes, sir, a straight A student."

"Welcome to Hempstead House. Allow me to introduce our dear friend Sir Arthur Conan Doyle," Mr. Whitfield said.

"This is an honor," Barzini gushed. "I'm sure you get this all the time, but I am one of your biggest admirers."

"Thank you," Doyle replied.

"Mr. Barzini, shall we begin?" Mrs. Whitfield asked.

"Yes, of course. Please be seated. Anywhere you like."

Mrs. Whitfield offered her arm to escort Doyle to his seat. Then she circled around the drawing room doing the same for her other guests.

"Ladies and gentlemen," she announced, "with much pleasure I present the Great Barzini and Leo!"

Barzini and Leo bowed as the group clapped. When the room settled down, Barzini began. "I believe that the spirits are looking upon us kindly tonight. They are surrounding us, always. Leo, if you would."

Leo made the candles in the brass candelabra burst into flame. The simple trick was very effective in the small drawing room. The audience members all inhaled, then let out intrigued laughter. The sound startled Leo for a moment and gave him a strange feeling in his chest, like riding over a bump in the road at a high speed. It was electrifying.

"I'm sure that all of us here in this room think about the unnecessary waste of young lives in this war," Barzini said. "It upsets me deeply. Many a night I lie awake thinking about what has become of all these fellows who have disappeared from our world. Where are they now? What are they doing? Have they dissipated into nothing? I choose to believe that is not the case."

Barzini took a seat at the end of the table near an illuminated lamp. Next to the lamp was a box with a hinged lid, and next to the box were a pencil and a pad of paper. The guests were invited to file past Barzini and examine the open box. It contained a telegraph key. A wire connected the key to a battery-powered buzzer, which reproduced the Morse code sent by the key. Barzini demonstrated that the objects were perfectly normal.

"It is my assertion that our modern technology is only partially understood. We can use it to a better end—to communicate with the spirit world. As you inspect the box, write down the name of a departed loved one and hand it to my assistant. He will then deposit them in the box. If the spirits continue to look upon us favorably, one of the notes will be read telegraphically."

When the dozen or so guests returned to their seats and Leo put the pieces of paper inside, Barzini closed the box. The telegraph key was tall enough that it sat just underneath the lid. Barzini paused for a considerable length of time. He then lightly put his hand on top of the lid.

"I feel their presence among us. Who here understands Morse code?" Barzini asked.

Doyle jumped to his feet. "I do."

As soon as Doyle approached the table, Barzini pressed his hand ever so slightly on the lid, forcing the key to engage and the buzzer to sound. Barzini pushing on the lid was impossible to notice, and the bright light from the lamp shining on his hands made a striking image to the audience. His slight movements created the dots and dashes of Morse code. Barzini had Leo memorize the code as well, in case he had to take over control of the box for some reason.

"Sir Arthur, are you understanding the message?"

Doyle's eyes turned steely, his face strained.

"That's the name of my boy! It's Kingsley, my son!"

"Your son's spirit is here tonight. Do you have a question for him?"

Leo suddenly felt uncomfortable. It seemed heartless to play with the man's emotions this way.

"Kingsley, are you at peace?"

The buzzer sounded out the answer, which Doyle kept to himself. Leo decoded it. At least here Barzini had showed compassion. His message was that he was in a good place and watching over his father. Barzini reached for the lamp and turned it off.

They continued to enchant the crowd with their Spiritualism act, peppering it with bits of information they had picked from the conversation. After a mind-reading game and spirit writing, Barzini knew it was time to end the performance. "Always leave them wanting more," he'd told Leo.

"Well, are you going to talk to her, or what?" Leo whispered to Barzini as they packed up the props.

"When she pays us I will hand her a letter detailing the act and a request for an endowment."

The stable hands reappeared to transport the boxes back to the car. Mrs. Whitfield and Barzini said their good-byes and exchanged envelopes. On their way to the car, Doyle intercepted them.

"I must thank you, Mr. Barzini. I am here in the States for a few more months working with my American publisher," Doyle said. "I will be staying at the Biltmore Hotel. Not to push the matter, but if ever you'd be interested in putting together a circle, feel free to ring me up."

"I am humbled," Barzini said.

They pulled out of the driveway and drove into the night. The car was cold and slow to warm up. A fine mist floated in front of the headlights like dancing ghosts.

CHAPTER 29

Enough Is Not Enough

For weeks they lived on bread and milk. Every penny mattered. The block in the icebox melted and was not replaced. They did not get new soap until the bar turned into a thin waxy wafer. Even Horatio felt their poverty. His meals got smaller and smaller, turning into scraps. His ribs showed.

Houdini had kept his word and had them booked into the Eden Musée. After a brief meeting with the theater manager, a cigar-chomping squat man named Irv, they booked a two-week engagement to begin in late March. It was a terrible month to début, long before the summer crowds, but they had no choice if they wanted to establish their act before Chung Ling Soo's arrival in New York City. And though Houdini himself would not be able to attend any of their performances, as he would be busy making an elephant disappear for a crowd of nearly six thousand people at the Hippodrome, Leo was not disappointed or jealous. To him it was perfect. Just two years earlier he'd sat in the very same theater, wide-eyed, watching a magician blow fireballs out of his mouth.

But it would all be for naught unless the check came through. Barzini's proposal to Mrs. Whitfield to produce the show went unanswered. Each day revolved around running down to the mailbox to check for that one letter that would change everything.

And then one day Leo opened the mailbox and found it—an envelope with the name HEMPSTEAD HOUSE embossed in bold black letters across the back. He raced upstairs to Barzini, who ripped open the envelope, nearly destroying the enclosed check. There was also a note. Mrs. Whitfield thanked him again and hoped that her donation would help the Great Barzini get his new theatrical production off the ground. The description of the show was nothing short of astounding, she wrote. However, she would unfortunately not be able to be the sole backer for the production. Neither would she be able to attend the show, as she would be traveling during that period. Future endowments would understandably depend upon reviews and the securing of a Broadway theater. She assured Signor Barzini that there were no strings attached to the check.

"How much?"

"Enough," he said. "But also not enough."

Leo took the check. It was made out for one thousand dollars. In her letter she said she would not be able to attend their début, but they had never told her when the show would be. Leo understood. Houdini had probably mentioned that the premiere would be at the Eden Musée. A woman like her would not want to brave the lower-class crowds at Coney Island.

One thousand dollars. That would take care of many of their debts, but it wouldn't clear the entire pile of past-due bills. Barzini had said it exactly right. It was enough, but also not enough.

Practice continued. Barzini and Leo performed each illusion over and over to the point that Leo could run them backward. He formed a bond with all the props. They became second nature to him, part of his life, like an old comb or a pocketknife. The pane of glass arrived just in time for dress rehearsals, and the trapdoor was oiled so there wouldn't be a squeak when Barzini fell through. And most importantly, the grand finale was so finely tuned that Leo knew his cues to the half second and could palm the bullet with either hand.

They arrived very early on the day of their début. Irv showed up at their dressing room to remind them that he was not liable for any disasters, and then scuttled back to his office. Barzini sat down on a chair in the corner of the dressing room. He said he needed to meditate.

Leo left him. As he paced the hallway trying to clear his head, he heard someone call his name. Penelope Martinka was standing at the backstage door.

"Long time no see," she said.

"Hey! I didn't think you would come."

"Wouldn't come? Of course I'd be here. My grandparents are saving me a seat. But Opa sent me back here to make sure everything was working properly."

Leo knew Penelope's grandfather had personally tested all the props just a week ago. All custom props from Martinka's got the same treatment.

"By the way," Penelope said, "you have a fan." She handed Leo an envelope. Leo flipped it front to back. Blank. Not addressed to him, no handwriting at all.

"Oh sure," he said.

"The kid who gave it to me said he didn't have money for a ticket, but that it was really important for you to read this before the show."

Leo thought he knew what this was all about. Penelope was playing shy. The idea that maybe, possibly, it was a love letter from her sparked his heart. He folded the envelope in half and stuck it into his back pants pocket.

"I'll read it soon."

"Okay. Want to take a walk?" Penelope asked.

Leo took Penelope on a stroll along the Surf Avenue boardwalk. It was a chilly morning and they saw a lady walking on the beach in a fur coat. Coney Island was quiet, with all of the rides and snack shops closed. He felt badly that he couldn't even offer to buy Penelope some cotton candy.

"The posters for the act look really nice. I saw them in Times Square and in some subway stations," Penelope said. "And of course inside the theater when I got here."

"Thanks. We have a few extras if you want one."

"I'd like that."

Barzini had hired an artist to sketch them during the moment in the illusion when the ghost appeared. Barzini's name was larger and bolder above Leo's. All the same, when they came from the printers it made the whole thing feel official, important. Leo kept one on the wall in his room. He looked at it every morning and imagined showing it off proudly when he was very old.

Leo reached into his pocket. "This is the bullet," he said.

Penelope took it from his hand. She squeezed her fingers tightly around it and clenched her eyes.

"That's for extra good luck," she said, and handed it back.

"Thanks," Leo said. He could hear a talker calling out his act on the boardwalk near the Eden Musée. "Well, I guess we should go back."

Inside the theater the stagehands were making some final lighting touches. People had started to file into the theater and take their seats.

"Break a leg, Leo," Penelope said.

She left him to join her grandparents as the house lights flickered on and off. It was almost time to start. Leo went back to the dressing room. He found Barzini in the same position as when he'd left. When Barzini saw Leo he stood up. They moved to the edge of the stage where the curtains shielded them from view.

Leo's stomach was in a knot and his face felt hot. His pulse throbbed in his temples. Seeing all the people in the audience was something he could not have practiced for. They must succeed. All Barzini had talked about in the past few weeks was the next step: moving from Coney Island to a Broadway theater.

Leo looked over the crowd, trying to find the person he would ask to mark the bullet. The first half dozen or so rows were filled with little people, Siamese twins and some of the guests Leo remembered from Houdini's New Year's Eve party. Leo was happy they had showed up. It felt like a welcome party. They brought many of their friends to fill up other seats. Leo saw a man with hair that looked like barbed steel who carried in another man with no arms or legs. A number of the back rows were still empty. The rest of the audience were locals who wandered in from the boardwalk. These were the people he had to ask to be part of the show. If he asked any of the Dreamland Circus Sideshow people, it would be too suspicious. The audience would think the act was rigged.

Some music started up and the show began. All other thoughts in Leo's head vanished as he focused on his performance. The candelabra trick impressed the theater audience as much as it had the Whitfields, as did some of the mind-reading illusions. But Leo could sense that this audience wanted more. He finally understood something Barzini had said long ago: a theater audience required the magician to work constantly to keep its attention. Minds wandered easily in such a big space. He realized how good Barzini actually was, and that the incessant practice had paid off. An interlude of a few minutes allowed Leo to change his costume. By the time he walked back on stage, the audience was ready for the bullet catch. The room was deadly silent.

Leo walked through the aisles, looking for someone to mark the bullet. An arm shot out and grabbed Leo's wrist. Leo looked down and saw a bulging cricket. Sweat dripped down his face. He wrestled his arm free.

"I'll have a look," the Mayor said loudly. "I know a thing or two about guns."

Spikes crawled up Leo's back. Blood pooled in his fingertips, making them feel like they weighed a ton. Leo glanced at Barzini. Leo knew there was no way for him to understand how dangerous this was, and now Leo couldn't just skip over the Mayor. The rest of the audience would question the whole act. He would have to make him look like a fool. The buzz of the lights corkscrewed into Leo's head.

"You seem a little young to know much of anything, let alone guns. I need someone with some knowledge," Leo said. "Are there any veterans present?"

Boris stood up from across the aisle. Leo hadn't noticed him before. He looked around but didn't see Murph.

"I'm a veteran," Boris said, stepping forward with a limp. Leo looked down at the Mayor.

"You already took what you wanted," Leo said through his teeth. "We're even."

The Mayor shook his head and spoke in a hushed voice.

"How can we be even when you owe us three hundred and fifty-seven dollars? Not to mention the pain of stabbing us in the back? That is a thing that cannot have a value placed on it, Leo. You are a liar and you have no honor or loyalty, and no amount of black hair dye or hocus pocus will turn you into an honest person again. You killed us."

"There was plenty of money to set up a better life, and you kept it all for yourself."

"But did I spend it?"

"Get on with the show!" somebody shouted from the audience.

"It doesn't matter anymore," the Mayor said. The smile left his face. "Now let's get on with this."

Leo gulped. Maybe Boris planned on gunning him down onstage. Maybe this would be Leo the Healing Child's first and last show ever. He had to think quickly, but he wouldn't call off the performance.

He showed Boris the gun and the bullet. Boris did as he was told, and verified both were real. He then marked the bullet, but before Leo could take the bullet and gun back, Boris loaded the revolver himself. This was a scenario they had not anticipated. Barzini had coached Leo on what to do in dozens of cases—if a drunk in the audience came onstage, if a heckler called out the truth behind the trick, if a sick person wanted Leo to actually heal them—but Barzini never told Leo what to do if someone loaded the gun. Barzini simply trusted Leo to not let that happen.

Boris held the gun sideways, looking at it intently. He lightly bounced the gun in his palm. Quietly he said to Leo, "Now I can see why you liked those magic shows so much. Is it a fake bullet? No, I don't think so. What would happen if I squeezed out a round into your belly right now?"

Leo forced a chuckle.

"Watch where you point that," he said, and grabbed Boris's arm, forcing it upward. "That's a loaded gun."

Leo reached for the revolver, but Boris snapped his arm free.

"Can this little freak heal himself?" Boris yelled to the audience.

He pointed the gun at Leo's head.

"What do you say? Can this wonder of the world save its own life?"

The crowd whistled and howled as Boris cocked the hammer. They had paid for a bullet show, and they wanted to see one. Leo looked into the blackness inside the barrel. He put his hand in front of the revolver, blocking the hole. He looked Boris in the eyes and stared for what felt like a year.

"Miracles are not cheap things," he said finally, raising his voice. "And neither is life itself. Even yours. Think about that before it's too late."

Leo's reflexes were quicker than Boris's. He thrust his knee where the stump fitted into the wooden leg. Boris flinched and Leo grabbed control of the gun.

"You came here expecting a magic act," Leo said, addressing the whole audience. "But this is real."

He had gotten control back, but the bullet was still in the gun. Leo tried not to look at Barzini as he approached the stage with the gun held high, pointed at the ceiling. Everything flooded out of Leo's head. The only thing he felt was the loaded gun in his hand. Onstage all sounds disappeared. Barzini was washed in light. He looked like a ghost already. Leo leveled the gun. Through the sights he aimed just left of Barzini's shoulder. He breathed in; his eyes watered and burned. The trigger dug into his finger as he squeezed.

The blast rang through the theater and Leo stumbled back. He saw Barzini drop through the door, saw the dummy revealed. Leo prayed to heaven Barzini was alive. The crowd exploded as predicted. Leo dropped the gun to the floor and stared into the blackness of the stage backdrop. He counted to four and waited.

Barzini appeared ahead of him offstage as planned. Leo slowly turned his body and saw Barzini reflected in the pane of glass. He let out his breath, and they finished the act without the final part of showing the bullet to the person who marked it. They took a bow together to a standing ovation. But none of it registered with Leo. He felt like he was underwater and the whole thing was a dream.

In the dressing room, Barzini dragged Leo to the corner. The veins underneath his skin bulged and warped the shape of his face. His eyes were wild and strange. He grabbed Leo by the throat, pinned him to the wall and squeezed.

"You almost killed me, damn it! Is that what you want? You couldn't have thought of someway to get the bullet?"

Through his tears, Leo said "I'm sorry" over and over.

"The bullet never enters the gun, damn it! The bullet never enters the gun."

Barzini smacked Leo across the face with his free hand. He smacked him again, harder. Then he let go. Leo slid down to the floor and wheezed. He couldn't talk or move or think. His vision was blurry. All he could do was breathe. Barzini stalked out and slammed the door behind him.

CHAPTER 30

The Bullet Catches Up

The following day, an uneasy tension settled in. Leo sat Barzini down at the kitchen table and finished all those half-starts he had tried before. After he explained everything about the Mayor and Boris, Leo was worried Barzini might be angry with him.

"I'm sorry," he said. "I wanted to run away from them, not drag them with me."

"We cannot pretend we can protect you from everything," Barzini said. "But they will not be seen on the boardwalk again. I will give their description to every talker and ticket-taker in Coney Island. A kid with a wooden leg next to a hulk with a cricket tattoo should not be hard to spot. From now on try to pick the volunteer ahead of time. Scan the audience, settle in on an older man or a woman."

After that, Leo and Barzini slid around each other in the apartment like they were opposite poles of a magnet. They waited courteously for each other to finish in the bathroom, ate together silently at the kitchen table and quickly got dressed. Their first performance was at noon. At nine-thirty they left.

On the subway platform a hunchbacked man sat on an overturned milk crate, strumming a guitar and moaning out a hymn. Leo dropped a dime into his hat. Barzini bought the morning edition of the *Tribune* and tucked it under his arm. In the subway car, Leo squeezed next to Barzini between a woman holding a baby and a man with a metal lunch pail. Barzini jerked his shoulders forward and held the newspaper close to his face. Leo could feel Barzini's hand shaking as he read.

"Why is your hand doing that?" Leo asked. Even though he'd felt relieved after telling Barzini about the Mayor and Boris, a knot remained in his belly. He could have killed Barzini.

"I had no choice," Leo said. "I'll apologize forever. But there was nothing I could do. It was the début. There were reporters in the audience."

"Were they from arts and entertainment or the obituaries column? A joke. We both learned a lesson. We move on."

"But I can't forgive myself. Look at your hand. It's shaking like a leaf. How can we go onstage when you don't trust me?"

"I do trust you. Now more than ever. You are the only person I can still trust."

"What do you mean?"

Barzini covered his trembling hand.

"You seem to forget that you had a gun pointed at your own head as well. Think of the future. Today is as important as yesterday. Tomorrow will be even more important. You watch. The début will be overshadowed by what comes next."

"I know. Every performance counts."

"No. Every performance is your last performance."

The weather on the morning of March 24 was overcast, and the foot traffic on the boardwalk was slow. The sound of the ocean exploding against the beach was overpowering. Leo looked out to sea. The water merged with the clouds into one gray backdrop.

Inside the theater all was quiet as well. The lights were off and none of the stagehands shuffled around backstage with boxes and props as they normally did. The theater manager, Irv, was nowhere to be found.

"Where is everyone?" Leo said in the dressing room.

Barzini sat at his table staring into the mirror. He applied light makeup for the stage and seemed to ignore Leo.

"What's going on?"

Barzini shrugged. Leo got up and wandered down to Irv's office. A crowd was huddled around Irv's desk.

"Hello? Doesn't anyone have work to do?" Leo asked. "Our show is in an hour."

Irv clutched a newspaper in his hand.

"The kid is right. Today it's going to rain money!"

Irv jumped up from the desk and shoved a talker out the door.

"You pump up the tip," he shouted. "Tell whoever you see that the bullet catch, the very same death-defying act performed by Chung Ling Soo, is on our stage tonight. You do that and mince no details. Got it?"

Then Irv grabbed Leo by the shirt and pulled him along, babbling on about publicity and the future and, most importantly, the crowds.

"So there was a write-up? Was it good?"

"It was like you were there yourself. Like you saw the bullet fly!"

"Really? In the *Times*? The *Tribune*? Wait, what do you mean? You *were* there!"

"The write-up wasn't about your act," Irv said.

"Then what's going on? What's everyone so excited about?"

"Chung Ling Soo died onstage last night. Took a bullet to the chest. I guess it finally caught up with him! Hey, wipe that look off your face, Leo. You guys are pros. Probably some freak thing. You could get run over by a bus just as easy. And get this! It turns out he wasn't Chinese at all. He was American. Imagine that."

Leo staggered back against the wall. Irv kept moving on, barking out orders to everyone around him. New advertisements needed to be made, a larger banner, more talkers planted around the boardwalk. The crowds were going to be beating each other to get in.

Leo ran to the dressing room. He threw open the door. Barzini watched him in the mirror.

"I read about it on the train, but I didn't want to tell you," he said. "I thought with all that happened . . . well, it would be best to wait at least until tomorrow."

"What went wrong?"

"I wish I knew," Barzini said.

"But you must have some idea. There's got to be an explanation."

"I'm sorry, I don't have one. I can tell this is upsetting you. I bet Irv has big plans, doesn't he? Leo, I want to tell you something. He's not wrong. We didn't get written up. Not a mention anywhere in any of the papers. Our début was a flop. But now there is a space in the world of magic that Chung Ling Soo has left. His death, though tragic, can only help us."

"Of course you'd say that. You hated him!"

"Let me ask you this: is our act better? You saw his act on film. I've seen it live. You don't have to answer that question. We both know our act is better. Though we had our differences, I would like to think he would appreciate our show. Remember, the bullet catch is an old trick. Billy did not invent it."

"It still feels . . . wrong."

"Listen to me, Leo. Maybe Billy and I didn't have a chance to reconcile. Who knows, maybe we never would have. But I would *never* want him to die the way he did. Yet in a way, this is bringing me—both of us—some sort of peace. Now come, we should do a run-through to make sure all of our steps are safe. That should assure you that nothing will go wrong during our performance."

So the show went on, and without a hitch. Leo managed to shake off his jitters, and found himself relaxed playing the part of the Healing Child: half Midwestern mystic, half earnest kid. Each performance was so full that the theater looked like a train station the day before Thanksgiving. When their fifth show of the day was over, Irv tried to convince them to go onstage once more—a midnight performance—but Barzini refused, saying it would be too much exposure. They followed Irv to the office where he counted out their cut of the box office. When the money was divided, Barzini put the cash into his breast pocket.

"I regret to inform you," he said to Irv, "this is our notice. We will no longer be performing at the Eden Musée."

Irv didn't beg Barzini to stay. He simply shrugged his shoulders. "Your choice. Just get your stuff out by morning."

"That's already been arranged."

When Irv walked away, Leo grabbed Barzini's arm.

"We did it? We're going to a Broadway theater? How did it happen so fast?"

"No. Not yet, anyway. But I am optimistic everything will fall into place very shortly. You'll see. I have a plan," Barzini said.

A plan. None of the plans in Leo's life ever led anywhere good. He wanted to trust Barzini, but something did not feel right. Their theater was gone. In the short period of time he had been there, it had started to feel homey. He tried to be optimistic like Barzini. Leaving Coney Island behind was surely a good thing, if they did wind up getting a bigger theater. He supposed this was all part of show business. But what bothered him was that he was not even asked how he felt about it.

CHAPTER 31

What's Fair Is Fair

Barzini placed the entire haul in the wall safe. When Leo watched Irv count out the cash, he'd felt like a million bucks. This was honest money, money that he earned by doing something incredible.

"So, how much are you taking out for rent?" Leo asked.

"Nothing is being taken out."

"Oh. That's awfully generous."

"You misunderstand. You haven't begun earning yet. You signed a contract. Refer to it."

"That contract had nothing to do with money. The only thing I agreed to was to keep whatever you teach me about magic a secret. Did you forget the terms of your own contract?"

Barzini ignored Leo. He slammed shut the door to the safe and spun the dial.

"Maybe you've forgotten that we're partners," Leo said angrily. "Why did you decide to quit without talking to me? That was the stupidest thing I've ever seen you do. Two days at Coney Island and you think some big theater producer is going to come looking for you. Well, so far I don't hear anybody knocking at the door. What you did makes no sense at all!"

Barzini floated past, still ignoring Leo, and left the apartment.

Leo went to the parlor and picked up the evening papers. The headlines about Chung Ling Soo's sensational life and death covered the front pages:

> A VICTIM OF HIS OWN MYSTIFYING ACTS. DEATH ON THE STAGE. THE TRICK THAT WENT WRONG.

Leo opened the *Tribune* first.

> One of those fatal accidents, which happily are so rare in stage life, is responsible for the passing of Chung Ling Soo, the Chinese magician. The artist was making his last appearance when Mr. Soo and his assistant prepared the plate and bullet act. The magician, it will be remembered, "catches" the bullet on a plate, but on this occasion there was something wrong, apparently with the mechanism of the gun. The bullet was not retained, but projected straight through the artist's right breast, fracturing the fifth rib. The bullet exited through his back, shattering the twelfth rib, and became embedded in the stage scenery. At first the audience was composed, thinking this was all part of Mr. Soo's act. The curtain was lowered and bioscope pictures of the war were shown to the audience while Chung Ling Soo was conveyed in all haste to the Wood Green Hospital. But, despite the best medical aid, within two hours the accident had a fatal termination.

Leo next opened the *Evening Star*. A passage tucked in the middle of the report must have made Barzini's skin crawl when he read it.

> It is said that whenever a conjuror anywhere in the world produced a new act Chung Ling Soo was very soon informed of it. It was not that he desired to steal anyone's tricks, he had too many of his own, but his interest in the business was so great that he desired to know whatever was happening.

The *Herald*'s account went deeper into Chung Ling Soo's life. The newspaper was able to get in touch with his wife, Suee Seen, or as her family called her, Olive Robinson. She was quoted as saying, "No one but my husband and the people who made the guns had any knowledge of the trick mechanism. These particular guns had been in use for twelve years. My husband dealt with the guns himself and never let anybody touch them."

Leo suddenly saw the barrel of the gun in front of his face. He knew that image would never go away. He folded the paper and put it on the table. He thought about how many times Chung Ling Soo must have seen the same view, and he wondered how long it would take to become comfortable with having a gun pointed at you every night. Just then the telephone rang.

"Hello, Leo, can you hear me?" Penelope asked.

"Sure. Loud and clear."

"I just wanted to check up on you. I know Barzini had all the props moved to the store. Did you get fired from Coney Island because of Chung Ling Soo's death? I mean, because they thought your act was too dangerous?"

"No. That's not it. It was Barzini's decision not to stay at Coney Island."

"Well, I'm glad everything's okay."

"Yes. Good night."

Leo was about to hang up the receiver when he heard Penelope shout, "Leo, wait, don't hang up!"

"I'm still here."

"I was curious about that letter," Penelope said.

"What letter?"

"The one I gave you yesterday. The kid said he was a friend of yours. Skinny kid, kind of jumpy."

Murph!

"You didn't tell me it was from a friend."

"Sorry, I guess I forgot. But I figured you would have opened it already."

Leo told Penelope he'll talk to her another time, then ran to his bedroom, where the pair of pants he'd worn was draped over the chair. The square outline of a folded envelope stood out in the back pocket.

> Leo, I need to warn you. Keep your eyes open. They are waiting for you in the audience. Please be careful. Need to talk to you, any night. Village Cafeteria, 2nd Ave and 10th Street.

Even if Penelope hadn't described Murph, Leo would have recognized his chicken scratch. Leo considered the note. He believed that the warning was sincere. If Leo had read the note when he was supposed to, the whole scene at the theater would never have happened.

It was nearly midnight. Leo grabbed his coat. He ran down the two flights of stairs to the street. Leo walked fast. Through the front window of the cafeteria he saw Murph slumped in a booth. Leo rapped on the window and went in. Murph looked sickly. He was pale and bony. His cheekbones stuck out. Leo slid into the booth.

"Are you okay?" Leo asked. "You look sick."

"I'm okay," Murph said. "But you should be worried."

"How did they know?" Leo asked.

"The posters are everywhere. The Mayor tore one down from Times Square. I told you they wouldn't leave you alone."

"We both made mistakes. After I saw you on the stoop to my building, I felt terrible. You were right about a lot of things. I'm sorry I didn't listen to you. I just didn't know if I could trust you."

"It's okay, forget it. Water under the bridge. I'm not here for your apology. I'm striking out on my own. I'm through with the gang. I woke up one morning and saw everything crystal clear. We're all going to get locked up sooner or later, with the kind of stuff he's pulling. That's why you didn't see me in the audience. Told the Mayor I wouldn't be a part of it."

Leo nodded.

"I didn't know what they were going to do. They just said they were going to mess with you because there was no money in the knapsack. I tried to talk them out of it, but it was no use. So I took a train to Coney Island after they'd left. I had enough money for the train ride but not enough for a ticket too. I had to warn you the best way I could. I hung around outside and asked some girl going to the show if she'd give you my note. When she said she knew you I figured you'd get it right away."

Could the Mayor actually be telling the truth about finding no cash in the apartment? Could it be that Robinson had someone break in and all they took was money? Which version was the truth? Or was Barzini making up a convenient story to cover for something far worse? Leo's stomach churned. He had a terrible feeling about what had happened to his small fortune. He knew the show was expensive and he knew how poor they had been.

"Leo, what are we going to do? I know it's a lot to ask, but I need your help. I need some way to land on my feet. You're the only one who can fix this. We always depended on the Mayor, right? So I went along with it when he set you up. The way he explained it, it made me think you couldn't be trusted. You gotta believe me that I didn't want to go through with it, but at the time it made sense. Now I realize it's just the opposite. The reason he's so mad at you isn't just about the money. It's because the gang can't do anything without you. You brought in the most money, you made sure we ate. When the fire was burning down the House of Providence, who was it the Mayor asked first to go along with his plan?"

"Me."

"That's right. Not even his own brother. And now he's got nothing. A cripple to take care of, and me, who he thinks is just a dope on a string. After you left I realized you were the only good part of the whole thing."

"I've got an idea, but I'm going to need you. Tell the Mayor you're sorry for complaining. Just do what you have to do to get him to trust you again. Let's meet back here in three days. Same time. But you have to keep the Mayor away until then."

They spat and shook, like they used to do back at the House of Providence. Then they left the Village Cafeteria, walking away in opposite directions.

Leo needed some straight answers from Barzini about what happened to the money. When Leo got back, the apartment was just as he'd left it. He went to his room and listened for footsteps, which did not come until the very early hours of the morning.

CHAPTER 32

Quiet as a Mouse

The front door opened. Leo heard shuffling inside the apartment. He cracked open his door to listen. Somebody began speaking in Chinese, but it was not Mr. Shen. Leo would have recognized his raspy voice. The conversation started off calm and collected, but soon the voices got louder and more excited.

From the bedside stand, Leo grabbed the small mirror he practiced with to watch his hand movements. He slowly pushed open his door. The hallway was completely dark. At the end of the hall, he carefully propped the mirror against the wall that faced the men and sat across from it. In the reflection he saw the back of Barzini's head and a man in a flashy suit with a diamond stickpin in his tie—Mock Duck, the gangster, known as the Mayor of Chinatown.

"Maybe your Chinese isn't as good as you think, Mr. Barzini. Let me speak to you in English so that you will understand. Mr. Shen is dear to both of us, so I broke my rule of never dealing with outsiders. I am only asking what is fair. Simple."

Barzini shook his head.

"You are asking for double, and I already gave you half of what you said the cost would be."

"There were many extra costs. What we call operating expenses. Do you know the term?"

"I am familiar. And *this* is what we call a shakedown. I know your reputation and I suppose I have no other option."

"No need for rudeness, Mr. Barzini."

Barzini got up from the chair and walked toward Leo, who saw that he had forgotten the mirror as he quietly scurried back to his room. As Barzini passed it, he paused. He looked down at the mirror and then into the hallway just as Leo disappeared into his room keeping the door ajar. Barzini went into the workroom. Leo heard the lock on the safe spinning and the clink of the door opening. Barzini slammed the safe shut and went back to where Mock Duck was seated. Leo stayed where he was.

"This is all I have at the moment. You will get the rest shortly. Now I want you to leave."

"Thank you, Mr. Barzini. I did you a favor and now you are simply repaying me. I will have someone come by next week for the rest. See? Simple."

Leo sat on the bed. He heard the front door shut. Barzini walked down the hallway. Leo heard him stop in front of his door and he expected him to walk in, but Barzini moved on and went to his room.

After a few hours of tossing in bed, Leo got up. Barzini was also up again and sipping espresso in the kitchen. Leo poured a glass of milk. "I think we have a mouse," Barzini said. "There was something scurrying around last night."

Leo sipped his milk.

"I heard something too."

"What you heard was nothing."

"It didn't sound like nothing. Why was Mock Duck here?"

Barzini paused and sat up straight.

"I have a debt with him."

"Yeah, I heard that. What do you owe him money for?"

"Leo, there are things about this business that you wouldn't understand. You're too young."

"I understand plenty."

Barzini finished his espresso in a gulp.

"You're right, you would understand. But you wouldn't like it. So the less you know, the better. Let's just say the costs I've incurred to get this production off the ground have been enormous. With only Mrs. Whitfield's very modest backing I had to scramble. Times are tough. There's a war on. The banks aren't giving out loans to magicians. So I had to turn to Mock Duck for help, and now I have to pay him back. But I have a plan. Don't worry."

"'I have a plan' doesn't make me feel better. You've said that before. I *am* worried, but not about that."

Barzini looked confused.

"Remember you asked me how I got the money to buy your Christmas gift?"

"Yes," Barzini answered.

"I told you I had some savings. Well I had a lot more money than what it cost to buy those chocolates. I had over three hundred dollars when I moved in, and now it's disappeared. What did you do with it?"

"Oh, that. Horatio had gotten into your things. He dragged the knapsack out and the money fell on the floor. I put it in the bank for you. And now it's earning interest. When you're old enough you'll have access to it. You should be thanking me that I took it, considering our house was broken into."

"But it's my money! You had no right to do that without asking me first."

"Can you look me straight in the eye and tell me that the money was earned honestly? Or did it come straight out of some poor soul's pocket? Consider yourself lucky that I didn't take it from you outright and donate it to the parish. Or use it for your keep. Feeding another mouth has not been cheap."

Leo thought about it. In a way Barzini was right. He had taken him in and turned Leo into something more than just a street kid. "Look, I know we're broke. If you need that money, I can give it to you. We can call it even and start from scratch."

"That's a very generous offer, Leo. But the reality is that my debt is in the thousands. Your savings would barely make a dent. And I wouldn't take it on principle. I'm not that kind of man."

CHAPTER 33

One Way Out

On the subway to Martinka's, Leo thought over how he would explain it all to Penelope. He couldn't just ask her to go along with his plan without letting her know what she was getting into. When he got to the shop, the door was already locked and the sign was flipped to CLOSED. Through the window he could see Penelope sweeping up. He knocked on the glass to get her attention. She put the broom aside and let Leo in. They stood in front of Walter the satyr. Penelope looked puzzled.

"Is everything all right?"

"No, not really. I'm sorry I couldn't talk to you last night, but Penelope, I need your help. I have some things to tell you. After you hear what I have to say, you can decide what you want to do."

Leo started from the beginning. He spared no details about his first two years in New York. Penelope's face turned white and her eyes grew wide. But Leo didn't stop. He confessed to her that he had stolen Barzini's wallet, and told her how he had been set up by his old friends and gone to jail. He explained that the Mayor and Boris were out for revenge. Penelope's hand covered her mouth as Leo recounted the close call at the first show at the Eden Musée.

"I have an idea how to stop them for good," Leo said. "But I can't do it alone. I'm sorry for lying to you. I understand if you don't want any part of this. Either way, I wanted you to know the truth about me."

She threw her arms around his neck and gave him a hug. When she let go she said, "Whoever you were before, that's not who you are now. I have to apologize too. I avoided you for a while. I guess I was a little jealous."

"Really?"

"Yeah. I mean, I meet famous magicians all the time, but that's just in the shop. When I saw you hanging out with Houdini and preparing for your show, I just figured you wouldn't want to talk to me anymore. And I think I reacted funny. Because I like you."

"Oh," Leo said. "I guess you know I like you too."

Penelope smiled shyly. They both looked at their feet for a long moment.

"So?" Leo finally said.

"So count me in," she said. "What's the plan?"

Leo told her. At first she thought it was too dangerous, and she questioned why Leo would trust Murph.

"Murph and I used to be best friends. People make mistakes, but what's important is if they try to fix it. I think I can trust him again. Come on, he's waiting for us now."

Penelope locked up the store and they emerged into the balmy early spring air. Car horns honked at each other as they walked to the subway. When they got to the Village Cafeteria, Murph was sitting in the same booth. The place was old and seedy, with floors so dirty that the soles of their shoes stuck with every step. Murph slid over to make room for Leo, while Penelope sat on the opposite bench.

"Hey, aren't you the girl from Coney Island?" Murph said. "Leo, you didn't tell me your friend was *this* girl."

"This is Penelope Martinka."

"Well, I'm glad you're finally here," Murph said. "The waitress said if my friends didn't show up soon, I'd have to leave."

"Why is that?" Penelope asked.

"She said I couldn't sit here without ordering anything, and . . ."

"Well, we'll have to fix that."

Penelope stood up and signaled for the waitress.

"We'll have three big pieces of apple pie with vanilla ice cream."

"You got money to pay for all of that?" the waitress asked.

"I certainly do, but you can forget about a tip if you keep speaking to us so rudely," Penelope said.

The waitress turned on her heel and headed for the counter.

"So what happened with the Mayor?" Leo asked Murph.

"I did everything you said. I told him you were a no-good snake and we should take care of you. At first he acted cagey about it. Why the sudden change of heart, he asked me. So I told him that while we're starving and freezing, you're living the high life. I talked about how you must really like having money to do whatever you want. I started to yell about it. And then I threw some things against the wall and I told him it was payback time. For real. And I stuck out my index finger and thumb and pretended I was firing a gun at you. You should have seen me, Leo. I was real good, just like in the movies. Maybe better. The Mayor was convinced. He doesn't suspect a thing."

"I don't like the sound of this," Penelope said.

Leo gave her hand a squeeze underneath the table. The waitress came with their pies and ice cream. Murph finished his dessert in a few bites. Penelope took one forkful, then slid the plate across to Murph.

"You know, I'm not that hungry after all. You finish it, okay?"

"If you're sure," Murph said.

"I'm sure, but eat it slower so you don't get a bellyache."

Murph wiped his mouth with the back of his hand. "Don't worry about me. I got a stomach made of iron. So what happens next?"

"Here's the plan. You're going to go back to the hideout and tell the Mayor you ran into me tonight in Times Square, or someplace, just do your good acting. Tell him that when you saw me your blood boiled, and you said unless I paid you off, you were going to break into my apartment again. Only this time it wouldn't be just to trash it. And that it can all be avoided if I make the payoff—only this time it's a cool five hundred bucks. He'll like that. And he'll believe it because he's desperate. Tell him I agreed, and that I said I would do it next Saturday night at seven o'clock at the hideout."

"And then what?" Murph asked.

"And then we're going to fake my death," Leo said.

"Are we gonna do like what you did at Coney Island?" Murph asked.

"Something like that," Leo said.

"Sounds like just the trick. Now tell me what I gotta do."

"Go back now and tell the Mayor exactly what I told you to say."

"And then, Murph, we'll practice the trick together, okay?" Penelope said. "You will need to know the timing to make sure everything comes off right."

She gave him the address of the shop.

"Be there tomorrow morning at ten. Can you do that?"

"Count me in. Say, Leo, one more question," Murph said.

"What?"

"You gonna finish your pie?"

CHAPTER 34

All Cops Are the Same

Leo didn't have to lie to Barzini, because by the time Leo got up he was already out of the apartment with Horatio. Leo didn't want Barzini to know anything about his plan. He wasn't sure how he would react, and he didn't want to be talked out of it.

At Martinka's, Penelope was waiting for him at the door. She grabbed him and pulled him aside. They were blocked from view of the rest of the store by a display shelf. The look in her eyes was serious. Leo thought that after what she'd said to him the other day, she was getting ready for a kiss. He straightened his back and closed his eyes. He leaned forward with a puckered mouth and kissed her lightly on the lips. His head went light.

Penelope gave him a shove. "*What are you doing?*"

"I thought you wanted a kiss?"

"There is a *police officer* here," Penelope said through her teeth. Her face was bright red. "*He is looking for you.* I wanted to warn you."

Leo slid farther into the corner.

"Leo, what is this all about?"

"I don't know," he said.

There were so many things it could be. The jailbreak, an old theft, something he had done and completely forgotten about. Or some kind of setup. A double cross. What if Murph really was the great actor he claimed to be and this was a trap? It was too late to run out of the store or hide.

"I guess there's only one way to find out."

Penelope pointed Leo to where the police officer sat leafing through a book. He wore a large baggy trench coat and shiny black boots. His bowler hat sat askew on his head. His face was dominated by flaming red muttonchops. The detective closed the book and looked up.

"Ah, the other half of the Great Barzini's act. You are the Wonder Child, I take it?" he said in a light Scottish accent.

"My real name is Leo. Penelope said you were looking for me. What's this all about? You don't look like a New York City cop. And you don't sound like one, either."

The detective stood up. He was easily the tallest person in Martinka's. He looked around the shop.

"Penelope, you have been such a help so far. Is there a place for me and Leo to have a quick chat in private?"

Penelope cleared it with her grandmother and then led the two into an empty workshop.

"My name is Inspector Masson. I am a detective at Scotland Yard. There is an open inquiry into the death of the magician Chung Ling Soo. I was in New York by chance when the death occurred, on my way to visit a relation in Chicago. Before I could board the train, I was contacted by the home office to interview magicians who are knowledgeable about the bullet catch. I understand this shop serves as a sort of magician headquarters. I came here to inquire about your and Mr. Barzini's address. Seems you've saved me a trip."

Leo was somewhat relieved, now that he knew he wasn't in trouble. Inspector Masson took out a pipe and a pouch of tobacco. The pipe had a stem that curved down and then up into a large flared bowl. He stuck the pipe in his mouth and lit it, making flames shoot out in a whoosh.

"Sherlock Holmes smokes a pipe like that in the movies," Leo said.

"Indeed he does. It's called a calabash. The missus gave it to me for Christmas. But in the books, Holmes smokes a churchwarden."

"Churchwarden?"

"It's a long-stemmed pipe about yay big," the detective said, holding his hands about sixteen inches apart. "Do you like Sherlock Holmes? I have to admit, I am a fan."

"Yes, me too," Leo said. "I've actually met Sir Arthur Conan Doyle. At a performance."

"You don't say. What's he like?"

"He believes in ghosts."

"Odd."

"He's nothing like his character."

"Well, I'll be honest with you, Leo. Neither am I. Yes, police work is very much like science. But where Doyle gets it wrong is that in both science and police work, the most obvious answer to a problem is usually the right one. In my experience, however unexciting, the heart of a crime is never some knotty tale where one minor clue uncovers the whole thing. But I suppose that's why Doyle is such a good writer. He doesn't have to tell the truth. Not like us."

"But you're here because of Chung Ling Soo. The reports made it sound like an accident. Not a crime."

"I am speaking hypothetically, of course. Did you know that the magician's real name was William Robinson and that he was born right here, in New York City?"

"I read the newspapers."

"Right. What do you know about him and his bullet catch?" the detective asked.

"Not too much. I know he'd been doing it for a long time. I saw him do it in a newsreel."

"Did Mr. Barzini have a personal relationship with the man? I know magicians often run in a small circle of friends."

"Signor Barzini is a quiet man. He knows a lot of magicians, but he doesn't have many friends."

"Understood, but that doesn't answer my question, Leo. Did Mr. Barzini have a personal relationship with William Ellsworth Robinson?"

"I think they knew each other a long time ago. But they didn't keep in touch. They were not friends anymore."

"I see," Inspector Masson said, puffing away at his pipe.

"You sure act like Sherlock," Leo said. "I mean it in a good way."

"Thank you. Tell me, Leo, in your bullet-catch trick with Mr. Barzini, do you use a prop gun or a real gun?"

"We use a real gun and a real bullet."

Inspector Masson raised his eyebrows.

"I see. Dangerous business, this trick," he said

"Can I ask *you* a question?" Leo asked.

"Go right ahead."

"Do those things itch?"

The detective took the pipe out of his mouth and smiled.

"I suppose my whiskers are a peculiarity in New York City. And yes, they do itch at times. I am considering shaving them to show my solidarity with the soldiers on the front."

"Huh?"

"British soldiers must be clean-shaven. The gas masks won't fit otherwise."

"Oh."

A few moments passed without either of them speaking.

"Do you have any more questions for me?" Leo asked.

"Not at the moment."

Inspector Masson gave Leo his card and the card of the hotel where he was staying. He knocked out the ash from his pipe onto his hand before sticking the pipe back into his trench coat pocket.

"I would be thrilled to see your version of the trick, Leo. Where can I catch it?"

"Sorry, you can't right now. We don't have a theater. We're hoping to land something soon." Leo gritted his teeth. Barzini had yet to proffer a new plan, and Leo was still very upset about the situation.

"Ah, just my luck. Well, then, I must be off. Tell Mr. Barzini that I will be calling on him soon."

Leo followed him back to the front of the store and watched him cross the street. When he was gone from view Leo went to the counter where Penelope and Murph were waiting. Opa was showing Murph how to shuffle a deck of cards when Leo interrupted. Leo looked at Murph. No matter how great an actor he claimed to be, even he couldn't fake such a genuine look of concern. Leo's lost trust was found. Leo had his best friend back.

"What was that all about?" Murph asked. "You ain't in trouble, are you?"

"He just wanted to ask me some questions."

"About what?" Murph asked.

"About the bullet catch and how it's done. Some magician died onstage in London doing it. You weren't followed, were you, Murph?"

Murph shook his head.

"You're sure?"

"The Mayor is in Brooklyn right now watching a boxing match. Boris went with him."

"Good. Let's go to the theater. We have a lot of practicing to do before Thursday."

CHAPTER 35

Performance of a Lifetime

"Do you remember it?"

"Which part?"

"The beginning."

"Yeah, I remember."

Leo lightly touched the pouch full of fake blood glued to his chest. It felt like a fat, rotten strawberry underneath his shirt.

"Good."

Murph gave the knock. Leo heard Boris's clumping approach. He checked to make sure the small tack in his sleeve was still in place. As the steps grew louder Leo's breathing became harder. He felt as if he were about to jump into icy waters.

The door opened. Murph pushed Leo inside. The Mayor sat in the middle of the room on an overturned wooden crate. Another crate was in front of him.

"Make yourself comfortable."

Leo sat down on the crate across from the Mayor. Murph and Boris stood behind him, blocking any chance of a quick exit. The Mayor let out a tense laugh.

"Well. Welcome back. I'm sure you are used to much nicer surroundings these days."

"You would know."

"Hey, I'm sorry about all that. Trashing the apartment, making a scene at your show. I was angry. You took a lot of money with you when you ran off."

Leo thought the Mayor was acting strangely. An apology? This was not the way Murph was supposed to have set things up. The Mayor was supposed to be in a rage, not calm and admitting he had been in the wrong. He was supposed to be unhinged, ready to pull a gun on Leo. Had the Mayor found out? Maybe he had noticed the difference in the rounds nestled in the revolver. What if Murph had pulled the wool over Leo's eyes once again? Leo sensed Murph and Boris behind them. He wanted to turn to see if they were up to anything. But he also didn't want the Mayor out of his sight, not even for a second.

"Leo, I can understand why you would want to get away from this. Not just this shack we live in now, but the whole lifestyle. But it takes a real low person to turn his back on his family when they need him most. To steal from his family."

"Families don't lock each other up and throw away the key," Leo responded. "Families don't lie to each other."

"*You* lied to *us*. You never trusted me. I was saving up for all of us. Did I spend one penny of that money? No. You assumed the worst of me, Leo. Maybe you don't understand this, but you hurt me. You were my brother. I got us out of that orphanage when it was burning to the ground."

"Stop acting like you were some kind of hero, because you weren't. The fire was just a good opportunity to leave. I did trust you, and we were once a family, but you changed all that. You held out on us. What were you planning on doing with all of that secret money, anyway? Run out on us when you felt you had enough?"

The Mayor shook his head.

"Fine. I guess I didn't really expect anything more from a guy like you. Where is the money? It's now five hundred bucks. Now that you're famous I bet it seems like small potatoes to you."

The Mayor still acted as if he had just been sung a lullaby and slugged down a glass of warm milk. Leo was waiting for the anger to surface. The seconds ticked away, and the Mayor patiently waited. Finally Leo had to answer.

"It's all gone."

"That's impossible."

"It's the truth."

The Mayor motioned over Leo's head. He felt Murph's and Boris's hands clamp down on his shoulders. He looked up at Murph, who betrayed no emotion. This was not part of the plan. The Mayor got up from the crate and rolled up his sleeves. The cricket twitched on his forearm.

"Where is the money?"

He slugged Leo in the stomach. The pain was immediate, but the panic overrode it. If the Mayor punched the bladder of fake blood and it exploded before it was needed, the whole game would be over. Leo tried to slump over to protect it.

"It's gone."

The Mayor struck again, harder.

"*Where is it?*"

The Mayor punched again, and again, and again. A tender spot in the shape of the Mayor's fist developed on Leo's stomach.

"He's lying," Murph said. "I know it."

Murph let go of Leo's shoulder. He went to the Mayor and leaned close, whispering something into his ear. The Mayor took in the information silently and then gave a nod. Leo followed Murph with his eyes as he walked to the hallway. When he returned, he was holding the revolver Leo had taken all those months ago.

Things happened very quickly, and not entirely the way Leo had planned them. The first surprise was Murph pointing the barrel at Leo's head—it was supposed to have been directed at his foot to begin with. The second was Murph allowing the Mayor to restrain Leo's arms behind the chair. The final surprise, the one that Leo had the least trouble understanding, was just how damn happy Murph looked.

Murph grinned ear to ear and cocked the gun.

"You're a lot of things, Leo. A dirty cheater, a yellow-hearted vermin, a phony friend. But most of all, you're a liar," Murph said. "So I'll ask you one last time. Where is the money?"

The Mayor's fingers wrapped around Leo's arms so tightly that Leo's hands tingled from lack of blood. Leo looked left and right. He couldn't see where Boris was standing, and he could only feel the Mayor behind him. He looked into Murph's eyes, hovering about a foot away, raised up all the phlegm he could find in his throat and spat in Murph's face.

Murph lunged forward, and Leo swiped his feet out from under him. The chair knocked into the Mayor's elbows, and he released Leo and grabbed his arms in pain. Leo grabbed for the revolver. Out of the corner of his eye Leo could see Boris helping the Mayor to his feet. Murph held the gun aloft and Leo reached for it, prying Murph's fingers off. A loud bang erupted into the room, scaring the pigeons above into a fury of wing flaps. Leo pushed Murph to the ground and without hesitation let another bang go. Murph lay very still. Leo dropped the revolver.

The Mayor looked like a marble statue, all white and frozen. His mouth hung open. Little squeaking sounds came out of it. He and Boris stared at the spot on Murph's gut where red liquid trickled out. And then the Mayor snapped to.

He ran for the revolver and scooped it up. With a shaky hand he pointed it at Leo. "You murdered Murph! This was your plan all along. You're going to pin this on us, aren't you?"

"I don't know what you're talking about," Leo said, backing to the wall. "I had to protect myself."

"You've been *planning* this all along! How could I have been so stupid? With us behind bars, you'll have that dough all to yourself."

"You've got it all wrong."

Leo groped behind him, finding only wooden boards.

"This one's for Murph."

The Mayor squeezed the trigger and the gun went off, just like it was supposed to. Leo instantly raised his hand to his chest and poked the tack into the pouch filled with fake blood, and the stuff came squirting out. He sank to the ground. He let his head swing in semicircles, let the lids of his eyes float shut. The performance of a lifetime. He shut his eyes and took only the shallowest of breaths.

A clunk on the floor. Leo imagined the Mayor dropping the revolver. Leo heard the sound of Boris hobbling over to his brother.

"What are we going to do?" Boris asked, barely audible. "Now you're a murderer."

The Mayor croaked half an answer and started to cry. Then Boris joined in. His eyes closed, Leo envisioned them when they were younger. The four of them taking turns sleeping to protect each other from the other kids in the night. Dodging smacks from nuns. Daydreaming together about running away. But that was a long time ago.

"What are we going to do?" Boris asked again. "We can't just leave 'em here to rot."

"We have to leave. Get out of this city. We'll call the cops on the way, say we heard gunshots. But we're on the next train to Philly. You understand? If the cops start poking around the neighborhood and asking who comes in and out of this building, we would be picked up in no time. This is serious."

Leo heard rustling. Across the room they were doing something. Leo's mind raced. He couldn't risk opening his eyes. Maybe they were crying crocodile tears and waiting for Leo to stir, only to administer the next round of pain. He heard them approach and held his breath. He prayed the pulse underneath his skin didn't betray him.

He felt their presence over him. Coldness fluttered down on him and covered him. They had draped a sheet over his body.

"Leo," the Mayor said softly, "I wish you had never walked away that night. Things could've been different."

The Mayor got up and walked away. Leo heard him and Boris packing up a few things. The Mayor was making promises again. He told Boris that they were starting over. He said that the tenement wasn't a home suitable for them, and that wherever they landed next they would be a step ahead of the game. After a few minutes of assurances, Boris interrupted. He had only one question.

"What are we going to do with this thing?"

Without skipping a beat, the Mayor said, "Just leave it."

And then they were gone. They left the front door open. The sounds of the street drifted in. Leo opened his eyes. The white sheet blocked his vision. He threw it off and sat up.

"Hey, Murph."

"Is it safe?"

"Yeah, they're gone. What the hell was that?"

"What was what?"

"I thought you said you remembered the beginning. You totally changed it."

"Well, it worked, didn't it?"

Just then Penelope came in carrying a bag.

"I saw it all from the window. I couldn't breathe the whole time."

"They're gone?"

"I've never seen anyone run faster."

Leo turned to Murph. They beamed at each other.

"I can't believe this worked," Murph said.

"We're free now," Leo replied.

"Your clean clothes are in the bag," Penelope said. "But first, I think a toast is in order."

She pulled three ginger ales out of the bag.

"Well, Leo," she said, "any words?"

He raised his bottle. He had never made a toast before, but the words somehow spontaneously sprang to his lips.

"To getting rid of your past to make room for your future."

"Hear, hear!" Penelope cheered.

They finished their drinks quickly, knowing that the police might be on their way.

"Murph, what are you going to do? You can't stay here," Leo said.

"Don't worry about me. I'll be okay."

"No, you won't. You've got no place to go. Come home with me," Leo said. "I'll explain everything to Barzini. What's he going to say?"

"He'll say that the stunt you just pulled was dangerous and stupid," Penelope said. "Opa already knows Murph and likes him. I'll take him home, it'll make things easier. And I've got an idea for you, Murph. Let me take a look at your hands."

CHAPTER 36

It's All Done with Mirrors

The sound of flags snapping in the breeze came from high overhead. Leo looked up. On the roof of the enormous brick building behind him was a row of bright banners. At each corner of the roof there was a structure like a miniature Greek temple with a steel globe on top. The Hippodrome was an impressive building. Leo returned his gaze to the street. A few hundred feet away the line was beginning to form for Houdini's performance. Showtime was still an hour off, but the weather was nice and people were enjoying the longer days. They could wait outside and enjoy a cigar and some conversation.

Leo and Barzini had the best seats in the theater, Houdini had seen to that. The sound of a packed house of five thousand people clamoring to find their places was like an ocean crashing on a beach, and it almost completely masked the soft tones of the calliope onstage. This was the sound of making it in the big time.

They were going to see him backstage after the show. Leo wanted to ask him then what he felt like after he made an escape. Surely it was something similar to what Leo was feeling now that the Mayor and Boris were out of his life for good. Despite the noise of the crowd behind him, Leo could pick out the sound of Barzini flicking his fingernails together nervously. He was clearly on edge.

Soon the lights dimmed. The calliope was wheeled away and

the orchestra, sunk beneath the floor level, began playing "Stars and Stripes Forever," a patriotic song full of horns and cymbal crashes. A line of trucks with actors dressed as soldiers sitting in the back drove from one side of the stage to the other. The troops all jumped out and were joined by chorus girls in red, white and blue sequined costumes. They began to sing and perform an elaborate dance routine, which went on for about half an hour. The vaudeville show was meant to raise the patriotic spirit of the audience. But really, war or no war, everyone in the audience was there to see Houdini.

After the five-minute sparkler-filled finale, the vaudeville troupe exited the stage. The curtain went down and a short man with an oversized megaphone walked to the center of the stage. "Welcome, welcome one and all to the Hippodrome, the pageant of a thousand workers, where everything is on a big scale except the prices."

This man was a trumped-up talker, and truthfully Leo thought the opening to their own act was better, more personal and mystifying.

"Settle back in your seats, enjoy our show, and don't forget to donate your change to the War Widows Fund on your way out. Every penny counts. Our ushers will be standing by each exit with collection cans. And now, ladies and gentlemen of all sizes and ages, I present the Great Romani."

Leo flipped through his program. The Great Romani's illusion was "The Mysterious Casket." Then there were two more acts before Houdini took the stage: the Zancigs, billed as *Two Minds with but a Single Thought*, and Lady Camile with her *Magical Horticulture*. When it was finally time for Houdini, the sound of mallets beating on kettledrums came softly at first, then built to a powerful crescendo. Leo and Barzini were sitting so close to the orchestra pit that they felt the vibrations. This was the signal to introduce the world-famous, the shocking and daring, the one and only Houdini.

The curtain rose again and Houdini walked into view. The audience erupted with cheers. It took several minutes for the applause to stop. Houdini stood patiently, calmly taking in the full house.

Leo realized how much had changed. The way he felt now was not at all like the first time he saw Houdini on the street. Leo had more appreciation for what was going on, the little details of lighting and the way Houdini stood. And then it struck him. Leo was watching the show as a fellow magician. This understanding made Leo feel very happy. There was something out there, bigger than him or Barzini—or even Houdini—that he was now a part of.

When the applause died down, Houdini walked to the edge of center stage.

"My dear friends," he called out.

His voice was the only sound in the gigantic theater.

"Thank you for joining me here today. Before I go on to present the greatest disappearing illusion of all time, I want to briefly talk to you about something that has been on my mind lately."

There were some uncomfortable mumbles from the crowd.

"A close friend of mine, a man I had known for many years, recently died while performing onstage. You may know him as Chung Ling Soo, but I knew him as Billy."

Leo looked at Barzini out of the corner of his eye. He had stopped picking at his fingers. He was taking short breaths.

"His dedication to his art permeated every single thing in his life. I often wonder what would have happened to Billy if he had chosen a less dangerous illusion." Houdini paused for a moment, as if to regain his composure. He looked up into a spotlight and went on.

"His death is a reminder to me of the dangers in letting yourself believe that what happens onstage is supernatural. That I, or you, are invincible against the uncontrollable forces of life. We are not."

The spotlight went off and Houdini looked back into the crowd. A sly smile came over his face. "I do not mean to upset any of you. We are here to be entertained."

Just then a large platform with a ramp on either side was brought out onstage and positioned above a tank of water. A long wooden cabinet on wheels was then rolled up onto the platform and settled in the center.

"But I want you all to be absolutely certain of one thing. While what is about to happen may not be supernatural, it is still magic."

Houdini motioned to someone offstage.

"Ladies and gentlemen, please welcome Jenny!"

An elephant emerged and lumbered toward the ramp. Each footfall made a deep thump on the stage. Its trainer led the way up the ramp and put the elephant into the cabinet. Leo looked closely to see if he could spot where the mirrors inside the cabinet were. The setup onstage was nearly identical to the schematics he'd seen in Houdini's workroom. It was arranged perfectly. Nothing seemed suspicious, even if you were looking for it.

The crowd applauded and a few people way up in the third balcony whistled.

"Jenny comes all the way from Africa. She is very sweet, but weighing in at ten thousand pounds, I don't think you would want to get on her bad side. You will notice that I have left the pool of water in its place, and have positioned Jenny's cabinet above it. I hope this will dissuade you from thinking that a trapdoor or secret compartment will be employed."

The trainer closed the door of the cabinet behind him. The audience could see him petting Jenny's large head in a soothing motion, like she was a housecat. A tympani roll came from from the orchestra. Houdini stood in front of the large cabinet. And then from nowhere, a small blast, a cloud of gray smoke. Leo squinted through it, and saw it happen. In half a second the mirrors moved into place and the elephant and trainer were no longer in view. It took a few more seconds for the rest of the crowd to see what had happened, and when they did there was a collective gasp, then cheering.

A group of stagehands soon appeared and wheeled the cabinet away. Houdini took a bow, and the curtain came down for a fifteen-minute intermission. Houdini returned to finish the program with a handcuff and chain escape and his trademark illusion, the substitution trunk known as Metamorphosis. Then the orchestra struck up a tune, and the curtain came down for a final time. As the audience spilled out into the aisles, Leo and Barzini lingered in their seats.

"So. What did you think?" Barzini asked.

"It's a cinch. A good illusion, but almost too simple. The mirrors in the cabinet do all the work. The elephant was a good idea because it captures people's imagination, but really, I think he should stick to escapes."

"Mirrors in the cabinet? Oh, right. No, I mean what do you think about his little speech?"

"About Billy?"

Barzini nodded.

"I guess Houdini was just being Houdini. Tugging at the audience's heartstrings."

"Perhaps."

When the last stragglers had left the auditorium, Barzini and Leo found the side stage door and entered. They walked past all the dancers and singers, still in costume. Barzini stopped one, a pretty girl whose sequined costume shimmered, and asked her where Houdini's dressing room was. She pointed to a door at the end of the hall. Barzini knocked. Houdini welcomed them in.

They settled down on folding chairs while Houdini took off his stage makeup.

"Thanks for making it," he said as he yanked at his tie.

He did not face Barzini or Leo, but looked at them in the mirror.

"Good crowd tonight. Very animated. I like that."

"Thank you for inviting us," Barzini said. "It was quite an impressive show. The opening act was . . . how to put it? Vivacious."

"People still love the old song and dance. What did you think, Leo?"

"Great show," Leo said. "Really great. But I've got a question for you. What do you feel like—I mean, what's going through your head—right after you break out of a set of handcuffs?"

"Well," said Houdini, "I suppose nothing at all. During the escape, I am very aware of my body and how I have to move it. But afterward, my mind just goes sort of blank."

"Interesting."

"Fruit?"

Houdini picked a few blueberries from a basket on his dresser and popped them into his mouth.

"No, thank you," Barzini said. Leo saw his impatience rise again.

"Listen, Harry, what I think Leo is trying to get at is, even though the disappearing elephant is a marvelous trick—large and impressive—you are known for your escapes. That's what people love you for. This patriotic vaudeville opening act you have now, it doesn't *go* with what you do. I have an idea and I want you to have an open mind about it. I know you had been planning a tour with Billy. What I am proposing is simply this: we take that spot. Me and Leo. Our bullet catch is fantastic. Coney Island is abuzz about it. Now, you don't have to answer this second, just think about it. I am certain you will arrive at the same conclusion. Believe me, it is a polished show. We are ready for the big stage."

"Franco," Houdini began in a strained voice, "it's not that. I'm sure your act is terrific. That's why I backed you in the first place. But a bullet catch now? After Billy's death? Don't you think that would be in bad taste? I couldn't have that on my stage."

Barzini looked crushed. But Leo understood, and couldn't disagree with Houdini. Still, Leo felt tremendous disappointment for Barzini. Leo could feel the coldness coming off him.

In a quiet voice he said, "But who will make that connection? It's just a magic show. You have personal feelings attached, that is why you feel that way."

"I do, Franco. I do have very personal feelings about this. Which is why I couldn't have it on my stage."

"I see."

Leo wanted to try to convince Houdini, but what could he say? Barzini looked at him. His eyes were the color of a frozen lake.

"I have another grand illusion, Harry," he said softly, trying to sound convincing but instead sounding defeated. "I won't need that much time to get it ready. We already have the rest of the show prepared."

"But unfortunately, you do not have the same big name that Chung Ling Soo had. I'm sorry, and I don't mean to be rude or condescending to you. But you have been away from the stage for too long. You may have created a stir in Coney Island, but what happens when we go to Chicago or San Francisco? No one will know you there. I need an opener that people will recognize. It's not about you, Franco. It's about filling seats."

"I see, I see," Barzini said. "Well, thank you for inviting us backstage and for the tickets."

They stood up and shook hands. All false smiles. Leo didn't know the words for what Barzini must be feeling. But he was proud of him. Barzini had shown composure, grace, dignity. Barzini had swung for the fences. He had ended up a little short, but in Leo's eyes he was a great man, noble and inspiring.

CHAPTER 37

Broken

By the time Barzini reached the apartment door, he was totally shattered. His face drooped. His back was bent. His movements had slowed down to an old man's shuffle. He went to his workroom and locked the door. He did not come out for dinner or for breakfast the next day. Leo left him alone. There was nothing he could do or say that would help.

On the third day, Leo found the door to the workroom ajar. He peeked inside. It reeked of sweat and licorice liqueur. Empty bottles littered the floor. Stacks of papers and blueprints of illusions were scattered across the work table. Barzini hadn't changed his clothes or washed since returning from the Hippodrome. Wisps of white showed at the roots of his hair. The black dye was fading from his goatee. Stubble spread all over his cheeks and neck. Horatio sat in the corner with mournful eyes. The scene broke Leo's heart.

"What do you want?"

"Don't lock Horatio up in there with you. He doesn't deserve your misery."

"Feed him and walk him, then, but leave me alone."

"Look, it's not the end of the world," Leo said. "What about that illusion you mentioned to Houdini? We could work on it now, together. Who's to say we can't develop a new act and find a new theater?"

"You don't understand a thing," Barzini said. "How could you? You're just a child."

"I understand plenty. I understand that you're just giving up. You're acting like Houdini promised you something and then took it back. Well, he didn't. The only promise he made was to get you a theater. He made good on that. The rest was your fault."

"Oh, was it?"

"You quit! What kind of a professional quits a run after two days? You quit because you assumed we'd just step into Robinson's shoes."

"Go back to the sewer I pulled you from."

"You're pathetic!" Leo shouted back. "You look like a Bowery bum. We could find other theaters or travel to different cities. Why does it have to be all or nothing with you? I don't get it. Why can't you just be happy doing magic? You were obviously successful or you never would have been living in this nice apartment all these years. We can do it again. Just say yes, take a bath and let's get to work. Okay?"

Barzini seemed to soften. But then he shook his head and grunted. "You still don't understand. We are *through*."

"I'm trying to help you."

"*You* help *me*? *You* lecture *me* about reality? Here is the truth: I had the idea for a new bullet catch. Ideas are not a dime a dozen; sometimes you only get one good one in your entire life."

Leo was angry, but he couldn't make himself hate Barzini.

"You took my money. And as far as putting it in the bank for my future, we both know that's a big lie. I understand that you would never have done it if you hadn't been at the end of your rope."

Barzini covered his head with his hands. He smoothed his hair down.

"I am sorry for the way things have turned out."

He got up and brushed passed Leo to the living room. He composed himself and picked up the telephone.

"Hello, operator. The Biltmore Hotel, please."

Barzini closed his eyes and sank into a nearby chair. "Desperate times call for desperate measures," Barzini declared. "Yes, hello. This is Signor Barzini for Sir Arthur Conan Doyle. Please patch me through. Hello, Sir Arthur. Gianfranco Barzini calling. I was hoping you were still in New York . . . you are . . . that's good to hear. I have been thinking a great deal about our conversation at the Whitfield estate. Are you still interested in hosting a circle? I believe my talents can be put to some good use in light of the newspaper headlines from London. . . . Really, you saw him perform the bullet catch at the Alhambra? Yes, next Friday is good. Your suite at the Biltmore. Midnight. Thank you." Barzini hung up.

"So you see," he said to Leo, "this is what it comes down to. Not all illusions are happy shows. Not all take place on a stage. Take Horatio for a walk. When you come back we will go over the basics of a séance. I am probably a bit rusty myself."

CHAPTER 38

A Magician, Not a Detective

Horatio barked at the door. Someone was standing on the other side, lightly rapping. Leo went over and looked through the peephole. The warped image through the glass was a tangle of flaming red muttonchops.

"It's that detective, Masson," Leo told Barzini.

"What detective? Are you in some sort of trouble?"

"No, I'm not in any trouble. He's from London. He came around to Martinka's a couple of days before we went to Houdini's show at the Hippodrome. He was asking me questions about Chung Ling Soo and the bullet catch. I forgot to tell you."

"Forgot?"

Barzini smoothed down his sleeves and opened the door. Horatio circled around Masson and sniffed his trench coat. Masson introduced himself, paying no attention to the dog.

"Inspector Masson, Leo tells me you've already met," Barzini said. "Come inside."

The inspector wiped his boots on the mat and hung his trench coat on the rack in the hallway. Barzini ushered him into the parlor. Masson packed his calabash pipe with tobacco. He tamped it down with a finger and struck a match.

"Leo, why don't you put on the kettle for tea," Barzini said. "And bring the detective an ashtray."

Inspector Masson shoved the pipe into his mouth and removed a notepad and pencil from his pocket. He dampened his thumb and forefinger with his tongue and flipped to a blank page. Then he put the notepad aside and rested his hands around the bowl of the pipe. His fidgeting seemed to make Barzini nervous. Leo went to the kitchen to make the tea.

"If I may ask," Barzini said, "what brings a Scotland Yard detective all the way to New York City to investigate the death of Chung Ling Soo?"

Leo filled the kettle with water and lit the burner. He came back to the room, placed the ashtray on the side table and took up a post leaning against the wall.

"We are working together with the New York City police department. The case has a number of loose ends both here and in England."

"Ah. We knew each other in our youth. But I've neither seen nor spoken to Billy in more years than I can count."

The detective jotted something down in his notepad.

"I've been told by one of the elder Martinka men—I'm not sure which one—that there is no such thing as a perfect magic trick. Would you agree, Mr. Barzini?"

"No, I don't think I would. I think there are perfect illusions, but the magicians executing them might be imperfect."

"Interesting choice of word."

"I don't follow."

"Execution. Do you believe that Mr. Robinson was the victim of foul play?"

Barzini laughed and lifted up his arms.

"I'm a magician, not a detective."

"Everyone in Mr. Robinson's production has been questioned, and they are all quite baffled. Not one of them could understand how a man who'd been performing the same trick for a dozen years without incident could have been killed."

"Accidents happen. Robinson wasn't the first to die doing that trick."

"I spoke with Mr. Houdini yesterday, and he believes Mr. Robinson may have been murdered." He let the word hang in the air, drawing a draft of smoke from the pipe and letting it out in a thin stream.

"His theory," Masson finally continued, "is that the only way Mr. Robinson could have died is if somebody substituted real bullets for the usual blanks. I think his notion holds some water."

"Inspector, you must take everything Harry Houdini says with a grain of salt. Unlike Mr. Robinson, I *am* on friendly terms with Houdini. He is genuine enough, but the man is fond of listening to himself speak and is prone to sensationalism. Why do you really think he's proclaiming Chung's death to be murder?"

"Enlighten me," Masson said.

"Harry Houdini's elephant disappearing act is a bust. Only those seated in the front orchestra section can actually see the trick. What's worse, he doesn't even make the elephant reappear. You see, the problem with Houdini always was that he's not really a magician. He understands nothing about the subtleties of timing, of misdirection, the essence of illusion. I've known Harry for years, and unfortunately he could never stand it when another magician upstaged him. Alive or dead. Even though he originally planned to tour with Chung Ling Soo, the fact that the newspapers are reporting on not much else except the sensational details of Soo's death makes Houdini jealous. That's his personality. He isn't getting the publicity he craves for his disappearing elephant act."

The teakettle whistled. Leo went to prepare a tray.

"I understand that Mr. Houdini paid tribute to Robinson at the Hippodrome. That seems contrary to what you say."

"That is true, but again, Inspector, as I just told you, everything that comes out of Houdini's mouth is calculated. The man is so full of himself someone should take a pin to him and pop all that hot air."

"I see. Funny, Houdini spoke very highly of you," Masson said.

"Well, in that specific case," Barzini said, smiling broadly, "he is a fine judge of talent."

Masson poured himself a cup of tea and idly stirred in the milk. Leo went back to his position against the wall.

"When you said 'unlike Mr. Robinson' just then, were you meaning that you were on bad terms with Robinson?"

"Pardon?"

"You said, just a moment ago, that *unlike* Mr. Robinson you were on friendly terms with Houdini."

"Oh? Did I?"

"Yes. And I'm still not quite sure what Houdini's celebrity opinion of himself has to do with his theory on Mr. Robinson's demise. Which, from my perspective, seems plausible."

Barzini shifted in his seat. His smile dissolved.

"I merely meant that Houdini might have hidden motives. I think he is attaching himself to a tragedy for publicity because he can't fill the Hippodrome. It's probably a blow to his self-esteem. I wouldn't be shocked if he were to do the bullet catch himself next, just to keep the headlines coming."

"He would have to learn how to do the trick first. Can you explain to me how your version works? Without giving anything too valuable away, of course."

"Our act is more like a short play rather than a standard magic show. I am killed onstage and brought back to life. The bullet we ask an audience member to mark is real and the gun is real. I can tell you that much."

"You have nothing to worry about from me, Mr. Barzini."

"I believe you. But whoever reads your report may not have the same scruples."

"Fair enough. Do you know how Mr. Robinson performed his version?"

"I have no direct knowledge of how his trick was done, but I can only assume it was with some sort of prop gun, based on the films I have seen."

"We assumed so as well. Both rifles were collected and taken to Scotland Yard for inspection. We have a department that deals with a new science. Forensics. Absolutely fascinating. We can now match the inner markings in the barrel of a gun to the little scratches on a bullet. It's as conclusive as a fingerprint."

"I see."

"No results yet. But everyone around Mr. Robinson said that only he handled and cleaned the rifles. They were secured under lock and key after every performance. Even his wife didn't know the secret behind the trick. But she did provide us with an interesting piece of information. The night he died they had to use a different kind of gunpowder. They'd been accustomed to using a coarse variety, but the new kind they obtained was fine, not as good quality."

"War shortage, most likely," Barzini said.

The inspector blew across the top of his cup and took a sip of tea.

"When I spoke to Mrs. Robinson, she claimed that when she went to his side after he collapsed onstage, the last words he spoke were 'Forgive me.' Why would he say that? It's so cryptic. I have been haunted by those words."

"That is an unsettling thing to hear. Perhaps his death was a suicide," Barzini said. "Maybe he was tired of leading a double life. Consider how many years he wore a costume and greasepaint and deceived the world into thinking he was someone else."

"That's another theory. There have also been rumors about extramarital affairs. I wouldn't want to tarnish his memory, but there may be some truth to them as well."

The two of them paid Leo no mind. They were evaluating each other like people haggling over an expensive vase. Barzini held his goatee and hesitantly continued.

"When I knew Robinson back in the old days in New York, he was with his first wife, named Bessie. They had an infant son. He abandoned them when he took up with Dot and went to England. Those rumors you mentioned are not new. He always had a wandering eye. So it's entirely possible that Dot felt spurned . . . and did something unfortunate," Barzini said. "That does not seem so far-fetched."

"That is yet another theory," the inspector said, "perhaps connected to Mr. Houdini's. Mr. Robinson's death was quite agonizing." Masson flipped through his notebook to get to the correct page. "The coroner's report reads that the bullet entered his body through the fifth rib and tore the right auricle of his heart, destroyed his liver and then exited through his back, shattering the twelfth rib and causing the bone to protrude four inches out of the body. There was nothing the doctors could do for him. He died of shock and hemorrhage. He bled to death."

Barzini cringed.

"Well, enough of the grisly details," the inspector said. "Thank you for helping me to understand your illusion."

"I am here to help any way I can."

Masson stood up and approached the door. "Oh, one final thing, Mr. Barzini."

"Yes?"

"Mr. Houdini told me to ask you about this." The inspector removed a piece of paper from his trench coat pocket and read it aloud. "*By three methods we may learn wisdom: first, by reflection, which is noblest; second, by imitation, which is easiest; third, by experience, which is most bitter.*"

He handed the telegram to Barzini. Barzini looked at it for less than a second and handed it back.

"There's nothing to say. It was a telegram delivered during Houdini's New Year's Eve party."

"And it was from Mr. Robinson?"

"You must know that it was."

"Mr. Houdini said you became agitated after he received the telegram. He said you were carrying on about threats from Mr. Robinson. So, Mr. Barzini, I'll ask you one more time to reconsider your earlier statement. Is there something about your relationship with Mr. Robinson that you have omitted? Perhaps your dealings with him have been more recent than decades ago?"

"I have nothing to add. Houdini had shared the details of my act with Billy. That was something he never should have done. I felt that the telegram was just another way for Robinson to upset me, to get under my skin. Whether that was his true intent or not, I felt fully justified in interpreting it that way."

"Shoddy behavior for a man you are on friendly terms with. Houdini, I mean," Masson said.

"I would agree. Harry should have never divulged what I told him in confidence. He has since apologized."

Barzini opened the apartment door.

"But if you are implying that I would directly benefit from Chung Ling Soo's death, then I suppose the answer is that I would. As would a long line of other magicians."

"I see. I may be back in touch with you if I have additional questions," the inspector said.

"By all means," Barzini replied.

Barzini closed the door and put his ear to it. The sound of the inspector's footsteps down the stairs melded into the other background noises of the neighborhood. Barzini turned to Leo and sneered.

"Slipped your mind? The next time an inspector comes along asking questions about foul play, you take note and let me know in advance. Hm?"

"He didn't say anything about murder to me."

Barzini left Leo behind and went to the kitchen. He sat at the table and tapped the servante open. He looked inside.

"What are you looking for?"

"Nothing."

Barzini sat back and let out a sigh. In his hands was a fresh deck of cards. He ripped the seal and began to shuffle them.

"Enough excitement for one day. Let me show you something new."

Barzini showed Leo how to make two cards, aces in this case, stick together in a deck no matter what. Once Leo got the gist of it, Barzini left him to practice, and Leo spent the rest of the afternoon happily perfecting the trick.

CHAPTER 39

A Circle of Ten

The two towers of the Biltmore climbed into the night sky. Low clouds scraped at the top floors of the building. On the street level, a bellboy opened the door of one cab after another as couples returned from an evening out on the town. Leo, Barzini and Horatio walked into the lobby. The séance to summon the spirit of William Ellsworth Robinson would consist of ten people. Doyle had invited three men from the Spiritualist movement, as well as reporter-photographer teams from both the *New York Herald* and the *New York Post*. The large clock near the reception desk showed it was nearly midnight.

They'd begun practicing for this night as soon as Doyle agreed to host the séance. Barzini explained to Leo that even though initially he'd been appalled by the idea of a séance, he realized that press coverage with a big-name celebrity was publicity that money couldn't buy. With any luck the story might catch the eye of a theater manager. Leo hoped that would be the case. He no longer confronted Barzini over his mismanagement of their act. He didn't bring up the subject of Coney Island at all. Nor did he badger Barzini into any confessions. However, the pressure of needing to turn their lives around in a hurry was constant and oppressive. Leo was happy to see that Barzini had picked himself up by the bootstraps and had thrown his despair aside. But they remained in a very precarious place.

“This will not be easy,” Barzini had told Leo. “The reporters are the ones to worry about. We won’t know beforehand if they will take the séance seriously, or if they will want to expose it as smoke and mirrors. And since we will have no control over the environment of Doyle’s suite, the few tricks we bring with us will have to go a long way. Our most important tool will be the power of suggestion. Given the right circumstances, which we will provide, a small audience can be forced into a light hypnotic trance. The whole thing should be over in less than half an hour.”

At Doyle’s door, Leo knocked twice. A moment later Doyle welcomed them in. A round table in the sitting room of his suite was draped with a floor-length white cloth. Set in the center of the table was a bowl of oranges, as a fragrant offering to the spirit world. Positioned in front of one of the chairs were three long candlesticks.

“Our medium has arrived. This is Signor Barzini, who has brought his assistant and his dog with him. Gentlemen,” Doyle said, turning to specifically address the newspapermen, “you may not be familiar with this fact, but animals are highly receptive to the presence of spirits.”

The reporters dutifully scribbled down Doyle’s words. Barzini took the seat behind the candlesticks and Leo sat to his right. Horatio lay on the rug in between them. The members of the circle claimed chairs around the table. Doyle reserved the seat directly opposite Barzini.

Neither Barzini nor Leo acknowledged the reporters. Barzini had made sure beforehand that Doyle told them there would be no questions and no pictures allowed while the séance was going on. Note-taking was forbidden during the ritual. Leo arranged the only visible prop they had brought. It was a Ouija, a spirit board made out of wood, with two curved rows of the letters of the alphabet, the numbers one through ten, and the words “yes,” “no” and “goodbye” printed around an image of a skull with roses wrapping over it. Leo made a great show of positioning the planchette, a pointer made from whalebone, over the skull.

“Please turn off all of the electric lights in the room,” Barzini said. “We are ready to begin.”

The group sat in darkness until Barzini lit the candles. He began to speak in a slow, mellifluous voice.

"We have gathered to contact William Ellsworth Robinson, known as Chung Ling Soo in the world of magic. I do not know if he has yet crossed over. I believe Mr. Robinson's spirit may still be earthbound, due to the violent circumstances of his death. He may be lingering, seeking answers from the living. If we make contact this evening, we must convince him to cross over, otherwise his spirit will wander forever."

"What should we do?" one of the reporters asked.

"You must open your minds, erase all negativity from your thoughts. Watch the flickering candles and think only of the deceased." This was how the room would be won over. Barzini had demonstrated on Leo in the workroom. After staring at the candle long enough, Leo's mind went completely still and he settled into a trance strong enough to keep him from focusing on anything else in the room.

"Watch the candles. Watch the candles. Form an image in your mind's eye," Barzini continued. "See the Chinese man standing onstage, a long queue down his back, dressed in a silk robe, with the porcelain plate shielding his chest. Feel the fear he must have felt every time he stood before the gunmen. Above all else, do not do anything to frighten the spirit."

"Should we hold hands?" someone whispered.

"That is not necessary. Watch the candle and let the light be your guide. Listen to my voice," Barzini said. "The spirit already knows that we are trying to make contact. Leave your hands on the table until the spirit acknowledges our presence."

Leo also stared at the candles, but he kept his mind busy with other thoughts. That way he would not be put into a stupor.

"Spirit, can you hear me?"

That was Leo's first cue. He dropped his hand below the table. He scratched Horatio under his jaw. Horatio howled loudly.

"He's here," Barzini whispered in a low, husky voice.

Second cue. Leo began to shiver and chatter his teeth. The others around the table did the same. This was also the power of suggestion. Just like laughs and yawns and hiccups, people in a trance would pick up and mirror body language. More importantly, they would believe that they felt whatever was being suggested.

Barzini took in several deep breaths, then stretched his neck side-to-side. That was Leo's third cue. He slipped off his left shoe and sock, and with his toes removed a small bell that had been secured under Horatio's collar. Leo grasped the bell with his toes and rang it a few times. Then he placed it in his other sock.

"We wish you no harm," Barzini said. "We seek answers. Have you crossed over yet to the other side?"

At this last cue, Leo started coughing loudly to disguise the sound of his foot striking a specialty match against the strip of sandpaper taped to his right calf. The trick match lit underneath the table and immediately extinguished itself. The smell of sulfur filled the room. He dropped the burnt-out match into his shoe.

"Tell us, spirit, how did you die?"

Barzini began to breathe rapidly. His chest heaved and fell. Suddenly he bent forward, just long enough to pull a vial filled with red ink from his sleeve and moisten the front of his shirt. When Barzini raised his chest, the men at the table gasped as they saw blood on his torso.

"Spirit, were you murdered?"

The whalebone planchette crept along the spirit board, moved by an invisible wire. It slid from the center toward the upper left corner and stopped on the word "yes."

"Can you identify the killer?" Leo asked.

The planchette slipped toward the upper right-hand corner near the word "no," but then shot across the board back to the word "yes." Flashes blinded Barzini. One photographer had shot a picture of the spirit board on the table, which prompted the other photographer to do the same. The planchette shot across the table and landed on the floor. Barzini blew out the candles. In the few seconds of darkness before the lights were turned back on, he slipped off the thin wire that was attached to the planchette and put it in his pocket. Barzini stood and faced the group. Leo quickly guided the loose sock on and slipped on his shoe.

"That was a mistake. You should not have done anything to frighten the spirit away. Robinson may now be doomed to never cross to the other side. I am sorry, Sir Arthur, but I feel quite drained. I don't think I can be of any further service."

Leo leashed Horatio and put Barzini's coat over his shoulders. They hurried out of the suite to the elevator before Doyle, a licensed physician, could insist upon examining Barzini's wound.

"What's going to happen now?" Leo asked in the elevator.

"They will probably play with the spirit board for hours and try to make it move. Things worked out well, just as we planned. I knew once you tell a photographer not to take a photo, then it's guaranteed he will. The timing couldn't have been more perfect. And Leo, you did a good job."

"So did Horatio."

"I told you that poodles were a gifted breed."

When the elevator doors opened, Barzini pulled his jacket tight to cover up the fake blood. The lobby had a few people sitting around and chatting loudly. They swirled dark liquids in snifters, and as Leo passed he overheard one man say, "There's no honor among thieves."

"Yes, but he was implicated in a *murder*, Charles," another replied. "That saying does not apply in this instance."

"In any event, and pardon the pun," a third man said, "that is exactly why he's singing like a bird. They found his records, everyone connected with him is going down and when Mock Duck gets the chair he will have to change his name to Roast Duck."

Leo and Barzini stopped at the same moment. Barzini approached the men. "Pardon me, do any of you gentlemen have the late edition?"

Barzini thanked one of the men as he took his copy of the *Times*. They moved across the lobby to read the front-page story. There was not much more information. Leo's imagination ran wild.

The ride home was infinitely long. When they arrived back at their apartment, Leo and Horatio trailed behind as Barzini bounded up the two flights of stairs. In the hallway Barzini let his overcoat drop to the floor. Leo picked it up and hung it on the coatrack. Barzini had collapsed into one of the parlor chairs. He unbuttoned the top three buttons of his stained dress shirt. Leo saw that his skin underneath was also stained red. Barzini shook his head back and forth.

"What happens now?" Leo asked. "Is it against the law to borrow money from a criminal? I mean, what if the money came from something illegal?"

"Borrowing money is not a crime," Barzini said. "But if the police find any records linking me to Mock Duck . . . then that will not be good."

CHAPTER 40

Gone

Mock Duck's grinning face stretched across the front page of every newspaper in the city. Barzini had gone out early and gotten as many different papers as he could find. None agreed on how many times Mock Duck had previously been arrested. Some claimed as many as fifteen, some as few as eight. However, all the papers agreed on one thing: the cops had evidence tying him to a murder in Chinatown, and to avoid the electric chair he was cooperating with them, naming names, but details were vague. The police were withholding information until the investigations were completed.

Leo flipped through the papers to the stories by the reporters who were at the séance. They had gotten decent write-ups from both. The article in the *New York Post* was titled MEDIUM CLAIMS CHUNG LING SOO'S DEATH A MURDER, while the *New York Herald* headline read ROBINSON'S SPIRIT TO FOREVER WANDER. Leo showed them to Barzini. He did not seem to care.

The next day Leo awoke to find only Horatio in the apartment. He was surprised the workroom was unlocked. The sounds of spring filled the apartment. Baby birds chirped, the first leaves of the season rattled in the breeze. Leo waited all day. He came up with scenarios about what must have happened. A manager from a theater probably read the accounts of the séance in the newspapers and called Barzini to discuss a booking. He might have gone to Martinka's to price out props for the next illusion. Or maybe he went to consult with a lawyer, just in case the loan he took from

Mock Duck wasn't so legal after all. At twilight, when Barzini still had not returned, Leo began to get nervous. He waited through the night, pacing the apartment. His worst fears surfaced. People disappear for two reasons only: they've met a bad end, or they've run away.

Sometime after midnight he went to the kitchen and saw something he hadn't noticed earlier. The servante was open, just slightly. Leo remembered Barzini rooting around in there after Masson's visit. He opened the servante wider and looked inside.

There were cards and palming coins, some folded newspaper articles, personal correspondence and a scrolled-up piece of paper. On the paper was a diagram of a stage. But there were no cues or design notes, just measurements and X's marking spots on the stage. Leo did not understand what he was looking at, at first. There was an arrow at the bottom with a note scrawled in Barzini's hand underneath it: *Stage exit WGHR*. The diagram meant nothing to him.

But then something tickled his brain. He found one of the newspapers recounting Chung Ling Soo's death. The magician was taken to Wood Green Hospital after being shot. Leo remembered the letter he had found in Houdini's workroom. The name of Chung Ling Soo's theater was also Wood Green.

But what was HR?

Leo took out Barzini's world atlas. He turned to the London section, and there, cutting through the northern part of the city, he found Wood Green High Road.

After a night of fever dreams and awakenings, Leo went straight to Martinka's. Murph was there to greet him at the door.

"Hey, Leo! What a surprise. Mr. Martinka figured that as long as I was staying with them for a while, he'd put me to work."

Murph was wearing an A-frame wooden sign advertising the shop.

"Penelope is a swell gal, just like you said. She convinced her grandparents to hire me. They taught me a few tricks and I'm going to do them on the street to drum up some extra business. It sure beats picking pockets. They even threw in lunch!"

Leo smiled. Seeing Murph happy made him feel good.

"That's great news, Murph. I'm real glad to hear it. You'll have to show me those tricks soon. But I'm here to see Penelope. Is she around?"

"Yeah, sure. Straight back."

The two friends shook hands and then Murph walked sideways out the door and began yelling at the top of his lungs, "*Nothing up my sleeves, nothing up my sleeves . . . come 'round, everyone, and see the show . . .*"

Leo went to the back of the shop and found Penelope dusting off the bookshelf. She saw him coming and stopped.

"Hey, Leo."

"Hi. Listen, has Barzini been to the store?"

"He was here yesterday."

"Did he do anything unusual?"

"Nothing strange. He settled up his bill for the props and for us storing them after you left the Eden Musée. He told us to destroy everything, so we did."

"He told you to destroy them?"

"The whole thing seemed odd, especially because he only owed about fifteen dollars. Oma offered to keep his tab going for the next show, but he insisted on paying. It wasn't a big deal. The props didn't cost *that* much, at least compared to a big stage production."

Sweat broke out and ran down Leo's face.

"Leo, you look like you're about to faint. What's going on?"

"How much did all of Barzini's props cost?"

"I don't know to the penny, but it couldn't have been more than two hundred dollars."

Leo backed away. He could have paid for their entire production himself. Why would Barzini need such a big loan from Mock Duck? And with Mock Duck behind bars, why would Barzini worry about a thing? There was no one to collect on the debt. And Barzini had said it himself—borrowing money was not a crime. Was he really worried about a tarnished reputation? Leo doubted it. More and more, lately, Barzini had been embracing Houdini's philosophy that all press is good press. The only possibility left made Leo shudder.

"I—I have to go," he stammered.

Penelope grabbed his arm. Her hand slipped down to his wrist.

"Is everything all right?"

"I don't know," he said. "But I need to find out."

CHAPTER 41

Death by Misadventure

Leo found Inspector Masson in the vestibule. He was speaking into the voice cone for apartment 3.

"Anyone home? Signor Barzini? Leo?"

"Behind you."

The detective from Scotland Yard spun around, his trench coat flapping.

"Ah, so you are. I've come to see Mr. Barzini," Masson said.

"He is working outside of New York City."

"Without his assistant?"

"Just this once."

"When will he return?"

"I'm not exactly sure."

Masson scratched his muttonchops with an upward flicking motion.

"I see. You wouldn't be hiding something from me, would you?"

The inspector put his hand on Leo's shoulder.

"You haven't shot him down for real this time, have you?"

"What?"

"Just a joke. May I come up anyway? I have some information you will be interested in hearing."

Leo prayed Barzini hadn't returned, but for all he knew he could be holed up in his workshop or relaxing in the parlor, simply choosing not to respond to Masson on the voice pipe. Going up the stairwell felt like swimming into a wave. Leo opened the door and found the apartment just as he had left it. The wave passed, and now he only bobbed in the ocean.

Leo showed Inspector Masson to the parlor. As they settled into the chairs, it took all of Leo's strength to control his shaking hands and legs.

"I only came by to say farewell. I have been called back to London. No time to see Chicago, unfortunately. Anyway, I wanted to apologize to Mr. Barzini. I feel I may have been too . . . forceful in our last meeting. The man had a certain suspicious way about him. Such is the way with magicians, I suppose."

"Yeah, I suppose," Leo said.

"Would you give him a message from me?"

"Sure."

"I think for the sake of closing a chapter in the past, he would be interested in hearing this news. Tell him that the forensics department at Scotland Yard disassembled the rifle that held the bullet which killed Mr. Robinson. The gun itself was a prop, as Mr. Barzini suspected. Once a bullet was loaded into the muzzle, it should have never left. The gun actually fired a blank charge from the ramrod tube beneath the muzzle. But on that fateful evening, one of the rifles discharged the actual bullet. The problem was twofold. After every performance Robinson unscrewed a plug to remove the bullet, when he should have been using a hook to remove it from the open end of the barrel. Because of his unscrewing that plug over and over again, some metal had worn through between the two chambers. Plus the fact that the new gunpowder used that night was thin and settled into the creases of the worn metal. When the rifle was fired, the main charge ignited and fired the bullet."

"So he would have died anyway?"

"What do you mean, 'anyway'?"

"Just that it was unavoidable."

"Oh, yes. That day, another day, who knows when, but it was definitely going to happen, by that rifle or by any one of the other prop guns that he rotated. It really was a senseless, tragic accident. The coroner has officially ruled it a death by misadventure."

Leo said the words over.

"Death by misadventure."

"Yes. Criminal charges will not be brought against the assistant who fired the broken rifle. He could not have possibly known the danger he held in his hands. However, there are still a few loose ends that need to be seen to. There were two men with rifles onstage as part of the show. One man with a rifle that functioned properly, and one man with the faulty weapon. But *two* bullets were found by our investigators."

Masson thrust two fingers into the air for emphasis.

"One of them was the bullet that killed Mr. Robinson. Its markings matched the rifle it was shot from. The second bullet does not match that rifle, nor any of the other prop rifles that Robinson owned. That bullet was found embedded in the scenery. It left a rather noticeable hole in the backdrop, which the stagehands swear was not there the night before. We have no idea where it came from or from whom."

"You mean somebody might have tried to kill Robinson but missed?"

Inspector Masson shrugged his shoulders.

"It's possible. Somebody could have been waiting in the wings. Nobody would have noticed, with all the actors and stagehands coming and going in such a large production. But I find that hard to swallow. More likely it was some other part of the act that we do not know about. But the case is officially closed now, and my feeling is that the truth about that second bullet will be buried with Chung Ling Soo."

Leo took it in. "Thanks for letting us know," he said gently. "I'll be sure to tell Barzini."

"I felt it was the right thing. And good luck to you and Barzini with your future shows. I have another few days in New York City and I'd like to relax a bit. Crossing the Atlantic is an anxiety-inducing experience these days. Never know when a U-boat might surface and decide to make you shark food. Interviewing all these magicians has gotten into my brain, and I'd like to see a magic show. Any suggestions? I recall Mr. Barzini saying that plenty of tickets were available for Houdini at the Hippodrome."

"You should go to Coney Island. You'll get more for your money."

“Good-bye, then,” the inspector said.

Leo locked the apartment door and went to the parlor to sit. His head sank. Horatio came and rested by his side. Leo felt the stillness around him. It became uncomfortable. Nothing stirred. There was no proof, no drop of a curtain, no reveal. But he knew. It was now so obvious to him. He calmly got up and took Horatio to Barzini’s bedroom and closed the door. Then he went to the kitchen and picked up the two golden lions. They seemed cheap now. He threw them hard against the wall. Then Leo hoisted up one of the chairs over his head and smashed it against the floor until it broke apart and splintered in his hands.

Far away and small he heard Horatio barking. He went to the workroom next and threw everything onto the floor. Glass bottles broke, mirrors shattered. Leo tore pages out of books and stomped on Barzini’s sketches. Through his tears he walked down the hall to his own room. Inside he noticed how bare and plain it was. The only decoration was the poster on the wall from their show. He stared at it for a while. What a lie it was. The drawing made the act look astonishing, as if ghosts existed and could walk onstage, as if Leo were part of something big.

He tore the poster down from the wall in one swift grab and ripped it until there was nothing left but little specks of paper blanketing the floor and the bed like flakes of colored snow.

CHAPTER 42

The Real Gianfranco Barzini

The stones gave off the earthy scent of moss and minerals. The smell of wet, old things. Leo crouched in the shadow made by the entranceway. The flat grave markers in the St. Mark's churchyard lay in front of him in orderly rows.

Important men were buried in the shade of the tall steeple. Leo recognized only one of their names. There was a sculpture of him from the waist up off to one side of the cemetery. His bald head and hawkish face were cast in bronze, but all Leo knew about Peter Stuyvesant was that he was a governor a long time ago, and he was a man with a wooden leg.

Leo got up. He walked between the wide markers, some with their corners chipped. His mind was blank. When he looked down at the rectangles of stone with names and birth and death dates carved into them, his eyes alternated between seeing the pathway between them and the pattern that the markers made. It was very quiet. No one came in or out of the church. Second Avenue was empty.

Dark thoughts filled his head as he looped through the cemetery. Leo left the churchyard and walked to Third Avenue. He went south to Chinatown. Inside Mr. Shen's shop, he turned over the OPEN sign and flipped the lock on the door. Mr. Shen watched him from behind the counter.

"I am sorry, Leo. I do not know where he is." Mr. Shen's face was long and his eyes seemed sunken.

"But you've seen him. I know it."

"Not for a few days."

Leo walked to the counter. He felt like he had fallen off the earth, like there was no ground for a million miles and he could just keep falling and falling and watching the only things he knew drift farther and farther away.

Leo thought he was going to pass out. Mr. Shen extended an arm and took him by the elbow. "Come with me." Mr. Shen led him into a small office in the back of the store. There was a round table and two wooden chairs. A gray cat slept near a radiator. Leo took a seat and Mr. Shen sat across from him. Mr. Shen poured himself tea from a kettle resting on a hot plate on a shelf nearby. He looked into the cup as ribbons of steam rose to his face.

Mr. Shen did not say anything at first. He blew at the tea and took small sips. Finally he put down the teacup. "You do not even know the man who you think is Gianfranco Barzini," he said. "What has he told you about his life? Family in Europe? Performing in front of kings and queens when he was younger than yourself?"

"What do you mean?"

"I have known this man for more than thirty years. He did not arrive in this city as a stowaway on a steamer. He arrived in a New York hospital. As he came into the world, his mother left it. No one knew who his father was."

Leo thought back to the car ride to the Whitfields' mansion. The story Barzini spun for him. It was all fake. Barzini had been conning him. There was no Barzini who snuck a dog onto a transatlantic boat and struck out on his own. Vanished was the person Leo had come to admire, replaced by a liar. Worse.

Mr. Shen continued. "He lived with different aunts and uncles for much of his childhood. He started coming to my shop and staying all day. He cleaned the glass for me and swept. I cannot recall exactly what first brought him here. But he was very curious by nature and I taught him some of the magic that I remembered. He spent much time here, learning everything I could teach him, including my language. As he got older we became good friends. I found him to be very talented. Much more talented than myself. So I encouraged him to pursue his dream of being an illusionist. One day he simply stopped coming by. I did not hear from him for many years. Then, just as suddenly as he'd disappeared, he walked back into my shop. Of course he looked different. He had transformed himself into the Great Barzini. And that's who he pretended to be."

"You introduced him to Mock Duck. You set him up."

"I am not following you, Leo."

"You could have done something to talk him out of trying to murder Chung Ling Soo. Maybe he wasn't there on the stage pulling the trigger, but Barzini paid Mock Duck for it."

"Murder? Franco never told me the exact nature of his dealings with Mock Duck, and I never asked. But I know in my heart he is not guilty of arranging a murder. He is incapable of that. He is neither brave nor cowardly enough, nor evil nor dishonorable. I don't believe he has abandoned you. Go home. You need to talk to him about these doubts in your heart."

As Leo left the office, Mr. Shen called after him.

"I had a feeling about you the first time I met you, that you were one of us. When you bought the firecrackers. But I knew for certain when I saw you spin the *baoding*. Leo, you are always welcome in my shop."

CHAPTER 43

The Curtain Closes

Leo stepped into the apartment and surveyed the damage. He was disgusted with the mess he had created. He could hear Horatio whining behind Barzini's door. Leo wanted to let him out, but he wouldn't until the floor was clean.

As Leo started to put things back in place, his head spun. The shock of Barzini's lies had worn off, and instead Leo felt sickened. He was alone again. His mentor was a monster. He had fallen for the same trick twice. He had an urge to just sit down on the floor, close his eyes and stop thinking. But something kept him standing. He went to the workroom to take stock of what Barzini had left. When he entered, his face turned ashen.

Barzini stood amid the chaos in the room.

"I'm sorry I left so abruptly, but this was hardly necessary," Barzini said, gesturing to the mess.

Leo's throat felt hot. He thought he was about to cry. "Why did you do it?"

"I had some business to attend to. It was urgent. I left you a note."

"There was no note."

"I left it in the kitchen on the counter. Did you open the window? Maybe it blew out."

"Stop lying to me. Stop talking to me like I'm some stupid kid. That's not what I meant, and you know it. *Why did you do it?*"

"Leo, it sounds like you are accusing me of something." Barzini cocked his head to the side and grimaced. "Why don't you stop tiptoeing around what you really want to say? Please, be specific. What I am guilty of?"

"The money from Mock Duck. You told me it was a loan to back the show. But what you owed him is a lot more than the few hundred bucks the props cost to make. What was the rest of it for?"

"Well, it wasn't all for the production. It was for the risk I was about to take."

Leo was repulsed by his callousness.

"You call what you did a *risk*?"

"Of course. I've been broke for quite some time. You know that. Years and years of performing the same tricks at the same cocktail parties for Park Avenue ladies provided me with a comfortable life, but my run ended. It was for the risk I was about to take on you."

"What about all those lies you fed me about growing up in Italy and living in China? About your uncle, and stealing the dog? I thought I knew you," Leo said. His face burned. "But you're just some fake."

"No more than you," Barzini said quickly. He raised a finger and pointed directly at Leo. "I have lied to you about my past no more frequently than you to me."

Leo seethed. Barzini was like a stone wall against the ocean. The pressure of small waves would not make it crack. Leo had to push over it.

"You failed, you know that?" Leo said. "As hard as you tried. His prop gun malfunctioned. He would have died that night anyway."

Barzini stared at Leo, not blinking, not moving a hair.

"I *saw* the diagram of the Wood Green theater. So I *know* what you did."

Barzini shook his head.

"The only thing you know is that I paid a lot of money to get a diagram showing Chung Ling Soo's stage marks. I am not proud of that. I am not a perfect man. Sometimes I say one thing and do another. But I needed that diagram."

Leo lowered his voice.

"I know exactly how badly you wanted that diagram. Inspector Masson came by. He said to tell you that the coroner ruled the cause of death as accidental. He said if it hadn't happened that night it would have happened another night. But the Inspector also said that a second bullet was found embedded in the scenery. A different kind of bullet. Not from one of Chung Ling Soo's guns."

There was a moment of silence then, for Barzini to mourn his long-estranged friend Billy, and Leo, his former distinguished teacher.

"I have this," Barzini said.

He handed over a piece of paper to Leo. On it was a rough sketch of an apparatus labeled "transmitter," a telephone and an empty cabinet.

"That is why I left. I needed to see a man about the equipment," he said in a soft voice. "The technology is very new."

Leo handed the paper back.

"You can't just keep reinventing yourself as you go along," Leo said. "It doesn't work that way, not when other people's lives are at stake."

Barzini held on to the paper tightly.

"*Say something!*" Leo yelled. He was surprised at the power in his voice. "For once, tell me the truth. Not a story. I need to know."

"I lived so many years," Barzini started hesitantly, "with my hatred burning a hole inside of me. And then, after he died, it became easier to admit to myself that I am only a skilled magician. I am not an entertainer on a grand scale. I never was. Alone, I will never be a sensation. Sometimes our dreams are not meant to come true."

"It was your dream to kill him?"

"My dream was to perform our illusion in front of many people and have them remember it for the rest of their lives. We share the same dream, Leo. But now I realize the bullet catch will always be Chung Ling Soo's trick. How could anyone possibly top dying onstage?"

Leo unexpectedly thought about the Mayor and Boris. Were their lives now going to be ruined forever, thinking they had killed him? Or would they move on, and mend themselves? Leo also thought about running after Masson and presenting all of his suspicions. He had no definite proof, just a long list of circumstances that pointed to guilt. If he did that would he be able to start over again? To cleanse himself and move on? But move on to where? To what? He knew he couldn't. He had signed a contract. Barzini's secrets were his own.

"I'm sorry if I let you down," Barzini said. "I am sorry for many things and I would like to try to make up for them. But I think you are wrong about something. You *can* reinvent yourself. You have done it before my eyes many times."

He was right. Leo had been an orphan, a crook, an ex-con, the son of an industrialist, a desperate nothing, a thirsty student. But always a showman. Barzini had taken a chance on Leo. Now Leo could take a chance on Barzini.

"But how can I trust you?" Leo asked.

"Because I need you more than you need me. Because I have taken you this far. Do not make the same mistake that I made, Leo. Is it so hard to forgive? With this new effect, the world is full of promise again. We will be the first to use this technology onstage. Leo, tell me, have you decided yet?"

"Decided what?"

"Who you want to be."

Leo thought back to his first night at Barzini's apartment. Barzini had asked Leo who he was. Leo did not know the answer then, but now it was clearer. He could be everything Barzini was not. He could be center stage, national tours, posters on every street corner. He could make thousands of people gasp at the same time like the roar of a steam engine. He could be Leo the Magnificent.

But he couldn't do it alone. He needed Barzini to help him. Barzini would lead Leo to where he rightly belonged. Leo's success would be his as well. Barzini would do it not for money or fame, but for pride.

Leo took the schematic from Barzini's hand. He looked at it more closely. The illusion was only roughed out. The details were not on the page yet.

"Who is on the other end of the telephone?" Leo asked.

"I don't know. I only had the general idea for the mechanics. None of the surrounding scenario has been developed."

Leo put the paper on the table and turned the two chairs back upright. He kicked the glass debris over to one side of the room. Barzini was watching him intently, his eyes glinting.

"So," Leo said. "Show me."